BLOOD
MOON

S.J. VERMILLION

SUNBURY
P R E S S

Mechanicsburg, Pennsylvania   USA

Published by Sunbury Press, Inc.
50 West Main Street
Mechanicsburg, Pennsylvania 17055

www.sunburypress.com

For information about special discounts for bulk purchases, please contact Sunbury Press Orders Dept. at (855) 338-8359 or orders@sunburypress.com.

To request one of our authors for speaking engagements or book signings, please contact Sunbury Press Publicity Dept. at publicity@sunburypress.com.

ISBN: 978-1-62006-569-3 (Trade Paperback)
ISBN: 978-1-62006-570-9 (Mobipocket)
ISBN: 978-1-62006-571-6 (ePub)

Library of Congress Control Number: 2015933711

FIRST SUNBURY PRESS EDITION: March 2015

Product of the United States of America
0 1 1 2 3 5 8 13 21 34 55

Set in Bookman Old Style
Designed by Crystal Devine
Cover by Amber Rendon
Edited by Allyson Gard

Continue the Enlightenment!

Dedication: To My Beloved Mother

The fog has descended with its silent burden;
Rendering nature uncertain and still.
The Sun is risen, piercing the curtain,
A welcoming warmth to disperse the chill.

Steve

CHAPTER 1

Ted Minnis scurried up the creaky steps to the marina manager's office with a mission. He would want an ironclad guarantee from Oscar Coleman the marina boss that he would be granted exclusive privileges in the event of the annual bottleneck debacle that occurred every Fourth of July in the Monnachawee Bay. His main objective was to secure the prime vantage point off the coast of Seaside, Maryland to view the fireworks display from the deck of his Sea Ray 440 with his mistress and his friends. He did not want to suffer the embarrassment of promising something to his friends that he could not deliver. Everything had to be perfect. Ever the opportunist, the forty-two year old successful hospital supply sales manager had even harangued the boatyard staff to ensure his craft, *The Rough Rider,* would not be bottled up at the Bay Marina as had happened in the past. After all this was the Fourth of July and as custom would have it, all boat owners desired to have the same prime viewing spot for the 9:20 PM display.

Minnis's tantrums were notorious and his reputation definitely preceded him. Unknown to Minnis was that Coleman was not on duty this morning. Instead his assistant Earl Carruthers was in charge. Carruthers had seen these self-important types before and was not going to be intimidated. He had a unique way that he had tweaked and perfected through the years. Call it Prozac induced maturity, but basically it was indifference. If somebody like Minnis tried to provoke him coarsely with an urgent request, 'Old Earl' would smile benignly and grant the party their wish. Earl adopted a new mantra—If it isn't important for me to remember then screw them and the Ferrari they rode in on! It beat heated confrontations and the lawsuits that ensued from his bygone temper laced confrontations over trivial matters. But most important, his sixty-eight year old heart couldn't stand such infantile altercations. Carruthers gave the jerk his way although the traffic would be light at the time that Minnis requested.

Arriving the next day in a 1990 BMW 325i convertible, Minnis and his *bimbo du jour* pulled sharply into a gravel parking space at the front of the marina. The black canvas top emerged from the trunk and engulfed the interior of the glossy white coupe while the windows rose electrically to seal the auto. The CD player was abruptly turned off in the middle of Bob Marley's, "We Jammin." The passenger door swung open delicately to reveal two perfectly manicured Gucci sandaled feet and a pair of long shapely legs. The heat and humidity coupled with the lack of any semblance of a breeze they had experienced in their ride to the marina dampened their faces. Minnis glanced at his diamond-laced Rolex and shook his head incredulously.

"Three forty-five! I told them three forty-five! Where the hell are they?"

" They'll be here, Ted. Relax!" his date consoled.

Octavia Bledsoe comforted the anxious sales manager by clutching his sun-burned forearm. A former Miss Baltimore runner-up, Miss Bledsoe was a stunning and accomplished African-American woman who worked as an assistant administrator at Baltimore General Hospital. Her appearance complimented her drug rehabilitated acquaintance to say the least. Minnis stood 5 foot 6 and Miss Bledsoe towered above her mate at 6 foot 1. On this day she was clad in short green khaki shorts and a maroon pullover. Her neck was adorned by a gold necklace with a solid gold heart pendant which hung above her ample cleavage. The necklace of course was a gift from her diminutive wife-cheating beau. Her black hair was styled long but on this day slicked back and kept from being swept in her face by a Baltimore Orioles baseball cap.

Minnis, bathed in British Sterling cologne and bath products, swatted away the increasing swarm of various flying insects attracted to his manly scent. At forty-two years old, Minnis's well-coiffed curly receding brown hair, tanned body, and gaudy golden chain around his chest hair-encroaching throat were testament that he was still a player in his mind. Like a knight preparing for battle, Minnis would preen his looks to perfection in front of a mirror prior to exiting his abode each morning for work or play but not before uttering his conceited anticipation of better looks for tomorrow to his reflection in the vanity mirror.

Minnis shuffled to the rear of his car to retrieve the two blue and white coolers which were in the trunk. The heavier of the two fell from his smallish hands and landed with a crash on the gravel lot. He cursed silently and opened it. To his satisfaction the Chivas Regal, Grey Goose, Jim Beam and the Kendall-Jackson Chardonnay were intact. He had used an old beach towel to cushion the spirits in the cooler while in transit along with plastic cups, plastic plates and plastic cutlery purchased at a gasoline station convenience store with his platinum credit card. The other cooler contained cold fried chicken, chilled steamed shrimp, potato salad and rolls along with ice he bought at a grocery store that morning before he picked up Miss Bledsoe.

Minnis's wife Anna as usual was unaware of her philandering husband's plans this day. She was out of the country administering aid to those ravaged from the effects of a war torn country in chaos, Somalia. If not from the constant pleading of her friends at the International Red Cross, she would be spending the holiday with Ted in Seaside, Maryland aboard the aptly named *Rough Rider*. (Aptly named because Minnis was born on the birthday of the 26th President, Theodore Roosevelt, and his mother proud of this distinction named him Theodore.) Ted in turn christened his Sea Ray 440, *The Rough Rider*.

***

Mrs. Ted Minnis was the daughter of a very prominent Baltimore importer. She was born in Frankfurt, Germany while her father was stationed there during the early years of the Cold War. Her father, Paul Kryshanski, was an average GI who assisted in installing listening stations that monitored Soviet communiqués from the Eastern Sector. He would spend his off duty time practicing his golf swing and soaking up the local atmosphere at hofbrau houses. He enjoyed the life of Frankfurt to the point of remaining after his enlistment expired and established himself with the local gentry with aid to the recovery of the war torn area. He was adopted by the townspeople, despite his country's occupational role, for his charity and dedication to youth development through the Lutheran Church and after his service ended, settled in Frankfurt and found administrative work in a popular brewery. His German friends would later become instrumental in his future import business.

Anna, influenced by her father's largess, adopted the philanthropic ways of her father as early as a young schoolgirl, by seeking donations from servicemen by selling cookies and fudge that her mother Alice Kryshanski had made, with all proceeds going to organizations set up by her father. Anna never lost the urge to aid those in need even in current times considering the destruction and rebuilding of West Germany she witnessed as a small child. Her selfless involvement to charity led her to all corners of the world and was considered by all....a saint except her noncommittal materialistic husband who sponged off her family's wealth.

Ted Minnis met Anna at a fundraising event for the building expansion of the Maryland Shock Trauma Unit. Ted, a master of influencing bordering on braggadocio, addressed the audience of would-be-donors. His speech, although coached by a better suited sensitive fraternity brother, wooed the checkbooks out of the pockets of the attendees and the event exceeded the donations quota sought by the Trauma Unit by nearly ten-thousand dollars. Anna had to meet this man!

The two hit it off right away. Anna, her deep brown-eyes, dark hair and tanned face, and slimly maintained-figure fell for the impact of Mr. Minnis's confident air. He was cocky, intelligent, and a maverick, an appearance that Minnis maintained to his advantage in all his dealings whether they be business related or personal. And now Ted knew an opportunity to strike hard was at hand.

The Kyrshanski name was gold in Baltimore, and Minnis was primed to strike hard. A gushing heart was all Minnis needed to pounce and take advantage of an opportunity. With this in mind, the shallow man went to work and lured the naïve Anna into her perceived image of him. So good was the charade that Anna was charmed to eloping with him despite the constant protestations from her father who saw through the masquerade. Anna, aware of her father's declining health, neglected his concerns and owed it to the fact that he would display one moment of clarity out of nine moments of incoherence. Anna's love for Ted would not be impeded, and she tumbled into the well of denial.

The one person that could have swayed her from this obvious faux pas was her mother. Sadly, Alice Kryshanski, had passed several years before from ovarian cancer, not witnessing the eventual success her daughter had amassed in her charitable dealings. Anna missed her mother and would visit her grave site regularly on Christmas, Mothers' Day and especially on her birthday when she wasn't away on her missions of mercy, ever praying to her for spiritual guidance from beyond.

At first their relationship flourished, and Ted accepted Anna's role as global envoy to the needy. She would depart for months at a time and write to her husband of her experiences from arid Equatorial Africa to the rain forests of New Guinea. Ted eventually grew tired of the missives and would manage to respond periodically whenever the mood struck, which became rarer as the marriage lasted. Ted's *me time* consisted of one night stands with women acquaintances at business boardrooms and bar rooms. After two years of marriage, Ted included an expensive cocaine habit to his repertoire and isolated himself from a rapidly declining social circle, eventually being released by his employer of 11 years.

Anna, feeling guilty for her lack of marital duties, shouldered the blame for her husband's condition and promised him that she would spend more time at home in the future. She would adjust her travel plans accordingly at once and have Ted admitted to an out of state rehab facility to treat his dependency on cocaine.

As Ted's condition improved to the point of an early release from rehabilitation, life inside the Minnis household returned to normalcy. Ted eventually found employment with a rival hospital supply company, Jenkins Hospital and Medical Supply Company, which knew of his reputation prior to his downfall and was desperate for someone who could make an immediate and course changing impact like Ted Minnis. After all, it was Minnis's aggressive salesmanship that caused the rival company to decline in stature in the first place.

Now Minnis was back in the fight to reclaim his territory, and his competition stood indifferent aware of his shortcomings. His dependency on cocaine gone and now replaced by support groups for recovering drug users, Ted employed that same dependent urge to catapult him back in the market place. Within the next six months Ted was back on top of the pyramid. His current company reaped what they had invested in Minnis. Ted, even more confident, was back to his cocky self. He wanted it all; fame and the Kryshanski fortune which he would eventually share when Paul Kryshanski died.

✷✷✷

Octavia Bledsoe's first encounter with Ted Minnis was rather memorable. Through Minnis's secretary he had arranged an appointment with the hospital administrator, Dr. Calvin Bracken. Minnis had plans of an aggressive plan to supply Baltimore General Hospital with their whole line of products and have it delivered expeditiously; better than the competition's turn around rate of one week. Minnis was determined to leave the administrator's office with a signed deal even if it meant endless hours of negotiation.

But at the last moment, the administrator left the hospital to attend to a family emergency and the matter was left up to the assistant administrator, Octavia Bledsoe whose hasty last minute instructions were not to agree to anything; just be cordial and postpone the meeting.

"Hello, I have a ten o'clock with Dr. Bracken," announced Ted to the receptionist in a domineering manner.

"I'm sorry, Mr. Minnis but he had to leave for a family emergency. His assistant, Miss Bledsoe, will speak with you," the fortyish receptionist responded in her professional tone.

"Why didn't anyone from your office contact me? I do not want to speak with a flunkey. I have important matters to discuss with the person in charge of supplying your hospital!"

"Miss Bledsoe is hardly a *flunkey* as you put it. She is a highly educated, respected, and knowledgeable professional in her field. I'm sure you will be impressed."

"*She?*"

The conversation between Minnis and the receptionist resounded in the office of Miss Bledsoe. Gritting her teeth, she stood from her desk and strode to the open door of her office.

"Mr. Minnis? I've been expecting you. Would you please come in?"

Minnis delayed a second before he assented to Miss Bledsoe's wish. He reluctantly moved past the reception area and walked the ten feet to Miss Bledsoe's office. Her office was like any other office. Various diplomas and degrees displayed in mahogany wooden frames hung from off-white painted walls, family pictures, plants, and accrued meaningful objects to Miss Bledsoe adorned a ledge that ran along the right side of her office. Her desk, neatly organized with the usual accoutrements one would find in any office seemed to evoke an ironical calm and serene presence by the one responsible for executing the administrator's urgent dictates. A soft jazz radio station added to the serenity of the office which Miss Bledsoe turned off as she neared her faux cherry wooden desk.

"Mr. Minnis, as you know I do not have the authority to approve any contracts unless directed by the board of directors, and that is, as you and I know, never ever going to happen," she stated pulling her leather chair back from her desk.

"Understood, but my company insists that a deal gets worked out today or else we are going to have to make efforts to drop any cost initiative that will benefit your hospital. Is there any way that I can contact Dr. Bracken at home or by paging him to discuss this matter? I mean, we don't have to conduct the meeting here. We could meet at his home or wherever is best suited for him. But, I insist to negotiate with him today!"

The young administrator sat incredulous to Mr. Minnis's demand. She played out the scenario in her mind before responding to the absolute coldness exhibited by Minnis regarding her boss's plight. How can I tactfully contact my boss while he is attending to his ailing mother on her death bed with a request to drop what he is doing and negotiate a contract with this idiot?

"Well... what's your decision Miss Bledsoe?" Minnis, still not seated, walked impatiently away from her desk and stared at a wall adorned with awards giving her time to squirm.

"Mr. Minnis my decision is this. Go out to the receptionist and reschedule the appointment! I'm sorry, but I cannot go outside of hospital policy and I will not burden my boss with such an absurd request considering his dire situation," the young administration assistant stiffened with anger over the salesman's overt insensitivity.

The expected tension purposely devised by the salesman as a ploy to stress out a party into capitulation to his terms lasted a few moments. Sensing he had no chance of sealing the deal from this bulwark of a woman, Minnis in his legendary shifting of facial expressions changed gears. After a brief pause studying a glossy photograph on the wall of Miss Bledsoe accepting her runner up trophy with flowers as Miss Baltimore, Minnis condescended.

"That's a real shame the judges didn't select you as Miss Baltimore. They did the city a real injustice. A woman with your beauty and brains! Just doesn't figure how you came in second place. The winner must have *known* one of the judges, if you see what I'm getting at. Do you enjoy eating crabs, Miss Bledsoe?"

"What?" the astounded assistant asked in amazed confusion bordering on rage. "Of course I like crabs! What does that have to do with your business here? I don't get it! You think you can bribe me with *crabs* so I'll sign a contract? Dr. Bracken told me about worms like you," she scolded.

"No, no," Minnis chuckled, "I just thought we could get together and start this all over. I promise not to talk business. My treat! Really, once you get to know me then you'll find I'm a bit more human than what you see here. Come on, now. The aroma of steamed crabs, the sweet buttery taste of back fin, the tang of old bay seasoning, the awakening of taste buds long since dormant since your last dealing with a Chesapeake blue crab plus the joy and ambience of a typical Baltimore crab house," Minnis coaxed. "I promise I'll be civil and a gentleman and accord you all the respect a woman like you deserves and more. What do you say, Miss Bledsoe?"

Bledsoe managed a slight smile and chuckled past her sternness towards the salesman. She pondered, sizing up Minnis to see if there were any possible ulterior motives lurking behind his gray and blue pinstriped Pierre Cardin suit. Minnis, after all, was known as a reputable businessman in the hospital community for years and did not pose a threat and was married to Anna Kryshanski, a member of one of Baltimore's elite families. After a few moments of tapping her pen on her outgoing tray, she acquiesced.

Minnis, as usual not completely satisfied with his failure to close the Baltimore General deal, did in fact negotiate a deal with a natural beauty, a Miss Baltimore runner up. One way or another he would leave a business with some sort of deal but not the kind his employer would approve. However, the overly confident hospital supply salesman knew deep down that the deal would be closed with the administrator when he returned. Using sympathy as a tool as he did with any human emotion that he was void of experiencing, Minnis made a mental note to stop by a nearby florist to have flowers sent to the home of the bereaved administrator. But his shrewdness did not stop there. He had to have Octavia. Knowing that Anna would be overseas administering aid indefinitely in Somalia with the International Red Cross, Minnis contemplated plans for himself and Miss Bledsoe. The fourth of July was around the corner and perhaps a trip to the beach and a ride on his boat could be arranged.

CHAPTER 2

The 1982 faded and rusty red Ford 150 pick-up roared into the marina parking lot stirring up dust and tossing gravel in its wake. Jimmy Castro, a boat mechanic, known to all at the marina as an expert in repair and a jack of all trades was on call to help out Oscar Coleman, the marina manager, in the event of an emergency with the hectic activity at the marina on the Fourth of July. Coleman's right hand man, Earl Carruthers had been given the rest of the day off due to a constantly convenient cardiac condition. Castro had been a fixture at the marina since 1984 and could always be counted on to help no matter what the emergency entailed.

Now approaching forty-nine years old, his physical features just recently began to betray his age. His moustache and his once jet black hair sprouted randomly gray strands. The bright sun highlighted the silver stubble on his leather-like unshaven slightly scarred face. On his head, he wore a worn blue ball cap emblazoned with the flag of the Lone Star State. The cab window behind him contained decals which conveyed his pride of being a veteran of Viet Nam. His license plates proclaimed that he was a Purple Heart Medal recipient.

His hands calloused and tough on the steering wheel veered the pick-up to the right next to a white convertible

BMW. He let the truck continue to run so he could enjoy
the end of Freddie Fender's "Rancho Grande" on his tape
deck player which he shared with the rest of the world with
his windows down. He had no air conditioning in the truck
and turned down the option when he purchased the
vehicle due to his tough Texas upbringing. The Seaside
summers were cooler than the ones he experienced in
Texas. Castro was born in Brownsville, Texas and a big fan
of Tejano music. He flipped the visor back up to the ceiling
of the cab, revealing a picture of his wife Sunny with their
son Danny. With no air conditioning in his truck Castro
kept the windows open partially as he leapt from the
littered cab replete with empty Lucky Strike cigarette
packs, half consumed Snapple tea bottles, screwdrivers,
and machine parts. He jumped from the cab wearing his
usual attire worn jeans, worn sneakers and a plain faded
pocketed orange tee shirt.

"Where's the fire, Jimmy?"

Castro blinded by the afternoon sun as he emerged
from the truck was surprised by the comment but
recognized that sarcastic tone. He froze in a brief disgust at
the poor choice of words. Shielding his eyes he looked in
the direction of the voice.

"Minus? Is that you?"(Castro always reminded Minnis
of the day he was paged as "Minus" by a marina restaurant
employee.) You back in town for the fourth?"

"Yes, Jimmy, it's me Ted with a friend, so please watch
your mouth!" warned the salesman knowing Castro's
propensity for salty language.

"Why? Will *he* get offended?" Castro joked.

Octavia emerged from around the BMW to join the
conversation.

"Me? No, I've heard it all. Nothing you utter will
surprise me," Tavia proudly announced as someone who
had escaped the vernacular of the inner city.

Castro recoiled. A more respectful conversational tone
was needed in the presence of this goddess. Deep down in
Castro's psyche was the urge to ridicule Minnis on how he
managed to land such a beauty. He fought back the urge to
question Minnis about the whereabouts of Mrs. Minnis,
but his instincts prevented him from doing so in

accordance with the unwritten rule from "The Manly Laws Of Discretion," an unpublished code that is instinctively ingrained in every males brain at birth not to question a pal when he sees that he is cavorting around with a woman other than his wife or girlfriend. Although, Castro mused silently, he would love to see Minnis squirm. Castro reached for the pocket in his tee shirt to retrieve a cigarette from the wrinkled cellophane pack.

"Jimmy, I'd like you to meet my *friend* Tavia," Minnis introduced clearing his throat. "Taves, this is Jimmy Castro. The best damned fix it guy in the world," Minnis proclaimed.

"If you say so, Minus. Please to meet you, ma'am," Jimmy said extending his left hand to a perplexed Tavia with an unlit Lucky Strike dangling from his lips.

"Taves, if NASA has problems, they refer their questions to Jimmy. Isn't that right, Jimmy?" teased Ted nervously. Tavia smiled as a generous ploy to avert her stare towards the right side of Castro's face which was obviously scarred by a fire.

"Minus, you butter me up anymore and I'm gonna feel like a stale bake potato at the Marina Bay Restaurant." Jimmy winked to show Minnis that his secret was safe with him. (Another reference to page one of "The Manly Laws of Discretion") While cupping his hands to light his smoke, Castro glanced at his watch.

"Well, I gotta get going. Boss man is gonna wonder where I am. See you all later. Nice to have met you, ma'am," Jimmy said gentlemanly interspersing his speech with a dry cough.

"Happy Fourth, Jimmy!" the couple chimed.

"Yeah. I hope you two have a *bang up time* tonight too." Jimmy turned towards the couple and waved pulling the cigarette from his mouth grinning from his insinuation.

"Is there something wrong with his right hand, Ted and why does he call you *Minus?*" the beauty queen runner-up wondered with a grin.

"Jimmy is the only one who has earned that privilege. He has done a lot of work for me in the past. Even though he looks as shaggy as he does, he's a gem, a real life saver! His right hand was injured in the war. He doesn't like to talk about it," Minnis responded while looking towards the entrance to the parking lot.

Suddenly a black Mercedes crept into the parking lot. Its occupants, a man and his wife scanned the lot slowly for an identifying feature. Tavia and Ted's attention were drawn to the cautious vehicle causing Ted to venture out in the middle of the parking lot to ascertain if it were his late guests. The driver of the Mercedes blew his horn to acknowledge that they saw Ted. Ted waved and pointed to an open space close to his car where his guest could park. The Chestertons had finally arrived!

Woody and Myra Chesterton were notorious procrastinators who wore large gaudy expensive watches for no apparent reason except only for prestige which was the foundation of all decisions in their materialistic purchasing. Punctuality was a term of which they were unaware. *The world waits for us, not visa-versa!* You would never see a Chesterton look at their watches unless somebody admired them and they would have to explain the worth of the item. Nowhere would there be an explanation regarding the practicality of the timepieces. Practicality was another word not in the Chesterton dictionary.

"We want to be noticed if not for our image but for our worth!" would be a suitable epitaph on their headstones. They were snobs of the highest caliber and too good according to them to even compete for their place on the social registry. Mr. Woodrow Chesterton maintained that his family could be traced back to the *Mayflower*. Historians often discounted the number of these assertions mainly due to the dwindling amount of survivors that endured the landing at Plymouth Rock from both ship borne illnesses and the harsh winter that ensued. Mr. Chesterton's boastful insistence of this notoriety was always questioned being that there was no actual documental proof connecting his ancestors to the *Mayflower* and nobody felt like going to the trouble to research the *fact* gathered around a bar. As for Woody's claim to be linked to William the Conqueror, Englishmen scoff at such a notion being that *all you bloody yanks think you're related to William the Conqueror.* Meteorologists had given thought of scrapping Doppler radar because they could accurately predict weather changes from the way the Chestertons noses were constantly pointed towards the jet stream. The presence of the Chestertons always preceded a cold front by the way. The Chestertons held little regard for their place on the social registry.

"If we are not number one, then why go through the aggravation of proving ourselves! The social registry is flawed. Even a man named *Kyrshanski* is on it!"

They were aware of Minnis's relationship to the Kryshanski family but were able to look past that because Ted was materialistic as well and didn't care about deplorable conditions in third world countries like Haiti. When it came to deplorable conditions in Newport, Rhode Island, the Upper East Side of Manhattan or the Hamptons then this would spur the Chestertons to action; but it would be in a chauffeur driven Bentley that would take them there.

They had made their fortune in questionable financial planning and later as a resort real estate team when their shady investment dealings with their elderly clientele started to unravel. It seemed that their clientele's profits rarely saw an increase while the Chesterton's firm grew to excess from an obvious accrual of material wealth. Still, they remained unruffled by the controversy and comported themselves as deserving of the same respect worthy of foreign dignitaries at a White House State function.

In fact they had experienced such a moment when they were invited to attend a State Dinner there by a remote friend of the President at that time, Ronald Reagan. They were never asked back after a social fiasco when Myra, after the consumption of a few martinis and to the dismay of her husband, complained bitterly about the lobster bisque lacking *originality* and the servants as having been shang-haied from a nearby International House Of Pancakes all within earshot of the First Lady. Nancy Reagan, as a favor for future administrations, had the Chestertons placed on the top of the blacklist of permanently banned guests outranking Sid Vicious, George Carlin, and any Soviet or East German Olympic judge.

Despite the tardiness of his guests, Minnis welcomed them and excused them for running late. Octavia stood by and rolled her eyes as Minnis did his about-face routine.

"Myra, Woody, I would like you to meet a good friend of mine. This is Octavia Bledsoe."

The Chestertons were not impressed and gave a lukewarm greeting to Octavia shaking her hand *a la* dead fish technique. Underneath, Octavia recognized this reception as one she has experienced over and over. She bit her tongue so as not to embarrass Ted. It was times like this that gave Octavia her inner drive to succeed, and she instantly recalled a biblical passage. "A camel will pass through the eye of a needle before a rich man enters the kingdom of God." Knowing this verse from the Bible gave her strength when it came to those who thought themselves better by the amount of material wealth they have accrued in their shallow and self-absorbed lives. She lived to outwit these types, and this was the reason she could rise in her profession so rapidly. Her superiors desired a woman who was cool under fire and able to think on her feet despite the occasional insult to her integrity.

Minnis fumbled through the difficult and uncomfortable exchange between his mate and the Chestertons. Not wanting to infuriate either party, Ted directed the Chestertons to his boat anchored three slips away. The Chestertons proceeded to the slip knowing they would not be carrying anything but what they brought, their massive egos. In other words, Ted would be lugging the coolers and other items fifty feet away and by himself. He knew he was going to receive feedback from Octavia if he asked her. But being the good friend, Octavia toted one cooler, the lighter of the two, and Ted managed to carry the heavier one balancing three plastic bags of items on top as a summer breeze toyed with the bags on top. The Chestertons, not on the boat for more than five minutes harped about the lack of comfort on the boat compared to the stately yachts that they were more accustomed.

"Ted, I was under the impression that your boat was the biggest in the marina," Woody induced surveying the marina. Minnis and Tavia struggled with the bulkiness of carrying the coolers onto the deck of the boat. The burden of the task went unnoticed by the Chestertons. Hearing his claim and not wanting to seem rude, Minnis dropped the coolers and exhaled.

"Well, Woody, if you look around the marina, it is bigger than most of the boats here."

And Ted's assertion was true for about the next ten minutes until a small yacht *All In* entered the harbor. Its owner, Richard Willard Evergreen, Esquire was a renowned New York corporate lawyer whose law firm represented half the advertising firms on Madison Avenue. This particular Fourth of July he ventured to one of his homes on the East Coast (one of them in Seaside, Maryland) to be feted by the Seaside Chamber of Commerce for his support of local businesses (a tax shelter loophole). His presence in town caused the local aristocrats to swallow their boasts of wealth as the ostentatious craft steamed down the main channel. It was a very humbling and emasculating for those of local fortune and they tried in vain to ignore its impressive chug through the main channel but it was trying to deflect attention from a charging rogue elephant hell-bent on spearing an abusive trainer with its tusks.

"Now *that's* a big boat!" declared Myra Chesterton, her balance shifting from side to side as she stood on the bow of *The Rough Rider*. In her uncomplicated and transparent mind, she was wondering why she was standing on the bow of Minnis's boat and not luxuriating on the bow of the *All In*. Her frail anorexic like figure swayed perilously in the breeze.

She was top heavy, but not because of her chest measurement which was hardly an issue, but due to the weight of excessive make-up that was built up on her face over the years. The heads on Mount Rushmore weighed less and required less maintenance! It would take a pressure hose to remove the yearly coatings of paint administered to Mrs. Chesterton's face and would require several appointments with a sand blasting contractor. The last time a job of this magnitude was attempted was with the restoration of the *USS Missouri* to remove years of neglected rusted steel which had accumulated in dry dock. Octavia prayed silently for a sudden gust of wind to sweep this witch off the deck and into the depths of the murky marina water ultimately providing an eco-friendly reef for underwater marine life.

"Well, Ted. Do you *still* believe you own the biggest boat in the marina?" Woody smirked smugly.

"No. But I believe that on this boat today, he can certainly claim he has two of the world's biggest as..." Octavia's words were cut short by Ted who anticipated what was coming next as Octavia defended her friend.

"Hey! How about a drink Woody and Myra?" Ted asked snipping the sparkling fuse of Tavia's ticking time bomb and giving her an admonishing look.

As expected Myra desired a glass of wine, a glass of Chateau Lafitte Rothschild and Woody's selection was a lot *less* demanding, Macallen Blue Label Scotch. Ted now was contemplating ditching these snobs at sea, but they were instrumental in a real estate deal for property that Ted treasured on Saint Johns in the US Virgin Islands, so he had to grin and bear these clowns for at least five more hours. And Octavia would need constant reminding to control her thoughts and actions; a difficult task, considering her obvious and immediate dislike of the Chestertons.

"Folks! I regret that I only have Jim Beam, Chivas Regal and Chardonnay to offer you. My bar below is not that well stocked. I mean it's not actually the *QEII,*" Ted explained weakly.

Myra looked at her aloha shirt-wearing husband for an appropriate snide comment. She would allow him to remark first and follow his lead to further aggravate the situation. Nothing for these two was above reproach. Everyone was fair game for their utter frankness, and they enjoyed this torture tremendously. This ploy was better than frustrating their servants at home. They loved to induce stress. Ted's hospitable offerings were likened to serving a bucket of Kentucky Fried Chicken to the Sultan of Brunei. Now Woody was ready to begin the game, and besides, Myra wanted to be standing on the deck of the *All In* across the marina. Precious time was being wasted with Minnis and his woman.

"Chivas and some random chardonnay from some vintner who specializes in producing wine in a cardboard

box in Ohio. Really, Ted? Tell me that you're being
sophomoric!" Mr. Chesterton intimated, "You must not be
in touch with our standing. You have really
underestimated us to be satisfied with an outing of this
sort to treat us in this fashion. I am truly insulted. You
have misled us and misrepresented yourself! Either you
make amends to remedy this downward spiral in our
relationship by providing us the proper respect or we
conclude the matter closed immediately!"

"No respect. No deal! Got it?" Myra snapped. She and
Woody employed this ultimatum tactic in getting
everything by intimidation except of course a re-invitation
to a White House affair.

Minnis's pride now was at issue, and now even he was
not going to bow to the outrageous demands of the
Chestertons. He was not one of their regularly abused
valets, butlers, or maids who were contracted out to accept
this abuse.

"Do they want me to drive to a liquor store to
accommodate them?" he thought.

A dormant super-volcano began to erupt in his insides,
not seen since Mount Saint Helens. He was surely being
tested and that force inside him, was beginning to build.
His temper was now going to be unleashed as had never
been displayed before. To hell with his dream of beach
front property in the Virgin Islands! There will be another
opportunity somewhere. This was not a vital life or death
decision. His face reddened. His heart raced and then the
unexpected happened.

The sky darkened suddenly even though there were no
clouds. A passing flock of gulls unleashed their fury on the
Chestertons as if it was ordained by a sympathetic God or
the prayers by Octavia for a divine intervention. Minnis
and Octavia were spared the gull downpour of partially
digested bait fish and French fries. The Chestertons took
the brunt of the barrage and stood speechless as if shell
shocked. The deluge of dung added an abstract design on
their designer clothing as if they had purchased his and
her matching outfits from a chic clothing boutique
promoting Jackson Pollock art. The styling mousse in their
elaborate and priced coifs by *Monsieur Claude de Prattville*

prevented any absorption down to the scalp, causing the
slime to run down their faces from their silvery white hair.

The pinpoint accuracy of the impromptu bombing was
worthy of a conspiracy theory. Have the engineers at
Lockheed Martin incorporated TV-laser-guided bird
droppings in sea gulls? Did the Chestertons pose a threat
to the US government? Was this some vast left, vast right,
or both wing conspiracy? Is this the successful experiment
result they were looking for? Imagine the possibilities and
the infinite amount of sea gulls! God bless the USA! All one
had to do was look at the Chestertons who were saturated
with gull guano to appreciate a concerted effort by an
entity with justice in mind to retaliate for their
questionable investment scams targeting the elderly.
Somewhere in the confines of the National Security Council
and AARP high fives were being exchanged.

Ted and Tavia, stifling their laughter, were awe struck.
Ted could not fathom that the bird blitz had not inflicted
any noticeable impact on his boat, not one direct hit!
Maybe I should rename this tub, *The Defiance*, he mused.
It was like a nautical neutron bomb!

"We're so glad that you think this is entertaining.
Would you please get us some towels so we may clean
ourselves off?" Woody postured sternly on the bow.

"I don't think my towels are good enough for you two.
My wife bought them from J.C.Pennys," Ted countered,
"You know I was reading a book about the Civil War that
kinda reminds me of you two," Ted recalled as his guests
looked at each other for affirmation of what had just
occurred.

"I don't get the reference, Ted," a grumbling and
confused Woody returned wiping his face on his shirt.

"Well, the reference is to the First Battle of Bull Run.
Did you know that the who's who of Washington travelled
to the battle site and considered the battle a *social affair*? I
mean they even packed picnic lunches."

"I don't get your point, Ted," snapped Woody crisply
wiping the slime from dripping down his face with his hand
and smearing it on his shirt. Myra stood frozen, her hands
outstretched as the goo ran off her bony arms. She knew

that a servant had to be nearby to attend to her predicament.

"Well my point is this, Woodrow. You and your wife My-Ra are just like those pretentious snobs who turned out for the battle, but complained because the cannons were interfering with your digestion of pheasant and amontillado and then suggested to the generals to move the battle to a more *peaceful* location," he dispensed wisely, "You two couldn't even enjoy a day in paradise without mentioning the most trivial of inconveniences, like the lime twist in your Margarita lacks pulp!" Octavia hung on Ted's every word until the coup de grace when she emitted the heartiest of laughter. She grabbed Ted around his waist in proud approval.

Woody's anger mounted at Ted's heartless comments directed at himself and his wife, "Ted, if there is any perception in your shallow mind that an apology will rectify this abhorrent display, you can kiss that notion goodbye! I am not going to stand here and be berated by a lying second class hospital supply salesman! You can consider any business deal DEAD! I don't care who you're related to! And, we don't imbibe Margaritas! Come on, Myra, we are leaving!"

The Chestertons, irate from the disrespect shown by their hosts, clamored to escape *The Rough Rider* colliding with each other exiting the boat in a comical way. Ted and Tavia grinned as the snobs negotiated their way up on the pier from the boat sniping at one another to hurry. Both were determined to get to the Mercedes first without being seen by any possible acquaintance that might be passing by the marina. Their haughty image was at stake and God help them if there was any local press photographer in the area to snap a photo which was not an issue for them at galas or social functions, but a photo here could be catastrophic in their standing with the Seaside social elite circle. They could already imagine the caption in the photograph.

"Chestertons bow to *pier* pressure!"

The Chestertons retreated slowly towards the parking lot. They tried to remain dignified keeping a stiff upper lip but caught the snickers from those they passed along the way to the parking lot causing Myra to sob uncontrollably. Of all the insults the two had deflected from the lesser of society, it finally took an act of nature to deflate their massive egos. They jumped into the Mercedes in their ruined and stained wardrobe briefly comforted with the knowledge of an imminent new car purchase now that the Italian leather car seats were now soiled with seagull residue.

Woody had no sooner started the car then floored the accelerator kicking up dust and gravel in his perturbed state, leaving bystanders in hysterics as he attempted to exit the parking lot; when one of Seaside's finest, Corporal Vincenzo D'Antuano, sounded his siren as he entered the parking lot causing Mr. Chesterton to come to an abrupt halt in front of the flashing cruiser. Minnis roared laughing at the sight.

"Well, Miss Bledsoe, I am certainly dismayed at your lack of control in the presence of my business acquaintances," Ted mocked. "Is that the way you deal with your usual clientele?"

"Of course it is, Mr. Minnis. I put on a stern façade and wait until they ask me out for crabs, and if that doesn't work then I pray for a sea gull attack," she laughed.

Ted smiled benignly and prepared to sail from his slip. He instructed Tavia to cast off the mooring lines. She struggled momentarily with the ropes, but determined as she was managed to slip the loops off the mooring posts without having to ask for assistance from her beau. As *The Rough Rider* cruised down the main channel, she joined Minnis at the helm of the aft cabin, admiring his seamanship and silently noting the surroundings of the marina as they passed by boats of all shapes and sizes. *The Rough Rider* proceeded calmly to the inlet passage and then Ted opened up full throttle causing Tavia to briefly stumble backwards, catching hold of a metal bar mounted in front of her. Ted, sensing Tavia's anxiety, ensured her that their destination would be only fifteen minutes away to Miss Bledsoe's delight.

CHAPTER 3

The marina manager's office was a two story wooden structure which was in dire need of a paint job. With windows surrounding all four walls, it resembled an airport control tower from the early heyday of aviation. Old venetian blinds hung at awkward and slanted positions because nobody had the time to fool with the ancient cords which were stuck in place by rusted metal caused by sea air. Even the blinds themselves were showing years of abuse with a sickly yellow tint. The windows themselves could have used a good washing every 10 years since that was the last time anyone washed them. A window air condition unit dripped rusty running condensate down the side of the building leaving a bright red and brown streak over the faded white paint.

Jimmy Castro made his way up the creaky splintered stairway to Oscar Coleman's office picking up the welcome mat which had flown down to the bottom step. The entrance door was in stark contrast to the rest of the building. It was new, but yet to be painted. The older door was so bad that the door knob kept falling off because the wood around it could not support the weight of the door knob. Jimmy flicked his half smoked cigarette off the top step and placed the welcome mat down on the landing. Turning the door knob he smiled because of his pleasure of not going through the usual routine of pulling the door knob from its jury rigged mounting and reattaching it. If not for the constant complaints by Jimmy, the doorknob would have remained unrepaired.

Inside he was greeted by Oscar's longtime assistant, Donna D'Antuano who was in the process preparing a fresh pot of coffee. The incessant drone of the window unit drowned out the creakiness of the front door. The BTU's of the window unit, uncontrolled due to a broken thermostat, could refrigerate raw meat if one had the mind to do it. If it got too cold, Donna would turn it off to regulate the temperature.

"Good morning, Jimmy! How ya doin, hon? Want some coffee?"

"Hey, Donna you do realize it's almost four o'clock right? Morning was over four hours ago. You know what I really want?" Jimmy implied slyly.

"Jimmy, Oscar will be back soon. I don't think we have time to fool around," Donna teased. "Ohhh, you want the brownies I made for you?" she asked coyly, "And I remembered this time to leave out the walnuts."

Jimmy's face lit up. Donna knew the right way to entice Jimmy to fill in for Earl was a bribe. Jimmy loved Donna's homemade brownies. To Jimmy, anyone who provided food in recognition of his friendship stood in high regard. He would frown on those who would buy him off with a hand shake, a twenty dollar bill, and a hasty and insincere *good job*, and then turn their backs on him and walk away. Castro appreciated the companionship and conversation with those he served. He refused alcohol as a reward due to his bad past experiences and if received he would give it to his coworkers after their shift ended. Jimmy just liked to be around folks. He liked helping others in need and would even come to their houses after work to repair plumbing, electrical, roofing, or other usual home issues. He never complained or showed anger. Jimmy just wanted to provide for his fellow man and receive friendship in return along with brownies, Snapple, and in rare occasions, a prized Italian meal.

Donna was Oscar Coleman's rock. She had been Oscar's assistant for eight years and seen the ups and downs of the life of a marina manager. She wrote the book on dependability since she could be counted on in dire situations; hurricanes, tropical storms, grounded boats, wild parties, impromptu jet ski skills competitions, firearms violations including gull target practice, sandbar parties, unsponsored and sponsored wet tee shirt contests, one neighbor pumping sewage into another neighbors slip, graffiti, strip Frisbee contests, keel hauling, vandalism, sloth, envy, a man dressed as the Energizer Bunny parasailing cartoonishly into a local radio station antenna tower, and decibel deafening music that could drown out the Apocalypse. She had seen everything! But since the advent of global warming, her hopes of witnessing a glacier inching its way towards the mouth of the marina faded dramatically.

Donna was a divorcee and swore she would never remarry. She enjoyed the single life and at age forty-three was definitely set in her ways. She was gentle with gentle folks, but cross her and you would have to deal with an attorney like repartee, and when she was finished with you, you began to question your existence and if Hell hath no fury than you would rather choose Hell than confront Miss D'Antuano in full rage. She was in the process of changing her married name back to Shea and clung to her Irish-American roots. Her auburn hair and green eyes were testament to her heritage and any notion of her being Italian went out the door and down the rickety steps.

She kept herself in shape by attending a kick boxing class and posted a picture of her ex on a duct taped punching bag at home. Although she had been divorced for five years, her trim figure was a testament to her betraying Lothario of a husband, whom she loathed. The punching bag in her den would be her second in two years! Coincidentally, it was Jimmy who helped her rig the new one to the ceiling after repairing the watermelon sized hole from where the first one was hung. By the size of the hole, Donna probably sent the bag through the wall and out to sea after her ex-husband policeman cited her for speeding in excess of nine miles per hour on the highway.

"Oscar should be back soon, Jimmy. Sure you don't want any coffee?" she insisted kindly.

"Ok, Donna. Yeah, it's going to be a long night. Might as well." Jimmy agreed.

Miss D'Antuano poured the coffee into one of the Styrofoam cups next to the Mr. Coffee machine and handed it to Jimmy to his right hand, and as Jimmy extended his hand he fumbled the cup briefly, managing to grip it before it spilled.

"Sorry, Jimmy. I forgot about your han..." she caught herself and reddened with embarrassment.

"It's okay, Donna. I have it under control!" Jimmy eased the embarrassment of those who noticed his deformity when he fumbled an object in his hand.

Jimmy gripped the cup with his thumb, index finger and middle finger because that was all he had on his severely scarred right hand. He had lost his fingers in a fire aboard the *USS Oriskany* an aircraft carrier during the Viet Nam War. Jimmy Castro served as an Aviation Machinists Mate 2nd class on the "Mighty O" and he was assigned to perform maintenance on F-8E Crusaders keeping them operational throughout Operation Rolling Thunder and other sorties in 1966. The VF 194 Red Lightning Squadron was an elite and legendary flight group that dated back to the Korean War and Jimmy was proud to be a part of it. The twenty-three year old was befriended by the aviators who risked their lives on these missions and Jimmy ensured these heroes that the least of the worries would be the condition of their F-8s. And that was a necessary and prevalent team spirit among the machinists who serviced the aircraft.

The door swung open and a red-faced, out-of-wind, heavy set, sweaty, man in his late forties entered. Oscar Coleman had returned and flushed with another unusual tale about the rapidly declining human condition. To quote any meteorologist/philosopher, all things are relative to relative humidity and heat indices of plus one hundred degrees.

"You won't believe this one! I just had to referee a tug of war between two adult women over a bikini top on the pier." He gasped and paused. "Both claimed the top was theirs. But when the weaker of the two let go causing the stronger one to fall off the pier into the drink, I had to award the one in the water the top. After all, possession is nine-tenths of the... bra!"

Jimmy and Donna groaned at Oscar's way of breaking the ice with his dry humor.

"How about some coffee, Oscar?" Donna offered again hoping to empty the carafe in order not to waste her vital need for caffeine.

"Sure, Donna," Oscar said as he approached the coffee pot, "Jimmy, you ready for this holiday craziness?"

Castro shrugged his shoulders to display his lack of concern of the anticipated evening of events.

"I really appreciate you volunteering to help out, Jim. You know old Earl's heart can't stand this *bravo sierra* every year."

"Yes, Mr. Coleman. I guess I'm ready. I told Sunny that I'll be tied up here tonight to help out, so she understands. I just don't know what to expect!"

"That makes three of us, right, Donna?" Coleman winked.

"Every year is different from the year before unless there is a variation on a previously *fun* trend from last year," Donna added.

Coleman stood at the window looking out towards the main channel of the marina sipping his coffee. He was elated that the traffic in the channel was running smoothly towards the exit of the bay. It truly was the calm before the storm because in less than an hour all hell would break loose with every boat owner vying to leave the marina at the same time. To complicate the matter, the National Weather Service had issued a severe storm watch from six to eight PM. The marine manager's serenity was short lived when he spotted the *All In* cruising out into the channel.

"Just where in the hell does he think he's going?" Coleman muttered. "Donna, better get me channel six!"

Donna complied with her boss and opened channel six to contact the *All In*. Oscar stretched the microphone cord to his position at the window.

"Marina manager to the *All In* do you copy, over?" Coleman asked sternly.

"Yes, sir. What can we do for you? Over," a smug disinterested voice returned.

Coleman's voice registered anger at the rudeness of the response. "You do realize it's still low tide in the channel, right? Over."

"Yep. It's low tide alright. Over."

"And you think you're going to steam through the channel with that huge tub of yours? Over," Coleman implied to create doubt.

"Our Captain is well aware of the navigational hazards and has explicit orders from his boss to steam ahead out of the marina. High tide comes in less than an hour anyway. While I got you on the horn, Mr. Evergreen is very unhappy with the way you people have let the trash accumulate in our dock. Over."

Donna and Jimmy stood looking out the forward window watching as the *All In* continued its treacherous passage through the channel, shaking their heads in shared disbelief at the exhibited audacity of the voice on the other end of the radio. Coleman now reacted with fury at the demeaning comment from the smug radio operator.

"*All In?* You have ten minutes to turn that boat around and return to port! I have the authority to order you to do that. If you proceed you will be fined and face termination of your privileges to the marina. Do I make myself clear? Over," the marina manager instituted.

"I will advise the Captain. Over," the radio operator replied realizing the ramifications of his failure to alert the Captain.

Sensing that the warning would fall on deaf ears, Coleman instructed Jimmy to take the skiff and race out to the small yacht to convince the owner to heed his command. Coleman's main concern was obvious. If the *All In* continued out, chances were excellent that it would run aground on a sandbar in the narrows just past the drawbridge. The marina manager had been experienced with this many times before and in most cases dissuaded boats of this size to proceed. If the *All In* ran aground at this location then the remaining vessels in the marina would be blocked from their excursions out of the bay. Coleman did not want to suffer the indignity from the wrath of the marina members. He would be targeted as the responsible party and not the owner of the *All In*.

Castro jumped at Coleman's instructions. He ran out of the office sliding down the metal railing as he had done in his naval days aboard the *Oriskany*. The weather worn wooden skiff lay docked in the pier near the staircase. After throwing the mooring line onto the dock, Jimmy pulled the starter cord frantically. After his fourth yank, the motor belched out the saved exhaust from weeks of inactivity. He sped out into the channel dodging other boats ignoring the five mile an hour wake rule. It would take Castro two minutes for him to catch up to the defiant craft. Meanwhile, Coleman continued his warnings demanding to talk to the Captain.

"Captain of the *All In,* I am sending an officer of mine out to board you. If you do not stop now, I will prohibit you from returning to port, that is of course if you make it past the sandbar which the odds are heavily stacked against you. Do you read me? Over."

After a minute pause the reluctant Captain responded, "We will comply. Over."

Below deck, Richard Willard Evergreen Attorney-at-Law was holding court with his usual Evergreen adorers. As he proudly proclaimed a recent bout with a litigant over a contested settlement allotment that he won, he was distracted by the sudden lurch of his vessel. Placing his martini on a nearby helm-shaped lamp stand, he rose and excused himself politely to his audience. Hastily he scaled the stairs up to the bridge burning from the inconvenience. Jingling the change in his pants pocket he emerged on the deck, wanting to unleash his fury on the Captain.

"Mueller? Who the hell told you to stop?"

"I'm sorry Mr. Evergreen. I've been ordered to stop by the marine manager. He is threatening us with fines and a penalty of being ousted from our port if we continue out. He is sending one of his officers out to us to board us. I believe that's him pulling up alongside of us," explained Captain Mueller nervously.

Castro slowed the skiff alongside the small yacht locating a ladder which had been placed for him by one of the deckhands. He grasped the ladder as the skiff clung to the side of the white hull of the *All In*. As he pulled himself from the last rung of the ladder onto the deck, he was met by Evergreen.

"You? You are the officer who was sent by that incompetent at the marina. You have no uniform, no badge! Why am I listening to some schmuck wearing jeans and a tee shirt? You're the *authority?*" Evergreen glared.

"Sir. Your captain here stopped his engines so I don't believe my boss is that incompetent. I am only here to inform you to turn around and wait when the tide is sufficient for you to proceed. You really don't know..."

Castro's words were cut off by an enraged Evergreen. One thing you didn't tell this stalwart of corporate law, was any sentence beginning with 'you really don't know.'

"Let me tell you what *you don't know!* I am Richard Evergreen and this will prove to you who has the power to influence!" Evergreen reached into his L.L. Bean khaki slacks and produced a wad of money containing bills of high denominations. He then flipped the bills rapidly in front of Jimmy's unimpressed face. Castro was not easily intimidated and any anger he harbored towards Evergreen was not apparent.

"Okay. Mr. Evergreen. You have shown me what you are all about and now I am going to inform you that if you continue to ignore our warnings, then you will certainly find yourself aground just past the drawbridge and then you are going to be in some serious shit! You will be putting your family, guests, and crew in harm's way at the cost of your own ego. Are you going to allow that to happen?" Jimmy stated resolutely.

"Nobody talks to me that way! You are nothing to me but a small menial man! I want you the hell off my boat now! And when I return you and your boss will be looking for jobs at the amusement park. I'll find a position for which clowns like you are truly qualified. Just for the record, what's your name and your boss's name?" Evergreen peered his intimidating glare into Castro's unimpressed face.

"My name is Castro. My boss's name is Coleman. You don't scare me, Mr. Evergreen," Jimmy proudly responded.

"Well, *Fidel!* You're going to find out how much pull I have around here when I return to port. Comprendes, Senor?"

"Loud and clear, Richard! Or should I call you Dick?" sniped Castro. He could see Captain Mueller wincing from the comment at the helm silently approving of Jimmy's brass cajones. To Mueller it was refreshing to see someone challenge this Captain Quigg of a boss with a taste of his own venom.

Castro turned shaking his head in defeat knowing that Evergreen was going to steam ahead anyway. He descended the ladder to the skiff as Evergreen peered angrily over the side wanting to spit at his adversary. He decided to swallow as a crew man observed Castro from the side nearby his boss. Using his hands, Castro pushed off the side and pulled the cord for the outboard which started immediately. He could hear Evergreen berating his captain.

"Mueller! Let's get one thing straight right now! I am the *authority* everywhere I go! You're only fear is to see if you still have a job at the end of the day. When I tell you not to stop, that means you don't stop. I don't care if there's a life raft with ragged refugees on board. You don't stop!! Got It?"

"Yes, sir. Loud and clear!" mimicked the captain trying to imitate Castro's courage.

From the office, Oscar and Donna stood speechless as they witnessed Castro's return. Knowing Coleman was training binoculars on him, Castro shook his head to signal that the exchange was unsuccessful in deterring Evergreen from venturing out of the channel. The *All In* was heading for the drawbridge which was already open as if the bridge operator knew the travel plans of Evergreen's boat. The drawbridge routinely opened on an hourly basis for the bigger boats to pass during the summer months. It was now five fifteen. Funny how things worked for one Richard Evergreen! Local police, dispatched to alleviate three miles of holiday traffic which was unexpectedly backing up at the bridge, were informed of a problem with the hydraulic system that lifted the bridge. Coincidentally as the *All In* passed through the lifted portion of the bridge, the hydraulic system became operational again and lowered. There would be no more *malfunctions* like this for three more months. Amazing!

Oscar turned to Donna and sighed, "Five fifteen and the bridge opens. That son of a bitch bribed somebody! I was hoping to hold him up before the bridge until the tide came in." Coleman placed the heavy binoculars down on the window sill.

Donna braced for the inevitable announcement from her boss.

"Well, Miss D'Antuano. Contact Seaside Sea Rescue and initiate Plan Alpha for rescue and recovery of a beached white whale at the entrance of the bay. Transmit that the entrance is being blocked by a grounded vessel and that we are closing traffic immediately. Also, alert Seaside PD to have someone here to curtail any violent and disorderly conduct from our malcontents here at the marina," Coleman instructed as he slumped into a squeaky armchair, cradling his head in his hands.

"God, I love the Fourth of July!"

CHAPTER 4

Jimmy Castro's life changed forever on October 26, 1966. While serving aboard the *USS Oriskany* as an Aviation Machinist 2nd Class, Castro motivated by sheer instinct rushed into the teeth of a fiery inferno on the hangar deck. Within minutes it was out of control and was spreading to the forward compartments where his fellow crewmen trapped by the raging flames and explosions pleaded in vain for rescue. The fire took nearly three hours to extinguish, but not before it claimed the lives of forty-four crewmen, including thirty-six combat pilots. The young machinist's mate raced to the blaze and without regard for his own life with flames feet away, aided others in throwing the heat sensitive explosive ordinance off the port side of the ship, preventing the perilous situation from escalating.

Prompted by the sounds of screams from men trapped in their quarters he devoted himself to prevent the fire from spreading. He locked out all his senses and felt as though he was submerged in a swimming pool. Everything was happening in slow motion and he could not move fast enough. Instructions were being screamed at him but he could not hear. His eyes looked but did not comprehend the sight of his crew mates ablaze. He didn't have time. His hands and face burned from the intense heat, but he could not feel the pain. The odor of burning flesh, clothing and

jet propulsion fuel, he couldn't detect. The sight of his
friends some ablaze in their quarters and on the hangar
deck would haunt him the rest of his life, not to mention
the physical damage that Castro suffered. The heat from
the fire blistered the right side of his face and seared his
right hand severely. The right side of his face including his
ear was singed badly. The machinists mate was evacuated
out of Subic Bay in the Philippines and flown to Honolulu,
Hawaii.

After enduring the nine long painful months of skin
grafts and rehabilitation, Jimmy was able to leave the base
hospital. He grew fond of his therapist, a California blonde
by the name of Victoria Rhodes. She was tagged by her
coworkers as 'Sunny' due to her love of life and positive
outlook on things. Many a wounded sailor or marine
credited her with overcoming the frailty and insecurity of
recovery by her optimism. The young therapist took an
interest in Castro due to her daily commitment *project* to
fruition to regain a normal and productive life. Not only
would she administer physical therapy, but unknowingly
she connected with the injured sailor because of a shared
sense of humor. Jimmy and Sunny shared a mutual vibe
almost from the start. It started when Jimmy complained
about his pancake breakfast in the hospital cafeteria one
Sunday morning.

"These pancakes are stiff and dry!" he announced to a
fellow hospital patient seated at his table dropping his
cutlery loudly on his plate in disgust.

"Reminds me of an old boyfriend I once knew," chirped
Sunny sitting behind him at a table with three female
coworkers. The nurses exploded in laughter.

"You dated an Admiral?" Jimmy replied his words
stifled by the stiffness of scars bordering his mouth, his
face swollen from numerous skin grafts. "I'll keep my
comments about the sausage to myself, knowing it might
trigger another romantic moment from your past." The
room erupted in laughter giving those in recovery a respite
from their daily anguish.

From this moment a bond was formed. Despite his
physical appearance, Sunny adored Jimmy. Sunny hoped
that Jimmy would provide the opportunity for them to get

closer despite her routine care of him. This was the soul mate she had dreamed of meeting. Their witty repartee could break the tension of any naval social event, and they became popular attendees. Gone were the days of being hit on by aged beach bums that Sunny encountered on her surfing exploits. She now had a number one fan in Jimmy Castro.

In her green and white VW Minibus, she packed away her Hobie long board along with her beau traveling from Waikiki to the North Shore. Still recovering from his wounds, Jimmy shied away from exposure to the rough briny sea water; number one on his doctor's avoidance list. Castro sat contently on the beach observing his curvaceous bikini clad therapist weave in and out of fifteen foot waves along with the regulars who frequented the same beaches. He marveled at her expertise from his beach chair positioned under an umbrella. A transistor radio blared out Top 40 music, including befitting surf music.

Jimmy wondered if Sunny could love him as much as he felt for her. He realized his physical appearance would be repulsive in a long standing relationship. His facial scars would eventually heal to a point of normalcy once the swelling reduced on his face, but that would be years according to his plastic surgeon, and his condition would require other surgeries as well. He could grow his hair longer to cover the damaged ear and some of the scars on his face. Thanks to Sunny's vigorous therapy sessions, he regained the use of his right hand despite losing two fingers. He was able to grip things however clumsily. The surgeon had done an exceptional job of grafting to repair his burned palms. But deep in his mind, as he watched Sunny paddle her way back to the pipeline, was what he could do to announce his love for her. Sunny adored his singing along with the popular songs of the day on the radio. He knew the words to every hit song especially the song, "Sunny" by which he tenderly serenaded her.

The fear of Sunny's rejection to his proposal would be life changing. If Sunny rejected him, then how would society react to him? He could always return to Brownsville to family and friends who would be thoughtful of his condition and that became obvious with letters from home.

His family was too poor to make the trip to Hawaii, and they waited anxiously word of his return. His mother and father wrote to their son every day. They had plans for their hero.

"Was Sunny taking me along for sympathetic reasons, or would she really be interested in spending the rest of her life with me," he postulated.

The petite summer blonde caught the perfect wave. She ducked under the onslaught of the crashing wall of water which enveloped her petite frame. Jimmy stood in horror expecting that Sunny was in extreme danger of wiping out and being tossed uncontrollably beneath the ocean surface. His fear diminished as the sprite Californian emerged from under the wave top, sliding laterally along the curl securely in charge. In control, she brushed her hand along the wave interior to show off her ability for Jimmy's delight. *What a hot dog!* Jumping off her board she gave a fist punch to the sky while in hip deep water. It reminded Castro of his rodeo viewing days in Brownsville, Texas when a cowboy busted a bucking bronco. He whistled his approval. Sunny slogged through the surf, clutching her surfboard in her right hand, grinned back her achievement at Jimmy who sat in admiration not only at her fete but her figure in the orange-white bikini. As she approached her friend she yelled,

"Hey, amigo! What did you think?"

"That was worthy of Wide World of Sports, but anyone can ride *those* ripples. When are you going to surf the big ones?"

"Ripples, Jimmy? I'd like to see you try!" Sunny's words were realized as she gently laid her surfboard alongside of Jimmy. Her face turned to sadness as she grabbed for a towel out of a beach bag noticing her man's frail condition.

"Sorry, Jim. I didn't mean that."

"Well, maybe one day," he said to comfort her slip. "Then I will get to teach you how to ride bulls."

Jimmy stood and helped his girl dry off her back. She turned and looked at her friend, her blue eyes tearing up. She looked up at him with a caring face and then hugged him.

"I love you, Jimmy. You know I would never say anything to harm you."

"I love you too, surfer girl. You're the hope I need to survive in this world! You can see through the bandages and see what I am inside."

From then on, it was true love. Jimmy found employment through a connection at one of the Naval parties that Sunny and he attended. The host of the party owned a shipyard in Honolulu. An ex-naval vet of the Korean War, Captain Nick Mazursky, or Captain Nick as he was known, took to liking Jimmy and assigned him to perform maintenance and some light mechanical duties with the knowledge that, if his handicap improved, he could earn more working on heavier tasks. Jimmy took classes at a nearby junior college to advance his knowledge in the electrician and plumbing trades. He grew fond of his work and soon accumulated enough money from both his work income and his disability income to purchase an engagement ring for Sunny.

CHAPTER 5

Ted Minnis and Tavia found the ideal spot. Anticipating the mob from previous years, Ted navigated to a point one mile off the shore to avoid contact with other boats, but still this was not a guarantee. It was like parking a brand new car in a remote space in a vast parking lot. Some dumb ass would eventually park in the adjoining space, even though there were numerous spaces closer to the entrance of the lot. There must be some scientific and psychological study to explain this phenomenon. Ted dropped anchor and stopped his engine. Tavia enjoyed the view and serenity of their location until Ted turned on his stereo which was tuned to a local oldies station playing "The Wreck of the Edmund Fitzgerald." Minnis emerged from the cabin clutching a Chivas on the rocks and wine glass containing the once dismissive Chardonnay. "Sorry, it's not Lafitte for the elite," Ted lamented.

"Well, you better do something to satisfy me or I'm going to hop on the first yacht that happens by, Ted," Octavia replied mimicking Myra Chesterton.

"Satisfy you? That will be later, my dear. There will be at least two episodes of fireworks tonight," Minnis forecasted confidently.

"Well then, baby, I better hold out until then," Octavia cooed. "I'll be looking forward to the Grand Finale!"

"How about some dinner, Taves?" Minnis offered in a host like manner.

"Sure, baby. I'm starved. Do you think we're safe out here? I mean the sky is getting dark," Tavia wondered craning her neck to the south.

"We'll be fine. I've seen these summer storms before. They're over in fifteen minutes and go on up the coast. No need to worry, Taves. And besides it's only a watch and not a warning," Ted assured his concerned date while attending to the food cooler preparing a plate of steamed shrimp, fried chicken, and potato salad. They both sat on the bench seat on the aft end of Ted's boat enjoying their meal as the breeze picked up. Tavia commented on how impressed she was with the gourmet touch to the simple dishes.

The small grocery store where Ted had purchased the food had on staff a gourmet prodigy who delighted in hearing praises from his appreciative patrons. The grocery store, a simple mom and pop operation, relied on the cook's talents to bring in business, and the store became popular among the locals with the cook's Southern type infusion in his dishes. It became a sleeper hit with its customers. Rich and poor, black and white, Asian, Arab, and Jew alike were drawn to the store for the tasty cuisine. The variety of the store's clients resulted in a utopian ideal image where social barriers crumbled and mankind reveled on top of the debris in unison proclaiming kindness and good will to each other as they awaited their meal order. There was a weak effort to have the cook nominated for a Nobel Peace Prize for bringing the world together briefly in the confines of the grocery store, but the humbled cook declined any heartfelt sentiment.

After a commercial break which included the usual overplayed inane jingles advertising resort bars, restaurants, pizza places, liquor stores, night clubs, candy shops, and beach apparel, the station returned to its play list beginning with the Dee Jay announcing the next tune, "Atlantis." Suddenly, Ted looked back towards the marina in wonder. There hadn't been any boats leaving the marina since he dropped anchor nearly an hour ago. There were, however, boats that had anchored prior to his arrival, but he knew something was wrong. By this time 5:30, as from past experiences, the marina should be emptying en masse and vying for that perfect vantage point. Although he couldn't view the marina since it was located about two miles away, and there were two left turns one had to negotiate around the south end of the barrier island, Ted stood rocking on the aft confused. Maybe it was the storm watch which was affecting his fellow marina mates from venturing out to the now choppy, wind-swept waters of the Atlantic. Moments after, Ted's concerns were realized by a stern directive announced over his radio.

"The National Weather Service has issued a severe thunderstorm warning for points North of Assateague Island to Lewes, Delaware from six pm to eight pm tonight. The storm is moving twenty miles per hour with wind speeds of up to 40 miles per hour. A small craft warning is in effect for these areas and residents are urged to take shelter immediately."

"We're going to have to ride it out here, Taves. Even if we tried driving back to the marina, we'll still encounter the brunt of the storm, and chances are we'll get swamped if the winds hit the port side when I turn into the inlet," he assured her nervously. "Better get down below, and you better put this on just in case," he commanded while handing her a life vest. Ted looked to the south as the winds whipped his hair back. An indigo blue sky was advancing his way accompanied by distant rumbles of thunder. Octavia, silent, looked as if begging for a decision from her friend. Ted turned and remained resolute as she clutched his arm. Tavia grabbed the life vest and struggled with the straps as Minnis secured any loose items on deck. Another thing she struggled with was her emotions which were now running amok with concern for the approaching storm and an anger she was harboring towards Minnis's overt nervousness on his ability to get them both through the impending tempest. The boat began to rock as the surf churned. From below, Tavia could hear Ted's frantic squeaky footsteps quicken on top administering to secure anything needing lashing down. The door to the cabin opened and closed. Minnis slipped on the stairs and caught himself on the railing.

"Well, we're as ready we're going to be! Hope you like roller coaster rides."

CHAPTER 6

As the weight of the October night squashed the sun into the horizon, the beach at Waikiki fell hushed. The waning moments of daylight had driven off the tourists and beach enthusiasts. Waikiki at night was a local domain again with chess games, lively chatter, and the drone of passing traffic. Romantic couples embraced silently on the beach admiring the beautiful Pacific sunset. A hotel employee commenced his nightly duty of lighting the numerous tiki torches. Among the admirers was an intimate party of four consisting of Victoria "Sunny" Rhodes, Jimmy Castro, Sunny's coworker Candice Middleton, and a local ukulele performer who appeared on a cue from Candice. Sunny stood confused unaware of Jimmy and Candice's plan and why a guy with a ukulele had joined their group.

Jimmy pitched his idea to Candice who in turn devised the plan. Knowing of Sunny's basic interest in astrology, Candice lured Sunny to Waikiki to witness a rare cosmic event based on Polynesian lore. The prime vantage point to witness this celestial sight with its astrological impact would be on Waikiki Beach. When Sunny inquired about the actual event, Candice informed her with double talk. "Venus is going to appear above the Moon which will mean all young women shall be fruitful and prosperous in their lives." She said it with such enthusiasm and forthrightness that Sunny fell for it. When Jimmy was approached by Sunny to confirm the legend, he simply said "Count me in! I want to be there, too! I'd love to see you and Candice full of fruit and prosperity!"

The ukulele player strummed island tunes as the trio watched the glow of the descending sun emit its last aura of orange from beyond. Flickers of flames danced on the tanned faces of the quartet. Jimmy nervously looked at Candice who stepped backwards which signaled the ukulele player to commence his rehearsed version of *This Guys In Love With You.* Jimmy dropped to his knees clasping Sunny's right hand.

"Jimmy, what the hell!"

Jimmy smiled and started to sing.

"You see this guy, this guys in love with you."

Confused and slightly embarrassed Sunny looked love with you." back at Candice who was brushing a tear from her cheek. Instantly, Sunny knew. She had been set up. Jimmy was proposing to her a la lounge lizard, but the lyrics were precisely what she wanted to hear. The ukulele player beamed benignly. Nearby, the remaining sunset admirers inched closer to the group drawn by the music and obvious proposal of marriage. A minute and a half had passed, the strumming stopped and Jimmy finished the song. Reaching into his denim shirt pocket, Jimmy pulled out a Marlboro cigarette box. Sunny perplexed. *Is he going to propose or offer me a cigarette?* Jimmy's scarred fingers fumbled briefly for the object he sought. He could sense the silent pressure of all knowing of his loss of dexterity. He cautioned himself mentally not to drop the object now that the area was dimly lit. Sunny's concerns were alleviated when a shiny ring emerged from inside the box glinting from the light of a nearby tiki torch and her beaux place it on her finger.

On the word "me" as in the phrase will you marry me, Sunny leapt and hugged Jimmy, kissing him to the appreciation of the small audience that had gathered.

"Is that a yes?" he joked. He looked at Candice whose smile betrayed her tears. "Hey, when does this Venus and Moon thing happen, now that we got this over with? I really wanna get you both fruitful!" Sunny ignored the remark choosing to relish in the elation of the special moment in any young woman's life extending her ring finger towards the distant light. Candice groaned at Jimmy and escorted Sunny to a more illuminated place to examine the ring. Giddiness ensued as Sunny and Candice shared the excitement.

The engagement would be short. Jimmy did not want to lose his love to one of the many that he would catch ogling her either at the hospital or out and about. Sunny was gorgeous inside and out. She radiated and transcended the stereotype of being just a blond which got her more respect with her peers than with her faux admirers who had one obvious thing on their minds. She was the All -American girl that shy wounded servicemen could confide their innermost feelings about the war and with life in general. In short, Sunny's role at the hospital took on an extra dimension of therapy; she listened intently and cared heartedly for her patients. Being infinitely modest, Sunny never realized the positive effect of her caring after a patient was discharged until years later when she received mail from appreciative veterans.

Soon after the engagement, Jimmy and Sunny announced their nuptials. The wedding took place at the base chapel at Pearl Harbor on December 27th. Sunny's parents Brad and Karen Rhodes flew from their home in San Mateo,California to attend while Jimmy's folks were too poor to make the trip. Captain Nick served as Jimmy's best man while Candice Middleton proudly accepted the role of maid of honor. Jimmy clad in his service blues uniform grinned as he watched his bride florally attired in a tropically appropriate dress strolling down the aisle with her proud father as a small quartet of island musicians strummed the Wedding March, projecting their island joy for the newlyweds from the side of the altar. As they started the walk down the aisle, Brad Rhodes whispered in his daughter's ear,

"It's not too late to change your mind, Vicki." Sunny nudged her father gently in the side to deflect his notion.

The Chaplain, Lt. Martin Avery USN, a regular at the base hospital as well as the chapel, stood under a crude steel crucifix, fashioned and welded from the remains of scrap iron from the attack on Pearl Harbor. It hung from a wooden beam that extended across the chapel. Lt. Avery had been at Jimmy's bedside during recuperation and had awakened Jimmy's long dormant soul; helping him to realize the inner spiritual strength he would need to garner to face the harshness of a real and cynical world regarding his physical appearance.

Sunny or Victoria as she would be addressed on this auspicious occasion would have made Queen Lili'uokalani proud of her attire this day. Her father kissed her and bade her his love as his daughter choked back the eventual tears. Mrs. Rhodes was already dabbing her eyes as they approached the altar. A gentle breeze cascaded through the chapel's open windows and doors blowing Sunny's veil and giving a cool relief to the small audience of forty on this typical eighty-two degree Hawaiian day.

A photographer contracted by the Rhodes roamed stealthily to the left side of the altar with instructions not to photograph the couple from the right side; a point conferred and approved by Jimmy. His mind drifted as Lt. Avery attended to the usual religious formalities of citing scripture and sermonizing. The reality of responsibility suddenly jabbed the groom in the gut. *How can I provide? Am I capable of being productive? I know I can't work at the shipyard forever. What does the future hold for me? Where will I be in two years?* His eyes darted about wildly focusing on the twisted and gnarled welded cross above his head. Sunny grabbed his hand again giving him comfort as if she knew the turmoil that was raging in his mind. He gulped and heard a faint scream deep in his mind.

Smoke billowed and he choked from the embers from a raging hell. An explosion rocked him to his knees. Blinded by the rapidly thickening smoke he swatted the clouds to find his way. His hand was on fire. When he came to a clearing, he felt the ocean breeze on his left; and on his right an intense blistering heat concentrating on his hands and face. He spotted an object, a Crusader engulfed in fire and then several crewmen ablaze. Aviators in their trapped quarters screamed for someone to extricate them. No, no this isn't happening! Not now! His thoughts were interrupted by a nudge on his right. It was Captain Nick deflecting his voice sideways.

"You okay? You're trembling".

"Yeah," Jimmy turned to see the audience for assurance of his whereabouts. *Yes, I'm on the altar getting married. I'm in Hawaii.* He gasped reassuring himself. Sunny beamed brightly. The chaplain instructed the couple to announce their vows. One helluva time for a flashback, he thought. Hopefully that won't crop up again! His episode over, he shook off the horror and returned his attention to his beautiful bride and the ceremony at hand. Beads of sweat formed on his brow. After being pronounced man and wife, the newlyweds embraced and kissed. The guests stood and applauded; Mrs. Rhodes still dabbing her eyes. Turning towards the appreciative audience, Lt Avery introduced the couple.

"Ladies and gentlemen, I present for the first time, Mr. and Mrs. Jimmy Castro. May God bless their holy union!"

CHAPTER 7

t took the *All In* exactly ten minutes to send out the
expected Mayday. Oscar Coleman and Jimmy Castro
monitored the transmission while Donna attempted
contacting the Seaside Police Department to arrange
extra security for the marina. The marina boat owners
were informed of the situation only moments before
the *All In* declared its emergency to the obvious
dismay of everyone with plans to venture out into the
Atlantic for tonight's fireworks display. The channel in and
out of the marina was closed indefinitely. In the distance,
the huge bullhorn like siren reminiscent of Civil Defense
Air Raid warnings blared. Emergency vehicles raced to the
scene of the accident located about a half a mile from the
U. S. Coast Guard Station in Seaside. Despite its proximity
to the grounding, The Coast Guard policy considered
matters like this as a municipal event and would not get
involved. Seaside did have contracts with commercial and
private boat owners to aid in rescue operations along with
a small flotilla of municipal craft. The emergency rooms at
local hospitals were put on alert also. Donna and Oscar
monitored the transmissions at the scene between a
Seaside patrolman and his dispatcher.

"Dispatch? This is unit 2-1-2. I'm on the scene. There is
yacht, grounded about a mile from shore and listing about
twenty degrees to the port side. I see about fifteen to

twenty crew and passengers on deck. No effort yet for
evacuation. Over."

"2-1-2, 2-1-2, any emergency water craft on sight?
Over."

"Negative. Over."

"2-1-2, what's your twenty? Over."

"Parking lot at Municipal Maintenance. Over."

"2-1-2, is yacht in danger of capsizing rapidly? Over."

"Negative. Right now it's just stuck and listing towards
the sandbar in middle of mouth of Bay. I suggest any
rescue attempt to use sandbar as base of operations to
retrieve occupants of yacht. Over."

"We'll consider that. Thank you 2-1-2. Stand by for
further contact. Over."

Oscar Coleman felt helpless as he sat and monitored
the transmission. What else could go wrong today, he
wondered, and then the fax machine went crazy. Donna
wheeled her way across the room in her ancient squeaky
office chair and glanced at the copy.

"Boss?"

"Let me guess, Donna. The Weather Service has
upgraded the watch to a warning."

Donna looked resigned towards Oscar as to share in his
despair. "Yes."

"Well, I hope they can get everyone off that tub, before
the storm hits," Castro offered. "Give me a radio, and I'll
take the skiff out there, Oscar."

Coleman, still thinking of options to aid in the rescue,
didn't hear Jimmy's request. He put his head in his hands
and stooped as if the pressure was all on him.

"Oscar, we did everything by the book to warn this ass
of what was going to happen. You shouldn't feel bad.
Nobody is going to blame you! Let me take the skiff now,
and I will keep you informed. Come on, Oscar!" Jimmy
pleaded loudly.

"Alright, Jimmy. I didn't want to use this way to put
your safety in jeopardy. Be careful, and don't do anything
stupid like risking your ass for some millionaire who will
end up suing you because you tracked mud on his teak
deck, and besides I don't want to have to face Sunny with
bad news," Castro's boss advised sentimentally.

"Don't worry, Oscar. I'll be okay. I've seen worse before," showing him his deformed hand and winking.

Oscar and Donna watched as Jimmy maneuvered the skiff down the main channel of the marina towards a darkening sky. The radio cackled non-stop with emergency vehicles reporting procedures and preparations at the scene. There was a commotion below Oscar's office and somebody was racing up the rickety steps. Hopefully Oscar thought it would be something less threatening like a bra tug of war.

CHAPTER 8

The wedding over, Jimmy and Sunny turned their attention to their honeymoon. Living in Hawaii presented a major quandary. When you live in paradise, where do you go for a honeymoon? Of course the natural inclination would be to explore and experience an exotic new land which would offer a lifetime of memories for a couple to reflect back on as the years of harmony grow. That is why Jimmy and Sunny chose Brownsville, Texas. It was time for Jimmy to introduce his bride to his folks.

Yes, Brownsville, Texas! Sunny wasn't sold on the idea at first until her husband mentioned that she could go surfing there on South Padre Island, a mere 40 minute drive from his home. Prior to the wedding, the couple agreed to flying to Brownsville in mid June when the air and water temperatures were suitable for Sunny in the Gulf of Mexico. In the meantime, they would have to "rough it" in Honolulu. Jimmy moved into Sunny's apartment, and life proceeded as usual with Jimmy working during the day and attending trade school at night and Sunny employed at the base hospital and surfing whenever she could get a break. Jimmy's disability pay coupled with his salary at the boatyard matched Sunny's pay from the hospital. The two saved to prepare for the eventual addition to the family. But, life was not all that grand. Jimmy was not sleeping.

The episodes occurred around two a.m. Once again, Jimmy experienced the on-going hell of his naval experience on board the *Oriskany*. Writhing side to side in bed, the violent shaking, his moans which amplified to an awakening scream of terror, his body soaked in sweat, catapulted him from the comfort of their bed, gasping for fresh air at the nearby open window. Sunny, too, of course was affected. She recognized Post Traumatic Stress Syndrome first hand at the hospital. Her husband needed immediate help. She had seen these incidents before at the hospital but was not prepared to have it be exhibited nightly in their home. The situation was nearly identical almost every night with Jimmy apologizing to his loyal and understanding wife who realized the importance of their wedding vows; *for better or for worse, and in sickness and in health.* He would go to the window and take deep breaths, heaving in the moist coolness of the Oahu night for about fifteen minutes. Now wide awake, he shuffled to the bathroom splashing his face with cold water to extinguish both the fire on his face and hands and most important in his mind.

He walked out into the kitchen grabbing a quart of Cuervo Gold from atop of the refrigerator, pouring three fingers high in a juice glass, then collapsing into the comfort of a wicker chair in the living room and switching on a dimly lit table lamp and the yellowing plastic Zenith radio. A pack of Lucky Strikes awaited his nightly visit on the table. He lit his first cigarette to the low volume tune of The New Colony Six's, *"Things I'd Like To Say,"* gazing at a framed autographed poster of Duke Kahanamoku which hung on the opposite wall. It was Sunny's prized possession. *Sunny, Best Wishes, Duke,* the legendary surfer endorsed. Under the poster stood an ugly mismatched bit of wooden furniture which served as a stand for family pictures. Jimmy focused on his mom and dad's photo. Rosa and Gilberto Castro were posed proudly looking to their left; their hard lives on display for the world. Though appearing grim, Rosa's petite left hand clasps her husband's right hand draped on her shoulder, a brief glimpse of truce in a once tumultuous marriage. Gilberto might have arranged the pose with the photographer so he could demonstrate his machismo; accrued from his rodeo experiences. An obtrusive six inch scar of heavy sutures laces the left side of his jaw; a wound incurred when a bar regular in Prescott, Arizona made a comment about drinking with Mexicans. The man attacked Gilberto with a broken beer bottle and slicing him just under his jaw just missing his jugular vein after Gilberto cooly responded with a one finger salute. This was the pinnacle of Gilberto's rodeo days for the wound nearly killed him. Gilberto's drinking, carousing, and lack of parenting had led to heated exchanges with his wife while young Jimmy cowered in the crowded confines of a staircase storage area in the basement. Jimmy tensed at the image.

As the announcer on the radio broadcast the time of 4:00, Jimmy took the remaining swig from his juice glass and returned to the bedroom, only to be awakened by the annoying shrill ring of Sunny's alarm clock at 7.

Jimmy never gave the details of his nightmares to Sunny; only to say they were related to the accident. Out of consideration for Sunny, he slept on the sofa in the living room granting her a peaceful night's sleep which would be his routine until the dreams ceased which they didn't. Finally noticing the strain on their marriage, Jimmy admitted that he needed help. With Sunny's connections at the hospital, an appointment was scheduled within two days with a naval psychologist.

Captain Nick granted the time off for his employee to receive treatment. He too had seen a change in Jimmy's attitude. Rudeness, lethargic behavior, and negative production began to wear on Captain Nick. His concern now turned sour towards his prized employee to the point of termination. There has to be a reason for this sudden change in character he surmised. He would plan to stop by the Castros after he closed up shop to talk to Sunny, knowing Jimmy was at school. As he walked up to the building, Sunny noticed him from the balcony.

"Hi, Captain Nick. What brings you here?" she cheerfully inquired.

"Sunny, I need to talk to you about Jimmy. Can I come up?" Hesitantly Sunny gave her approval knowing that Jimmy's condition was probably affecting his work. She waved him up and proceeded to the door to let Captain Nick inside. Her smile turned to anguish as she expected bad news from his employer. Captain Nick reached the second floor landing as Sunny greeted him ushering him inside the apartment. His face showed the concern she was expecting. This would not be a pleasant drop by to just to say hello.

"You both have a nice place here. Mind if I sit?" Captain Nick scanned the room to look for anything that would explain Jimmy's sudden personality change. Sunny offered a seat at the dining room table.

"Sunshine, (Captain Nick's formal address to Sunny) what's happening with Jimmy? Are you two having trouble?"

"Nick, we're having trouble, but not the kind you think. Jimmy can't sleep at night. He's reliving his accident at sea every night. It's horrible. He wakes up trembling and sweating. Sometimes he screams. He never told me what happened, but I can tell it was traumatic," Sunny openly admitted.

Nick recalled the scene at the altar when Jimmy seemed removed from the wedding and was trembling. "Sunny, is he getting help?"

"I have him scheduled to meet with a psychologist at Pearl on Thursday. It will be his first appointment. I guess he forgot to tell you. Did he do anything bad?" she asked cringing.

"Nothing harmful or bad. It's not the Jimmy I know. But, I've seen this before with returning vets. War doesn't end for a lot of these guys. Like Jimmy, I was also stationed on a flat top, *the Essex* which *The Oriskany* is modeled after. Fortunately I didn't experience anything that Jimmy faced!" he segued realizing the matter was being addressed and glancing at his watch, "Well, listen, Vicki, I'm glad our boy is getting help and I will give him the time off he needs to recuperate. When he gets better, have him stop by."

"*Stop by?* Does that mean he won't be working for you *now?*" Sunny posited confused.

"Yes, Sunny," Captain Nick stood, "Look, I can't have a guy walking around in a fog. It's dangerous at the yard especially when I am training him to weld. When he gets better then I will rehire him. I'm sorry. Have him call me tomorrow, and I will tell him."

"Captain Nick. Jimmy owes you a lot. He considers you a friend and knowing him, he will understand your decision. We will always be in your debt," Sunny affirmed grasping Nick's tattooed hairy arm.

"Are you two going to be okay financially?"

"We'll be fine." Sunny smiled confidently as Captain Nick proceeded down the stairs. She closed the door and wondered how Jimmy would handle the news. The ring of the phone broke her concentration. It was Candice Middleton.

"Sunny! I'm leaving," she gleefully announced. Sunny could not understand how somebody who was leaving Hawaii could exhibit such joy.

"I'm going back East. My application got accepted at Democratic National Headquarters in DC. I'm going to be working for the Humphrey-Muskie campaign! I can't believe it!"

"That's great, Candice! I'm happy for you. How did this happen? I didn't know you were into politics," Sunny asked trying to seem interested after hearing Captain Nick's bad news.

"Well, my dad has connections with Senator Muskie, you know, me being from Maine and all. He asked me if I would be interested. Little did I know that he was serious. So, I sent the application in. So now, he calls me and tells me that I've been hired. I'm so excited! I'll be backing the NEXT President of the United States! Just think of the opportunities and powerful people I will be meeting!"

"If Jimmy was here, I'm sure he would like you to send his *regards* to LBJ. After all he was drafted on LBJ's watch."

"I hate to be short with you, Sunny, but I got to call everyone else! I had to tell you first! I'm so excited! I'll see you tomorrow at work. Bye!"

"Bye, Candice. Congratulations!" Sunny was sure her friend did not hear the last word she uttered and wrote it off due to Candice's excited state. Her best friend and confidant would be leaving. Now, it was just Jimmy, her job, and her surfboard that would remain in Honolulu.

CHAPTER 9

The winds from the tempest roared across the ocean surface reminiscent of on Oklahoma dust storm from newsreels of the 1930s except on water. The first gust nearly raised the stern of *The Rough Rider* pitching Ted and Tavia to collide with the wall divider in front. Several objects scattered and fell onto the cabin floor. Tavia gathered herself and raced to look out the porthole. The sky now appeared dark gray and green. Rains were driven horizontally strafing the craft as if being riddled with small caliber ammunition from an angry God. The gale howled hauntingly non-stop. To both of the occupants, a silent mutual fear gripped them to the point of paralysis. Neither would admit their fret wrought feelings. There was no time. The winds and waves twisted the boat tugging at the iron chain entrusted with anchoring the boat. Again the frequent motion from the wrath of the storm sent Minnis and his mate to bounce and ricochet off the inner walls of the boat. Above the persistent howl of the storm, shrilled high pitched voices pierced the cabin walls of *The Rough Rider.*

Ted peered out the nearest porthole in the direction of the horizon trying to pinpoint the direction from where the voices originated. Tavia looked through a porthole nearest to her. Through the wind churned waves and rain drenched porthole, Ted noticed a bobbing out of control boat steaming towards *The Rough Rider*. It appeared to be the same size as Ted's boat but darker and ominous as it smashed through waves on a collision course with Minnis's craft. There were no visible lights emanating from the encroaching vessel. All he could make out was a silhouette. His concern heightened, Ted reached for his life jacket and retrieved a flare gun and an air horn from a locked box inside the cabin. Tavia frozen in fear and praying aloud to Saint Anthony to deliver her safely from thunder, lightning ,and storms, watched Minnis struggle with his life jacket as he instructed her to remain in the cabin with the radio and monitor distress calls from the nearby boat.

"Ted. Don't leave!" Tavia pleaded in terror. "I don't know what to do if something happens to you." Her plea was interrupted by the sound of children crying hysterically in the distance.

"DADDY! DADDY!! SOMEBODY HELP! HELP US, PLEASE!"

Minnis dashed up the steps, placing the flare gun in his belt and air horn in his jacket, he knew he would have to force the cabin door open due to the strength of the wind on the outside. With all his effort driven by the concerns for the safety of his boat and the now persistent cries of the children on the other boat, Minnis managed to force the door open on his first attempt. The cabin door slammed shut after he emerged on deck. Fumbling on deck with the flare gun and air horn and trying to maintain balance from the violent rocking of the boat ,Ted now added frustration to his ever escalating list of concerns as the air horn dropped from his life jacket and was lost on the deck awash with sea water. He cursed aloud as he fell back towards the cabin entrance while holding the flare gun. He was immediately consumed in the surge of sea that cascaded onto the deck. Once righted, he held his right hand up and fired the flare at once. The flare soared dramatically above him but a gust drove the flare north of his position, piercing a cloud and falling insignificantly into an engulfing wave.

The nearby boat now was fifty feet from collision. Ted would have to pull anchor, but he knew this would be fruitless using the motorized winch in this storm and time would be an issue since the distressed craft would be crashing into his boat at any moment. In vain, he tugged the chain holding the anchor, but was sent reeling by the constant ocean onslaught. As if Providence had interceded, the air horn washed up to his crotch as he lay on deck gripping a handrail, exhausted. He grabbed the air horn, blasting the warning in a staccato series of randomness as if it were an improvised Morse code intelligible to all. Meanwhile below, Tavia was comforted that the sound of the horn meant Ted was still on board hopefully not signaling her on deck.

The shrieks and cries continued from the distressed boat. It now became apparent that there was a woman and at least two children on board, but not one of a father or an adult male. And then another sound unlike any one would hear in the middle of a storm like this, a yelping dog obviously in some distress. A tired and weak Ted, pulled his way to the side of the ship, clutching any hand holds he could find to navigate his way and prevent him from falling into the sea. Staggering from the violent way *The Rough Rider* was being tossed about, Ted finally arrived to the rail closest to the sound of the whining hound. His eyes squinting from the sting of the sea spray and rain scanned the churning stormy sea. Although the poor animal could be heard nearby, he was unable to pinpoint the exact location as the dog's pleas faded into the rapid pull of the tumultuous tide and the undulating waves. There would be no way to rescue the poor animal due to the distance and incredible quickness of the ocean current.

And then a voice, the male voice he was hoping to hear earlier, echoed from the darkness, his tone punctuated by the intermittent gulping of sea water. It was a surrendering sentiment he valiantly tried to convey to his loved ones; his final words before the inevitable force of the ocean dragged him below the surface.

"I can't make it! I will always love you!"

Ted could hear this man's final farewell, but doubted those on the nearby boat could not have heard him over the fury of the storm. He scanned the ocean for the man as he watched the distressed boat stop abruptly nearly ten

feet from *The Rough Rider*. Ted, despite the impending
collision, put his hands to his mouth in the manner of a
megaphone and cried out to the father, "SWIM IN THE
DIRECTION OF MY VOICE!"

Ted pulled the air horn from his life jacket. This time he
had made sure it would not fall out of his belt, so he
jammed it further inside his jacket to inside his shirt. He
blasted the horn continually hoping for a response from
the father or those on the boat nearby. He grabbed the life
preserver which hung near the cabin door, holding it in
case the father appeared in Ted's throwing range. All that
was heard in the next moments was the desperate and
mournful wailing of a mother and her children; nothing
from the sea. *At least I can save them*, Ted thought. The
winds curtailed from the initial intensity and the rains now
were steady but not blinding as they were before. The
storm was proceeding north and out of the area but the sea
was still churning from the storms wake.

"HELLO.... I WILL COME TO YOU!" HOLD ON! HELP IS
ON THE WAY!!! STAY PUT!"

Tavia struggled with the cabin door. Her weak frame
pushed hard against the wind closed door but now she was
motivated by an inner drive. After spending the last
twenty-five minutes being thrown from side to side in a hot
and humid boat cabin which was continually rocking back
and forth, Miss Bledsoe could no longer withstand her urge
to expel her lunch. No sooner had she exited the cabin, she
grabbed hold of the handrail, and vomited what she would
later declare as "everything I have ever eaten in my 26
years on Earth." Minnis approached her and steadied her
as she convulsed, patting and rubbing her back, gently
consoling her.

"Tavia, are you ok? I need you to help me!"

"What can I do, Ted?" she said choking back.

"Tavia, there is a boat over here with a family in
distress." He pointed to the other side of *The Rough Rider*.
"I'm going to need you do some things so we can rescue
them. It's urgent. We need to do this, now!" Ted directed
her as he toggled the winch switch hoisting the anchor.
Tavia, suffering a headache to accompany her stomach
woes managed to turn her attention to the dark shadow of

a boat where loud mournful cries could be heard about ten feet away. The boat rocked as Minnis started the engine thus drowning out the desperate wailing from the nearby boat. The breeze was refreshing to Tavia and coupled with the beads of perspiration provided a cooling effect, lessening her seasickness momentarily. With the anchor free from the sea floor and the engine roaring, Ted turned *"The Rough Rider"* towards the stranded boat. After seconds, he arrived along the side of the distressed boat.

"HELLO? HELLO? I'M HERE TO HELP YOU! DO NOT BE AFRAID! I'M COMING ABOARD YOUR BOAT!" Ted figured that the mother with her children went down below and huddled safely until they knew Minnis was to be trusted. This, he thought would explain the sudden silence on the unlit boat. Ted turned to Tavia to instruct her on how to keep his boat steady while he went aboard the other boat. The two boats already were trading paint as they were tossed into each other by the violent waves. Tying a rope to a centrally located spot on his boat, Ted leapt up to the deck of the neighboring boat with the other end of the rope and secured it to a handrail. Ted inspected the craft for any possible damage. He could always tow the boat back to the marina with the surviving family members on *The Rough Rider*. He continued his inspection on deck. First, he checked out the stern and noticed nothing unusual. The sky began to lighten from the passing storm and the rain had all but stopped. As he passed the cabin to inspect the front of the boat, he noticed the name of the boat on a faux wooden life preserver near the cabin door. The name of this boat was *Donovan's Pride*. The life preserver painted in the colors of the Irish flag indicated that the boat hailed from Seaside, MD. Minnis knocked on the vinyl cabin door and got no response. He was surprised that the door opened when he turned the knob.

"Hello? Anyone here? I'm Ted Minnis. I'm here to rescue you," Minnis slowly and cautiously descended down the steps to the cabin below; his right hand searching for a light switch. "Hello?"

A sudden jolt and thumping noise from the jostling of the two boats caught Ted's attention and now he was getting angry.

"Look, I am here to help you! Don't be afraid! If you don't come out now, I am going to leave. I don't think you want that after all you've been through," Ted announced as he scanned the room. Now the sun finally broke through just as it was setting and Minnis walked through an illuminated cabin, opening bedroom and closet doors, looking under beds, inspecting the engine space on deck, checking the bathroom, the door swinging freely. *There is nobody here! Where the hell did they all go?* Minnis mumbled as an overwhelming eerie sense pervading his entire body. The feeling of dread followed him up the steps to the deck. With each step he took into the darkness, he felt an imposing presence that would reach out and gouge out his soul. While inspecting the deck of the bow, he abruptly stopped at a stirring image which culminated his escalating dread. The anchor had never been dropped! *How can this boat be so still and not drifting with the tide?* He peered into the surrounding waters to see if the family had abandoned ship. *Nothing!* Another jolt from the choppy seas reminded Ted of the damage his boat was incurring from his make-shift mooring. Untying the rope aboard the *Donovan's Pride* he jumped in terror back on the deck of his own boat in a panic scurrying around the damp teak deck trying to formulate a plan with his mind jarred by his recent bout with a foe of fearsome repute, the unknown.

He quickly pushed away from the aqua marine hull of the *Donovan's Pride* with the aid of a pole. As the two boats separated, he noticed a white streak of the paint from *The Rough Rider* running lengthwise along the hull of the ghost ship. He immediately bent over the railing and inspected his hull. Smatterings of aqua marine paint scraped the hull along with dents and scratches; a reminder of the jostling between the two boats. Tavia held the wheel steady while choking back gags.

"I'll take it, Taves," Minnis commanded as he restarted the motor.

"Where are they, the people we heard on the boat? What happened?" Tavia cried.

"Tavia, there is nobody on that boat. They probably jumped in to save their father. I'll contact the Coast Guard and have them look into it. We got to get out of here! I plotted their position," Minnis stated crisply shifting his attention to driving the boat away from the haunted scene. Tavia once confident in her mate's seamanship now saw cracks in his venerable façade. Minnis's eyes darted wildly in every direction trying to rely on his manual skills alone to no avail as he shifted the controls on the helm without noticing the harm he could be doing to the motor. Motivated by ultimate fear, he wanted to escape the scene of the ghost ship as soon as possible.

Tavia, free from the helm, walked to the side of the boat where moments before the two boats hugged side to side. She was on the verge of another bout with seasickness when she screamed in horror.

"OH MY, GOD!! IT'S GONE!! THE BOAT'S GONE!!! TED!!! TED!!!

Minnis shifted into neutral and stood next to Tavia both swaying from the force of the choppy water. It was true. There was no way the boat could sink in less than the two minutes that Ted had exited. *Donovan's Pride* had disappeared, unbeknownst to the two... once again. Incredulous of what they had witnessed, they stood in shock trying silently to compose a logical reason as to the sudden disappearance of the *Donovan's Pride*. Both scanned the surroundings as if maybe a distant shadow of a boat on the horizon would give them closure in their search. Physics and logic would cement their belief that the boat just simply vanished from some unearthly force. There was no evidence of any flotsam one would see after a sinking or a wreck at sea. An eeriness as thick as the recent storm clouds now hung over Tavia and Ted. The setting sun in his face, Ted turned to Tavia and asked,

"How do I report this to the Coast Guard?"

"You have to do it, Ted. I'll stand by you. I saw it too, remember?" Tavia pleaded grabbing her mate's arm to stress her willingness. "That family is out there!"

"OK. I better get you back home. Any paler and you'll have to change your race on your driver's license. If you can hold out, I'll stop by the Coast Guard Station on the way in. I'll note the coordinates."

Tavia nodded as another wave rocked the boat triggering another urge to vomit. Minnis returned to the helm and turned the rocking boat back towards the marina. There would be no fireworks for the two tonight. As the sun waned in the west, the full moon emerged on the horizon in the east...a full red moon. The two remained silent on the return trek back to the marina. Both were trying to comprehend the trauma they had just witnessed.

For the first time since his early teens, concern swept over Minnis like a tsunami. He was badly shaken to the point of temporary forgetfulness of his directional skills back to the marina. If not for Tavia's reminder, *The Rough Rider* would have missed the turn towards the marina and continued in a southerly direction. Ted was obviously affected; a light was switched on inside of his dark and cold indifferent persona. A battle was being waged in his dormant conscious with Ted stranded in limbo as forces collided in his gut. He was exhibiting concern, an emotion he had rarely experienced.

CHAPTER 10

By now, the cramped Marina Manager's office grew even smaller as Oscar Coleman and Donna D'Antuano collided with each other to address the emergency in the channel. This was no time for manners, and they both respected each other's attention to the situation non-verbally. No instructions were necessary. They had experienced situations like this before and the bumping was considered an occupational routine. A mutual respect developed in these years and in a weird way, they both looked forward to these events. After all the two considered adrenaline rushes as invigorating, comparable to a dip in a hot tub in mid-winter. If there was any of those sarcastic signs hung in the standard office environment, it wouldn't hang here. The only sign was one hung on the opposite wall from the front door. In dark red letters, the sign announced:

CHALLENGES WELCOMED HERE. BRING THEM ON!

Suddenly, the squeaky office door swung open. A five foot nine inch man of Mediterranean origin, sweating and clad in a police uniform stood silently in the doorway and examined the commotion occurring inside the tiny office. Respecting the activity, the local police officer awaited an acknowledgement from the two. There was a slight amount of eye contact as Donna shook her head in dismay to recognize the officer as she received updates from Jimmy who was at the scene. Oscar Coleman furiously leafed through a red vinyl folder entitled **Procedures**. He peered momentarily and greeted the officer by his first name, Vinny, and returned his focus to his folder. As Donna signed off from Castro's transmission, while scribbling notes on a filling legal pad, she mumbled a somewhat memorable reference line from the movie "Casablanca."

"Of all the emergencies in this town today, they sent you!" she murmured preoccupied with a rolodex on her messy paper strewn desk.

"Donna, if it was my choice this would be the last place I would like to be now. I won't be here long," he assured his ex-wife. "You all know there's a lynch mob forming downstairs? I recognize half of them as usual customers of the town jail. I know I'm going to have a busy night here. Any word on how long the marina will be closed?" Vinny asked concernedly.

"Still initiating Plan Alpha. The rescue units are on site, but that stupid boat is unstable due to listing. We're still waiting on when and how to evacuate the craft. Oh, and there is a storm brewing if you haven't heard. Other than that everything is peachy keen," Donna responded rudely. Then, correcting her attitude, she added, "Plan Alpha is in effect which we have to rely on contracted commercial vessels to respond to the incident and being this is a holiday, you can imagine the delays in response time. Tell the mob, it won't be until... Oscar?"

"Twelve noon, tomorrow. Of course, it won't take that long, but we come out as champs when this is resolved earlier. The *children downstairs* will be happy and forgetful of this inconvenience," Coleman added referring to the mob's actions as an infantile display of holding your breath until a parent caved to their demands.

Suddenly a gust of wind rattled the ancient windows of the Marina office, sending the mob below scurrying back to their bayside homes ironically resembling rats evacuating a sinking ship. The winds whipped clouds northerly at an incredible rate and soon the rain peppered the side of the office and as expected the cacophony of radio transmissions increased proportionately including an update from Jimmy Castro.

"Donna. This is Jimmy. I'm going to head over to Colletti's Bar and wait out the storm. Nothing's happening here. The *All In* has been warned to stay on board and wait for the storm to pass. I will be able to watch and report from the deck overlooking the scene at Colletti's. I'll contact you once I arrive there. Over."

"Hmmmm, Colleti's? How convenient, Jimmy. Bring me back a hunk!" Donna kidded knowing her ex was still in the office.

"A hunk of what?" Jimmy misinterpreted naively as he was never used to the term *hunk* in his vernacular unless it referred to a portion of cake or other food item.

Seeing his presence being neglected due to the current state of affairs, Corporal Vincenzo D'Antuano exited the office quietly without an announcement as his ex-wife and the marina manager tended to procedures and monitored the frequent transmissions of the emergency dispatchers with their contractors. Plan Alpha, as expected, was taking precious and critical time to implement in tracking down key personnel by the contractors. So far, only one commercial vessel, a dredge barge, responded to the call with an estimated time of arrival in one hour. Out of ten contractors, Drake Dredging and Salvage or DDS, for short, had respected the urgency of any emergency situation and had planned accordingly with management to schedule a crew to be on standby on all shifts 24/7.

Emergencies were never scheduled and always occurred at inconvenient times. The barge was moored at a job site down the coast about 10 miles and could be manned in a matter of moments thanks to the implementation of a military type management style by a Korean War veteran supply sergeant, Blanton C. Drake, the owner and president of DDS. Failure to respond to Mr. Drake's appeal would result in termination of service or as the owner called it *dereliction of duty*. Naturally, Mr. Drake like Captain Nick would employ veterans who recognized and respected a military environment up to the point of a court martial and subsequent firing squad. Drake took

pride in his response time and would reward his crews
handsomely. The cavalry was on the way!

The storm erupted. Aboard the *All In*, Evergreen raged
at his Captain in private as his guests donned life jackets
and worried. Their outing was now a life and death matter.
To thwart a possible capsizing, the crew of five was busy
transferring ballast along with the guests to the starboard
side of the boat. Winds rocked the grounded yacht, and
with each gust driving the ship to list even more, moans of
women and children in terror emanated from the lounge
where they had taken sanctuary. The five crew members
slid and tumbled while moving any weighty portables to
the starboard side. The crew, clad in drenched white
uniforms, were not only driven by the thought of an
impending capsizing, but by the security of their
employment from the unyielding and impossible demands
of Richard W. Evergreen, Esquire.

To face this man in a heated rage was likened to being
pierced by a laser in the solar plexus. His cold steely eyes,
unblinking, would penetrate the thickest of skins. The crew
and any employee would know when Evergreen was on the
warpath. He would storm through an office, a yacht, a
boardroom, with a steely grimace jingling change in his
slacks. He was a coiled rattler and primed for striking no
matter if you were an executive or a recently orphaned
child with a bad limp. This guy took no prisoners and
enjoyed in humiliating subordinates to satisfy a sick
visceral urge for perfection. He demanded not only service,
but your soul in the end.

Many a man questioned his existence after an
encounter with this monster with some of the unfortunate
meek souls believing this man's bellicosity resorting them
to taking their own life. Unofficially, Evergreen's antics had
claimed at least the lives of six of his subordinates and an
endless tally of disjointed and broken spirits. He never
accepted responsibility for those that had taken his abuse
of personal brow beatings even in his personal life.

His own son Richard Jr. was not excluded from his
vitriol. At the age of fifteen, young Richard suffered a
nervous breakdown from his over analytical, perfection
seeking father from whence he never overcame. Being

named after his father carried with it the burden of excelling in all endeavors. He was being groomed from an early age to be a razor and when he didn't succeed at finishing first, he felt the heated harshness of Richard Senior's typical intimidation and taunting. The youth developed a stammer from the constant reproaches until he broke from reality. Life had closed in on him from all sides causing him to stare down at the ground and deafen the sounds around him even though he felt the lashes from the venomous rantings hurled at him. The lack of self confidence carried through his brief teen years causing him to shun the coming of age that normal kids would recall with fondness through their adulthood.

For Richard Jr. every day living consisted of another descent into the swirling abyss of depression. Once esteemed by his friends at school, he became an object of scorn and cruelty, an easy target of abuse. After months of denial that her son could be suffering severe mental illness Mrs. Helen Evergreen capitulated in having him visit a psychiatrist to her husband's dismay. The doctor's aggressive technique to probe into the youth's inner self only complicated matters causing the Evergreen's only child to withdraw completely. On a beautiful spring day morning Richard Jr. dressed in his usual school attire; navy blue sports coat, blue tie, short sleeved yellow pin striped shirt, gray slacks and brown suede saddle shoes. He hardly spoke to his mother before his solo mile trek to St. Martin's Prep School in Manhattan. Reaching the corner of a busy intersection in front of the school, he placed his book laden bag down on the sidewalk and waited. A noisy restaurant supply delivery box truck raced to beat the changing light. The youth stepped from the sidewalk into the path of the speeding truck. Both did not stand the chance of avoiding the collision. Richard Jr. died instantly. The driver of the vehicle claimed the boy stood sobbing in front of the vehicle just seconds before impact. Witnesses attested that the driver had no chance to avoid the accident. Richard Senior thought differently by suing the driver and his company for all its worth enlisting the services of John Kasimir, a ruthless prosecuting attorney. Kasimir exemplified the rage in the elder Evergreen's determination to find guilt. It was as if Evergreen himself was prosecuting the case with Kasimir serving as a proxy. Despite Kasimir's harsh attack on the driver, the jury found him innocent of manslaughter charges due to Richard Junior's psychological problems. Complicating matters with reliving the accident nightly, Kasimir's foray into the driver's soul left a resounding and unrecoverable effect. He never drove a truck again and finally succumbed from alcoholism directly attributed to the accident. Evergreen felt vindicated, even elated that the driver had died but cheated when he was denied his claim for damages in a subsequent multi-million dollar civil suit against the driver's company. Although Kasimir had failed in both the criminal and civil trials, Evergreen was satisfied that Kasimir had represented him zealously especially with the tortuous cross examination of the driver that killed his son. From this point onward, 'Kaz' was Evergreen's sword of retribution and ever loyal mainly due to a handsome retainer, negotiated of course.

The boy's father's transparent greed outweighed the grief during this trying time and Mrs. Evergreen had finally seen the light realizing her marriage of seventeen years was actually to a soul consuming callous, greedy monster. She was appalled at her husband's lack of remorse. He never shed a tear for his son's demise for fear it was a sign of weakness. She filed for divorce (contested of course) immediately after her son was buried never wanting to see her despicable spouse ever again.

Evergreen's main modus operandi was to reach inside and extract the soul of the average guy. He despised anyone with a smile. Humiliation was made in public to ensure the other guy wouldn't make the same mistake. The listing of the *All In* was secondary to survival in the minds of the crew. Not facing Evergreen's tyrannical wrath was number one.

His confidence crushed and left in a limbo of indecision as others had experienced, Mueller emerged from the crew's quarters shaken. Not only was his job in dire jeopardy, but his seventeen year career as captain of any ship would be scrutinized by Evergreen with his power elite connections, who promised him that he would not even be allowed to rent a paddle boat in a duck pond! Mueller was a broken man, and when he was approached by one of his crew he stammered incoherently to the seaman. Another victim chalked up to the ego of Richard W. Evergreen, Esquire! This would be his first yacht captain. But, someone would have to command the crew and save the ship and its occupants. He wondered if he could muster what was left of his shattered self-image replaying the episode of Evergreen's tirade continually. Would this be the first victim of the storm and eventual capsizing?

The tide came in coinciding with the storm front. The sandbar, once prominent when the *All In* went aground, was now all but totally submerged. Jimmy Castro stood on the screened-in deck of Colletti's with several patrons intrigued by the developments in the bay. His radio reverberated with the ramblings of updates from rescue vehicle units and dispatchers. Castro sighed, *Now, if the occupants of the* All In *can stay put during the storm and not do anything stupid, everything will go to plan!* As the drinking crowd continually pressed Castro about developments in the bay, the jack of all trades turned and politely deflected the repetitive and annoying interrogations. He had to contact Donna. Drake's barge was entering the mouth of the bay an hour after notification!

"Donna. This is Jimmy. The barge has arrived," Jimmy gladly reported from the parking lot as the storm was ebbing. A steady drizzle was now falling and the once gusty winds had lessened. The thunder crackled up the coast like a distant artillery exchange. Donna immediately contacted the *All In* to inform them that rescue is imminent. Making his way to the skiff, Jimmy was faced with a stark reality. The skiff was inundated with rainwater. In his haste, he forgot to cover the small boat. He would never hear the end of it from Oscar and Donna.

"Heh! Forgot to cover your boat didn't you?" a mildly intoxicated fisherman chuckled as he passed the perplexed boat mechanic. "Hey, don't you work at the marina?"

"Yeah. Hey, buddy you got a bucket I can borrow?" Jimmy asked sheepishly.

"I'll do you one better than that. I'll loan you my bailing pump," the jolly fisherman whistled and strolled down three slips to his moored trawler and after a few minutes returned with a bailing pump.

"Hey, thanks," Jimmy said as he reached for the commercial sized pump that would rid the skiff of rainwater in minutes.

"I recognize you now. You're a mechanic. You must have been in a happy hour mood to forget about covering your skiff. You do good work," he continued belching the effects from a recent downing of several draught beers imbibed at Colletti's.

"Jimmy? Jimmy?" the radio holstered on Castro's hip reverberated.

"Go ahead, Donna," Jimmy responded dropping the pump.

"What's the progress with the barge?"

Both Jimmy and the fisherman craned their necks towards the listing boat. The barge made its way to the scene at a speed of 10 knots and slowed as it neared the site of the grounding awaiting instructions from the Seaside Fire and Rescue.

"Donna, they're maneuvering into position. It won't be long before they evacuate," Jimmy assured confidently.

"Thanks, Jimmy. Over."

On board *All In* Captain Mueller was receiving procedures from the Seaside Fire and Rescue Service on evacuation. The barge would pull alongside the listing side of the yacht, preventing it from the possibility of capsizing. Once that position was stabilized, the marooned occupants would be lowered into awaiting rescue boats on the other side. The process would take about an hour or two, depending on the depth of the tide above the now submerged sandbar.

Captain Mueller, despite his recent reprimand from Evergreen, now concentrated his attention in the hopes of a successful rescue and to not add to his obvious navigational error to the escalating crowds on the shore; even though he felt the entire blame fell on Evergreen. A ladder was secured to enable the passengers to access the rescue craft below. In the lounge, Evergreen consoled his guests with promises of complimentary five star restaurant dinners and outings at a future date to ease the morale of his disgruntled and inconvenienced guests.

The bailing almost complete, Castro's attention turned to a familiar boat entering the area. It was *The Rough Rider*. An oddly shade of green paint, scratches and dents indicated a collision of some sort along the port side as Minnis pulled into dock near the Coast Guard station. Jimmy knew he would be servicing the boat soon. His curiosity risen, Jimmy gave the bailing pump back to the fisherman with a brief appreciation and headed over to *The Rough Rider*.

"Minus? You alright? What the hell happened?" Jimmy grabbed the mooring ropes that Tavia threw to him as Minnis cut his engine off.

"Jimmy, what are you doing here? What's going on over there?" Minnis asked pointing to the *All In*. Tavia's interests were peeked also despite the obvious signs of seasickness.

"A yacht ran aground. They are getting ready to pull everyone off. What happened to your boat?" replied Jimmy underplaying the grounding.

"I don't know how to tell you this, Jimmy, and I don't think the Coast Guard will believe me, but we collided with a boat out there that disappeared," Minnis conveyed as Tavia nodded her head in agreement.

"Hit and run during the storm?" Jimmy suggested.

"Not exactly. I responded to a boat in distress. I could hear people screaming for help and when I got to their boat and inspected it, there was no one aboard! And then when I noticed that the anchor wasn't deployed and the boat wasn't moving, I got the hell off. After I started to return, Octavia shouted that the boat was gone!" Octavia nodded again her approval of the story as Jimmy turned to her. "It was a matter of five minutes. You ever hear of a boat sinking in five minutes?" Minnis quizzed Jimmy for moral support.

"Did you get a position?" Castro stressed intensely.

"Yes. I was on the way to report it to the CG," Minnis said pointing to the station house.

"You got a description? A name?" continued Jimmy in an unusual concerned state.

"Well the paint on my port side will bear witness to the description. As for the name it was called *Donovan's Pride*," Minnis revealed.

A stunned Jimmy stood as if he had been punched in the gut. His mouth agape with awe, he reiterated Minnis' words, *Donovan's Pride*. It was yet another account of an unsolved mystery of eight years past that sent Castro reeling backwards, his back slumped on a splintered weathered piling. It had been two years since the last encounter with this mystery ship which had all been forgotten until now; written off as some wild imagination to create an urban legend. And here it was presented again directly to Jimmy Castro as if it were intended by some master plan from beyond the grave.

Jimmy examined the paint on the side of Minnis's boat. The shade of aquamarine paint, a rarity on marina boats which Jimmy was familiar with, evoked a memory of the day Michael Donovan came to the work shop to confirm his choice of paint to be applied to his boat. The paint had to match the original which was now fading. Castro was contracted to do the painting. Since, this was a special color, Castro ordered extra to have on hand in the event of damage to the *Donovan's Pride* and the difficulty in obtaining this particular shade; a shade of green to emphasize Mr. Donovan's proud Irish roots. Castro recalled petting the Donovan's family pet, Paddy, an anxious Irish Setter while discussing plans for the painting of his boat. Paddy went everywhere with his owner.

"Jimmy, does that name mean something to you?" Minnis asked Jimmy noting his puzzled expression.

"Are you sure it was called *Donovan's Pride?*" Jimmy asked to assure he had heard the correct boat name.

"Yes, I'm sure. There was a wooden life preserver on the deck with that name painted on it, hung right outside of the cabin! Painted with the colors of the Irish flag," Minnis explained.

"You said you heard screaming, sounds of distress. Can you describe them?"

"I heard a woman and children screaming from the boat. There was a dog and a man in the water. Never did see them. All I heard were screams, and the man saying a farewell to his family. It really sank a hook in me. I don't think the CG will believe me or my friend here when I mention the boat's sudden disappearance. What do you think I should do?" Minnis nervously inquired needing assurance from Castro.

"I would tell them, Ted. Make sure you tell them exactly what you told me. Also, give them the position coordinates. And most important, do not remove the paint and damage from your boat until your story is investigated thoroughly! In other words, cooperate and don't be difficult!" advised Castro sternly gently reminding Minnis of his shortness of patience.

Minnis agreed and helped Tavia off the rocking boat to her eventual delight. Her legs wobbled uncontrollably from the rough seas, her seasickness, and above all fright. They appreciated the advice from the jack of all trades and headed into the bustling Coast Guard Station to convey their account of their eerie experience. Castro knew the Coast Guard would regard this story as a low priority considering their records on actions taken two years before on a costly and fruitless search. The file on the missing of the *Donovan's Pride* had long been closed with no desire in reopening it. It was now considered comparable to the sightings of the *USS Cyclops*, a ship that went mysteriously missing in 1918 and has been seen at different times through the years aimlessly adrift.

He knew Minnis's story was factual. He pictured the Donovan family. Mrs. Joanne Donovan was the perfect wife. Her brown eyes bore the color of newly minted pennies. She was a devout mother always abiding and living life to the fullest like her adventurous husband. She and Michael bought Paddy as a Christmas gift for their daughter Kate and their son Mike Jr. They were a loving and vibrant family that always enjoyed a Christian family lifestyle and would participate in church and charity events like manning a refreshment stand at church carnivals or sponsoring a clothing and food drive for the needy in the county. Heaven was their eventual destination when they sailed from the marina on July 4, 1984, but one wonders why they return to haunt those that experience and share in their tragedy, a thought which confronted Mr. Castro. Or maybe, it was to impel Jimmy to investigate the sighting and bring both closure and the truth to the mysterious surroundings of the sinking which would clear his name from being linked to its disappearance.

CHAPTER 11

The crowds began arriving soon after the storm had passed. Families with blankets, chairs, coolers, strollers, and assorted sundry items in plastic bags made their way down to the beach to establish a point in the sand to settle a temporary land claim in viewing the fireworks display.

Meanwhile up on the boardwalk, shop owners enticed the passing crowds with aromas of pizza, funnel cakes, hamburgers, hot dogs, fried chicken , caramel corn, and of course french fries. Beach apparel shops announced fifty percent savings on the usual family and unusual profanely worded beachwear. Game arcades echoed loudly and band music performing in bars enthralled those briefly as they strolled by. As crowds looked towards the sea and as others approached their sandy destination, a full red moon elicited their attention like a pre-fireworks performance. People stopped abruptly on the boardwalk and marveled at the scene; some never witnessing a spectacle as this. They took out cameras and photographed this unusual phenomenon.

A clamor developed in front of *Casa Del Sol Beachwear* as folks commented on the rising red orb hanging over the horizon drawing some casual attention to three lonely figures advancing from the shore. Lured by the commotion outside her store, Carmen Zavala meandered around the throng to see what was so compelling.

"Dios Mio!" she blessed herself instantly. "Diego! Diego! It's The Blood Moon, close the store!"

Her husband finishing a sale on the cash register looked at his panicked wife who was busy moving merchandise away from the entrance door. Clothing fell off hangers in the overcrowded store as Carmen swiftly closed one door. She ran towards the back and fanatically gestured the remaining patrons to leave now. Her husband perplexed as to why she was ushering prospective buyers from the store on a particularly profitable evening. Customers reacted with taunts as she escorted them some by the arms out of the store and slamming the exit door shut while locking it.

"Carmen, what the hell are you doing?" he asked as he finished a sale with an astonished female customer who looked back at the small round panicky woman.

"*Diego! La Luna Sangre! La Luna Sangre!* The Blood Moon! She is here!" she informed Diego in her raspy voice as she switched off the lights in the rear of the shop. She then clumsily raced back to the front of the store brushing stacks of various apparel items from their stuffed cubby holes onto the floor and peered through the store window masking her round face with beachwear on display. Somewhat infuriated, Diego shook his head, stood, and curiously scanned the scene in front trying to see the horizon as the mob passed in front. He removed the fancy amber colored cigarette holder from his mouth and cradled it in the ancient ash tray by the register. In the distance, he saw what caused concern with his suspicious Filipino wife.

"Carmen, we are in the United States, now. This superstition doesn't exist here! There is no lady with no face coming to drag you to Hell with her and besides if she has no face, how does she know where she's going? Look if she doesn't come by in the next ten minutes, I'm going to reopen the store and if she does I will sell her a tee shirt and some Coppertone," he offered in a sardonic Hispanic tone.

"Diego, you shouldn't make fun of her. She represents the justice, blind justice like the lady with the scales."

Outside the *Casa Del Sol*, a group of three stood falsely riveted to the spellbinding findings of Reynolds their *friend-in-nerd* who was seated on a bench. It seemed as if the only one interested was Carmen Zavala whose face peered from the sales window behind Reynolds causing the three friends to chuckle as if the frightened store owner closed up shop just to eavesdrop on Reynolds's stark revelations on life.

"You know I timed last year's display here and compared it with the previous one held at the Washington Monument. You know the ones here were three minutes and twenty-two seconds longer than the ones held at the Mall?"

"Wow. I'm amazed, Reynolds," one of his cohorts said in a mocked appreciation of his friend's dedication to detail.

"I couldn't believe it myself. I contacted the National Park Service and they said they would monitor both events from now on. Isn't that something?" Reynolds boasted proudly.

"No, Reynolds. I'm amazed you *timed* the fireworks in the first place, you dweeb," his friend informed.

With the booms announcing the initial stage of the fireworks display, the crowd silenced and focused their attention on the show. Diego pleaded with the vigilant Carmen to turn the store lights back on so they could conduct business. Carmen turned her head back to her husband and shushed him. She was amazed at what she saw when she peered through the store window again.

She gazed into an image that immediately entranced her. It was if she was watching an old home movie of her Filipino childhood. There she was in a red and black checkered dress playing tag with her friends, Emilia and Lily. Her mother was hanging clothes on a rope line as the three frolicked in the backyard dodging around the bed linen undulating in the Manila breeze. Carmen, enraptured, managed to smile at the images. Her heart warmed as she absorbed the scene. The joyful images of her childhood were magical compared to the harshness of her adult years of reality.

The brief elation filled her soul until strands of blond hair whisked about in the foreground of the scenes. The image pulled away from the window and grew smaller as if watching an old black and white television fade to a tiny white aperture. Carmen gasped in horror, her eyes rolling back in her head and then she fainted, falling face first into a waist high wire basket of multicolored Nerf footballs, knocking over a rack of Tee Shirts which proudly touted the rally cry of the current generation, "Weed is the Word!"

For the past few moments she had been gazing into the void of the Woman With No Face who was on the outside of the window looking into Carmen's curious face. As the avenger stepped back, Carmen realized her worst dread. She had been face to face with God's messenger on the night of the Blood Moon. Diego leapt over the counter to attend to his collapsed wife.

Outside the mysterious woman proceeded to walk shrouded in the shadows of darkness down the boardwalk shielded by a blind old man with a seeing eye dog, a badly fur matted German shepherd . From behind, the woman appeared lonely in search of someone; perhaps an old flame from years past; Elenore searching in vain for her poet whose adoration of her was never realized by her while on Earth. Her light flowing skirt concealed her feet and she had the appearance of gliding along the rough hewed planked surface of the boardwalk. The blind man with a banjo slung over his right shoulder was returning home after a twenty years absence *to entertain* the patrons on the boardwalk courtesy of the Blood Moon. The blind man caught some familiar glimpses by adults and they stopped and craned their necks backwards for validation. *Isn't this the same blind man I saw as a child? How can it be him? I'm older but he hasn't changed!* But here he was again in his usual unchanged garb, the ragged brown tweed sports coat, his eyes sealed by the burden of aged eyelids, his gruff weathered countenance, his frayed checkered cap, the gray baggy pants, and his nicotine stained hands. The inquisitive shrugged their shoulders after a brief summation and continued their trek unconvinced that this was a different man. Even his dog appeared the same, downtrodden and weary from earlier times.

CHAPTER 12

ctivity was at its zenith at the site of the grounded yacht. The barge now anchored next to the stranded vessel, stretched beyond the fifty foot yacht by ten feet which concealed the predicament. Rescue boats galore darted back and forth to the shore bringing with them the relieved passengers of the *All In* and escorted them to awaiting emergency personnel on the shore to examine if they would require medical assistance.

One woman clutching her chest and complaining from a shortness of breath was whisked from the site immediately. The paramedic unit exiting the parking lot was trailed not only by her concerned husband but also by Milton Craddock, the town's notorious and literal ambulance chasing attorney. The trip to the nearby hospital located outside of the city limits would take the unit usually 15 minutes. Since the majority of traffic was concentrated in town due to the fireworks , the paramedic unit arrived at the hospital in a record 11 minutes; a point only relished by the driver and his 2 man crew.

However, Milton Craddock could not claim the same result. He was stopped by one of Seaside's finest about three miles from the city limits on the apex of a hill that rose noticeably in contrast to the vast coastal plain. Craddock cursed silently as he pulled to the side and readied himself with the standard credentials and inevitable lawyerly intimidations. A floodlight from the patrol car illuminated the worn body condition of his 1983 weather beaten Chevy Impala. What seemed like an eternity and an opportunity to cash in on the victim of the grounding by somebody's negligence slipping away, the impatient attorney lowered his window and urged the officer to "get this over with."

The officer obscured by the bright lights approached the Impala examining cautiously any possible threat to his well-being. Noting the license tag, he scribbled it into his citation book and strolled to the anxious driver leaning from the window with his license and registration.

"Officer, I am an attorney. You might have heard of me, Milton Craddock?" stated the lawyer in a rushed manner.

Pulling the required identification from the hand of the inquiring violator, the officer whose face was unseen by Craddock since the focus of the floodlight shone on him, showed little attention to the lawyers request for recognition. Taking the cards, he returned to his squad car. Craddock could hear his identification being transmitted by radio to police headquarters. As this process was taking place, the lawyer resigned himself to losing a prospective client to another rival. He sighed and suddenly replayed the image of being pulled over. The sound of the siren, his heartbeat racing, and eventual embarrassment by being seen by random passing motorists all raced in his mind as the precious legal opportunity ebbed in the time the patrolman processed his information. Finally, the officer emerged from his vehicle and returned to the usual frustration of facing a traffic violator caught in the act of speeding.

"Mister Craddock. I recorded your speed in excess of twenty miles per hour. I have you clocked at sixty miles an hour in a 40 mile an hour speed zone. You have thirty days to appear in court if you wish to present your case before the judge. I need you to sign at the bottom here to acknowledge you have been cited and advised of your rights," the patrolman instructed.

The lawyer, not willing to aggravate his sudden inconvenience, signed the citation without complaint hoping to get to the hospital before some vulture descended on his prospective client. The officer tore the citation from his notebook and handed the copy back to the driver.

"Craddock? That name is familiar to me now. Are you related to Stanley Craddock?" the officer asked politely.

"Yes. He was my father. I'm following in his footsteps. I took up his law firm after he died. Look, officer, I don't mean to be rude but..." Craddock's request was cut short.

"Those are big shoes to be filled. He was a councilman and mayor, right? He made his name in railroads afterwards if I recall," the officer infused.

"That's right. About twenty years ago. He never was involved with railroads though. Listen, officer...I'm sorry I didn't get your name," Craddock requested squinting his eyes.

"Officer Ken Dillon," replied the policeman in a distinctive voice leaning on the car door "Badge number eight-thirty-one," he enunciated for effect.

"Yes, uh, Officer Dillon. I really need to get to the hospital to visit with my client. Can I go?" Craddock asked politely.

Still unable to see the officer's face from the bright glare of the floodlight, Craddock surveyed the uniformed figure for some sort of identifying feature: hair color, facial hair, scars, eye color something, but to no avail.

"Yes. You can go but drive safely when you get back on the road. Have a good night, Mr. Craddock. Maybe I'll see you at the courthouse soon."

An icy coldness crept up the back of the neck of the lawyer as he fumbled to place the citation in the glove compartment. Officer Dillon's voice inflection revealed an image of familiarity that he wanted to convey deeply to Craddock and this puzzled him. "Should I know this guy?" he thought.

The lawyer's car once illuminated by high beams, floodlights, and red and blue flashing lights on top of the police car was plunged into complete darkness. There was no crunching sound from the patrol car leaving the gravelly berm to return to the asphalt of the road. Craddock sat up, his eyes adjusting now to the total blackness of the area, checked his rear view mirror. The patrol car was gone. Opening his door, he exited to scan the highway; first east and then west. A vehicle was approaching about a half a mile to his west, but he discounted that it could be Officer Dillon. He waited only to see that it was a minivan on its way to the beach loaded with kid's bikes and cartoon colored inner tubes. Where was the patrol car, he pondered. From his vantage point on the top of the hill he could see for miles in either direction, but the minivan was all he saw. He looked for tell-tale signs of headlights and tail lights. Officer Dillon had disappeared without a trace. All that could be seen was a full red moon in the eastern sky.

CHAPTER 13

Seaman Second Class Christine Millard typed furiously on her keypad the facts of the sinking of the *Donovan's Pride* as relayed by Ted Minnis and Octavia Bledsoe. With the coordinates of the missing vessel in place, her Commanding Officer, who randomly oversaw any data entry, reacted with scorn as if a cruel hoax was again being played on him. He looked at Minnis and his sea sick mate with the intent of uncovering of who these people were in relation to the hoax player. His face reddened and commanded S-2 Millard to cease processing the data at once. He glared at Minnis and Tavia with an intense fire in his eyes. The young clerk, confused, replied to her superior with an official "Yes, sir." Her commanding officer, Master Chief Gerard Thibodeaux, left his bespectacled female aide in a haste shaking his head and cussing inaudibly to explain to the two of the abrupt cessation of the report without an explanation. Nervously and regretfully, she managed some professionalism not exhibited by her boss to inform Minnis and Bledsoe of her instructions if the two had not overheard the order directed by her CO.

Nearby sitting in a fabric covered waiting room chair, a woman wearing faded jeans and a black blouse complemented by sandaled feet preoccupied with jotting the details of the incident in the bay on a legal pad, lifted her head. The mention of the *Donovan's Pride* shifted her attention to the activity at the counter where Minnis and Bledsoe stood in disbelief of the Coast Guard's reluctance to get involved with the sinking of a boat off the coast.

"What? You don't believe us? I have paint on the side of my boat from the sinking boat! I'll show you it! It's right outside!" Ted announced to the S-2, hoping his voice would be heard by her commanding officer. "There are people who possibly drowned out there! You gotta do something! We're not making this up! We're not leaving until we get some action!"

Finally, frustrated with the scene at the counter Master Chief Thibodeaux summoned Seaman Millard into his office. Moments later, she returned rattled after receiving an admonishment from her boss in her failure to evict Ted and Tavia from the premises. She also produced a document, a computer print out with the words "Ha Ha!" scribbled on it with a red Sharpie.

"Please read this!" she stated somberly.

The computer printout was a copy of a Coast Guard Search and Rescue report dated 12 September 1986. A dynamic red circle drew Minnis and Tavia to the summary.

```
    "Donovan's Pride"//Lost at Sea: 4, July
1984. (storm) // No Survivors
    Family of 4: Michael (father), Joanne
(mother), Kathleen (daughter), Michael Jr.
(son)
    Physical Evidence: None// Vessel not
recovered
    David J. Bennington, Lt. Cmndr. USCG.//
Washington, DC
```

The two gazed into each other's face as if they had awakened from a nightmare. Seaman Second Class Millard gasped as she witnessed the silence and the inability of the two to comprehend the report. If this was an act, Minnis and Bledsoe were worthy of Hollywood Oscar status. Ted again read the report to assure himself he wasn't misinterpreting the report. As if suckered punched, Minnis slowly paced to a nearby chair across from the counter and collapsed in shock. Tavia followed and sat in a neighboring chair sandwiched between an ancient black compass on her left and Minnis on her right. The gray -haired woman was now piqued by the escalating events in the lobby of the Coast Guard Station. The activity in the bay was now secondary and her attention now focused on the pair seated to her right.

"I don't mean to pry, but did I hear you mention the *Donovan's Pride?*" the woman stated softly placing her hand gently on Tavia's shoulder.

Tavia, waiting for Minnis to respond, nodded her response politely to the inquisitive woman with a caring face that urged support for their account of the evening's horror. Seaman Millard stood at the counter her womanly instincts honed in on the conversation among Minnis, Tavia and the curious woman seated next to them. Knowing she would be scolded for her lack of detail to her assigned and expected tasks, Millard, clad in her snug blue fatigue uniform, hung on the anticipated response by Minnis. The gray haired woman knowing she would have to do something to elicit a reaction then announced to the shocked pair.

"My name is Gwen Blasingame. I write for the *Seaside Daily News*. I'm here to cover the situation outside. I had to get out of the rain," she proved by pointing to her wet blouse, "but I think I can help you figure out what has happened if you don't mind. You two look like you deserve an explanation."

"Does it show that much?" Minnis asked dejectedly with a slight grin gazing at the freshly waxed tiled floor. "I know what I saw, and my friend will back me up! This isn't a damn prank!"

"Yes. Do you want me to explain what you saw?" the reporter offered.

"Well, I'm sure we can agree on an explanation from *someone* who knows," Minnis offered sarcastically.

From outside the entrance to the Coast Guard Station, a loud confrontation ensued. Threats intertwined with cussing and intimidation audible to the habitants of the Seychelles Islands echoed through the foyer of the station walls. Any conversation in the office would have to await the turmoil that was entering the counter area, reminiscent of a New York Precinct house after a mass prostitution bust. The Coast Guard Station rarely was the scene of these type of exhibitions, but then again it was not the usual haunt of Richard Evergreen in full battle mode. His reputation definitely and literally preceded him. Master Chief Thibodeaux not averse to conflict and aware of the impending confrontation strode in anger to the counter and stood next to Seaman Millard crossing his arms.

"May I be of assistance to you, sir?" the Master Chief asked sardonically in a Cajun drawl.

"You are really overdoing it with all these rescue boats out here! It isn't necessary, you know. This is really embarrassing!" Evergreen exclaimed.

"You must be Evergreen. We've been monitoring the radio transmissions here. That's quite a mess you created out there!" the Master Chief condescended. "Those rescue boats are dispatched by Seaside Fire and Rescue, sir. We have nothing to do with it unless the problem gets worse. This is a city matter! I don't know how many times I have had to tell you people this tonight!" the short stocky man cried out in frustration addressing a few of the locals in the lobby with the same complaints as Evergreen.

Evergreen was stunned by the announcement by the Master Chief who began to grin at Evergreen's misfortune and bad seamanship. He didn't know how to respond to the news and swallowed the threatening venom laced speech he was going to unleash on the CO. Feeling the fruitless attempt of intimidating the Coast Guard, he exited the station pushing on the glass of the door so hard he left his oily handprints on the glass panels. The other deflated complainers followed him languidly out of the lobby. All that remained were Minnis, Tavia, and the reporter.

After the dust had settled from Evergreen's encounter at the counter, Gwen Blasingame reminded Minnis and Tavia of the disappearance of the *Donovan's Pride*.

"Obviously, what you saw was real. You're not the only ones. About four years ago, a man reported the identical situation to the Coast Guard. However, he did not board the boat nor did he report the location. He just gave sketchy details. He had no navigation skills. So, when the

Coast Guard went out to investigate his claim, they could not zero in on the exact location. They wasted a week in another costly and fruitless search.

"There is also a rash of bad practical jokes usually made around Halloween about this particular *ghost ship* so the Coast Guard regards them as meaningless. So that's why the CO here treated you that way.

"The man who reported the sighting was later institutionalized because he was so certain in what he saw, it became an obsession and he would routinely harass the authorities with his rants. His name was Ben Jacoby. I believed him, and when I came to his aide my editor told me to drop my contact with him or risk termination. You see, the townspeople got tired of the story and regarded him as crazy by his ongoing crusade to prove his story. He went on radio, TV, Geraldo, disrupted public meetings and city holiday functions, and the most heinous crime; upsetting vacationers!"

"Now if you two have specific coordinates, then we can skip the Coast Guard. I have contacts with people who do deep sea diving. Wouldn't you like to see this nightmare resolved before it becomes a preoccupation?" she posed.

"Of course we would, but why are you so interested?" inquired Minnis.

"Well, I'm looking for the big ticket out of here. You know there are only so many flounder and white marlin tournaments you can report before you feel it's the same story every year. I'm a writer looking for the *big* story, and I think I have one. You'll get mentioned in my book!"

"Ted! Just think of it! You and me mentioned in a Pulitzer Prize winning novel!" Tavia declared excitedly.

"I don't think my wife will like it, Tavia" the guilt ridden Minnis snapped. "Look Miss Blasingame, I believe this would bring closure to family and friends, but you are going to have to keep my name and the name of my boat out of it for the sanctity of my marriage."

"Agreed!" She grinned at the irony of the mention of *sanctity* from the obvious two-timer. "The coordinates?" She gave her notes on the yacht grounding over to Ted for him to record the latitude and longitude of the missing boat. Ted complied and in bold blue ink noted the location.

CHAPTER 14

Jimmy returned home from trade school an exhausted man. He promptly placed his books on the coffee table and walked towards the kitchen. Sunny adorned in a sheer black negligee, softly and silently sneaked up behind her tired husband who was pouring a cool glass of guava juice from the wax carton. She wrapped her arms around his waist caressing him.

"Hey, sailor, buy me a drink?" she wooed in a deep sensual voice.

Jimmy grinned and gazed at the wall above the sink. "Sure, baby. What'll it be?"

"I want something in a long tall glass, something that will take me a while to enjoy. A drink so hot, ice doesn't stand a chance!"

Jimmy placed his glass down on the drain board of the sink and turned facing his hot sexy wife. Not saying a word, he pulled the spaghetti straps of her negligee down her arms. As the straps reached her elbows, the negligee slid to the floor revealing Sunny's toned and tanned naked body in the glow of the flickering fluorescent light over the sink. The pale flesh from her bikini line stood in contrast to her dark Hawaiian tan. Her breasts round and firm were magnetic drawing Castro's hands to fondle them in a gentle motion driving Sunny wild in anticipation. She hugged him closer and slammed her mouth against his as Jimmy caressed her lower back, pulling him into her. Jimmy swept her up in his arms sustaining the kiss all the while and proceeded with his bride down the hall to the bedroom. Moans of passion echoed through the apartment. A window fan prevented the embarrassing chorus from emanating out of the window in earshot of neighbors. The lack of intimacy over the past month was evidenced by the intensity of the love making. The drought of non-restful nights for Jimmy was over temporarily. A collective sigh registering about five minutes was attained after the lengthy and longing passion performance culminating in a shared Lucky Strike even though Sunny didn't smoke.

At seven the next morning Sunny fumbled with the alarm clock as it vibrated with its annoying ring. She lay motionless staring at the ceiling, recalling her evening of absolute joy. Jimmy stirred next to her. He did not leave to sleep on the sofa. Did this mean no nightmare? Man, she thought, if this is the cure to his post-traumatic stress disorder then I am going to be worn out before I'm thirty! Now, I have to tell him the bad news. Jimmy turned to her side of the bed and winked.

"God, I feel great. That's the first time I've slept peacefully in over a month." Jimmy declared, interrupted by yawns and stretching. "I don't feel like working today. Let's do something together."

"I thought we did last night, Jimmy," Sunny reminded him while hugging.

"I mean go someplace and do something. I'll call Nick." It was the perfect time for Sunny to relate to her husband the conversation with Captain Nick.

"Honey? There's something I got to tell you now. Promise me you won't get mad," Sunny said shyly.

"Okay baby, what is it?"

"Captain Nick came by here yesterday. He told me to have you call him this morning. He doesn't want you back until you get treated for your stress. He regards you as a safety risk and doesn't want you to get hurt on the job," Sunny stated frankly.

Jimmy stared off in wonder trying to stem back a rising temper. Noticing the anxious look on his wife's freckled face, he swallowed the anger and sighed gazing at the ceiling. Moments passed as he contemplated his options. Taking it out on Sunny was not one of the options. He loved her too much.

"Jimmy with your disability and my pay, we can make it. Once you graduate from trade school you'll find another job. Captain Nick is just looking out for you." Sunny pleaded to comfort Jimmy.

"I owe a lot to him. He gave me a job when nobody wanted me. He was my Best Man. Really, I shouldn't be mad. I think I'm just confused trying to get my life off to good start after the Navy and facing obstacles everywhere I go because of my physical appearance and now my mental state!" Jimmy related convincing himself to be positive.

"I know it is hard Jimmy. But, I love you and I know you'll be successful. It's what inside you that made me marry you. You'll beat this thing. I'll be by your side all the way," Sunny squeezed her love for solidarity.

"All right Mrs. Castro. I'll call my ex-boss and then we'll head up to Hale'iwa. What do you say?" Jimmy turned to his blond mate and smiled his affection for her.

"I'll call work and wax up my surfboard." Sunny happily obliged.

CHAPTER 15

Tyrone Boston and his three homeys had had enough of the fireworks display. Collectively they had devoted eight minutes to the celebratory illumination. They wanted what every unsupervised teenager wanted; to wreak havoc and have a good time doing it. Now the time was at hand. There were perhaps 15,000 innocent victims on the boardwalk with diverted attention. The pickings were easy. Items of prey included purses in strollers, bulging wallets in rear pockets, bicycles, mopeds, skateboards, headphones, and the usual bumping and groping of females. So, the quartet marched abreast down the boardwalk, seeking to steal from and annoy as many boardwalk patrons as possible, while their heads looked towards the flashing sky.

Dion Jones the fastest of the four nabbed the first purse from a stroller. With no witnesses seeing his quick jerk of the strap, he nonchalantly proceeded to a side street rummaging through the leather bag searching for cash. He tossed the non-important contents including credit cards on the ground until he saw the familiar green legal tender; the object of his desire. Then, out of true thug consideration, he threw the bag in a dumpster. He stashed eleven dollars in his baggy pants pocket and as planned would go solo for a while to avoid any law called to the scene.

Meanwhile, Tyrone's remaining two miscreants, Fart (pronounced Faht) and Antwuan weren't so lucky. They too had seen a stroller containing a purse. Approaching the stroller like lions preying on a lone elk, they awaited the moment of the strike. Unbeknownst to them were two undercover policemen who had staged the scene pretending to marvel at the colorful shower bursting in the sky. While Antwuan kept watch, Fart moved in to grab the purse from the collapsible carry-all stroller. Unseen by the two thieves was a transparent monofilament fish line tied to the purse connecting it with the stroller, laden with a 16 pound bowling ball wrapped in a child's blanket. Fart clutched the handbag and sprinted with the stroller and bowling ball bounding behind in tow. The cops divided with one corralling Antwuan who could not have moved any faster because he was laughing heartily at the image of his homey trying to free the purse from the stroller which was dragging and thumping sideways down the boardwalk behind him.

The force that Fart yanked the stroller sent the bowling ball in motion picking up momentum as it careened wildly on the boards causing spectators to jump in unexpected unison. It looked like a continual human 7-10 split with the ball exiting the boardwalk down a side street to the expressed amazement of a group of senior citizens who were strolling up the inclined sidewalk to the boardwalk; not expecting a ten pin ball in full bowling alley velocity as a regular occurrence on their nightly trek to the boardwalk. As the other policeman caught up with Fart, an easy collar, expressed his displeasure of being set up by *the man.*

"You got nothin' on me, man. Let go of me! I was framed! This is entrapment!"

Not aware of the commotion three blocks behind him, Tyrone had his sights set on a demure *sista* walking behind a blind man and a seeing-eye dog. Her windswept hair blew into the darkened void of where there was once a face and she was moving slowly behind her escort. She kept her head down obviously shy and insecure of her appearance, but to Tyrone she was worthy of his instant *charm and tactfulness;* proven points that have worked for him in the past with *the hos in de hood.*

"Hey, baby. I'm Tyrone. What you say me and you get quainted? I'm a lot of fun to hang wit," he proclaimed blocking the woman from her pace placing his right hand on her left shoulder. Suddenly a searing of burning flesh caused the urban and urbane home boy to jerk his hand back from her shoulder. His hand went coldly numb as if he just thrown his umpteenth snow ball barehanded at passing motorists from a freeway overpass in Buffalo following a moderate lake effect snow of 50 inches. Cradling his injured hand with his left hand, he was awestruck as the woman nudged by him and continued on her way.

"Hey, I wouldn't hang wit you anyhow, bitch! I'd probably get frostbite on my lips if I kissed you! I'd have better luck wit a ice cream sammich!" he yelled catching the attention of spectators.

The blind man registered an approving grin of the brief encounter and continued his labored walk with his dog leading the way. In front of a vacant shop he plopped down a bag and slung off his banjo. The woman with no face patted him on the back as she passed appreciating her escort.

"Good luck with your mission!" he stated in a gravelly throaty voice.

As if planned by a military entity, an idling police car awaited her presence. Officer Ken Dillon opened the rear door making sure she didn't bump her faceless head on the roof of the car, appearing as if the woman with no face was being taken in custody. Officer Dillon adjusted his rear view mirror catching sight of his passenger in the rear seat. Her face appeared in the mirror. She smiled content with his company. Freckles, blue eyes, dimples, straight perfect teeth, and tanned skin with a hint of make-up betrayed her image of a divine avenger. Her face could be altered to accommodate her comrades from beyond or terrorize her human targets worthy of the wrath of an incensed God. She was assigned the code name "Ermengarde." Her mission was to see to the annihilation of Richard Evergreen and to be executed with extreme prejudice in accordance

with the Supreme Contract of Human Conduct, Chapter 12
Section A. Article 5; which states:

> Any individual conducting himself in the
> manner of the deliberate and unremorseful
> destruction of human souls to dignify his image
> and stature in a vindictive and spiteful
> manner, shall be held in violation of The
> Supreme Contract of Human Conduct. The
> destruction of human souls is hereby described
> as those individuals whose spirits have
> suffered the lifelong effects of damages
> thereby limiting and stunting their joy of a
> true life which was directly the result of
> cruel and callous acts committed by humans who
> validate their actions of those that they have
> victimized.
>   It is then that the Supreme Council will
> exact revenge upon those in violation of the
> Contract to the fullest extent of the law in a
> manner befitting the crime. The vengeance will
> only occur when the Moon is Full and Red from
> the blood of the innocent. Those responsible
> for callous acts resulting in suicide will be
> destined to suffer an ETERNITY of punishment
> from which there is no pardon.

Agent Ermengarde opened a two inch thick dossier on
her target that was placed in a satchel on the rear seat.
Officer Dillon had turned the dome light on for her to
peruse the material. The dossier contained case histories of
all those disjointed and wandering souls that lay in the
destructive wake of the effects of Richard Evergreen,
Esquire. The color coded files ranged from red (suicide
related) to blue (just cold cruelness). Her head shook in
amazement. Never before had she been assigned such a
menace. The manila folders slid across the bench seat as
Dillon turned onto the main highway. Her instructions to
"execute with extreme prejudice" now made sense. The
sheer magnitude of the case histories alone warranted an
extreme and instant visceral reaction. This case would
summon all the creative juices she could fathom to

administer to this walking plague of society. She counted six suicide folders in the dossier attributable to Evergreen.

But, there was a reason she was assigned. The Supreme Council was confident she was the right agent. It would take a cool calculated plan to humble this monster. The objective of the plan was to get Evergreen to beg for mercy from those he victimized. Mercy was not an emotion inherent to his psyche. She sighed at the enormity of her mission. It would be her biggest project to date.

"What do you think Agent Ermengarde?" Dillon inquired glancing over his rested arm on the back of the driver's seat.

"I would like to drag this guy straight to Hell, but that would be too good for him. He needs to realize what he has done," she responded gritting her teeth. "It's going to take some doing, but I have a plan to terrorize this scum. How is your assignment going, Ken?"

"Well, I came in contact with the son of the man who railroaded me. He didn't understand the connotation when I mentioned it, but I'm sure I left him wondering," the ghost officer said adjusting his rear view mirror. "He's going to be instrumental in revealing the truth about what happened to me and all the shenanigans that took place in City Hall."

"Did you hear about the couple that came across the *Donovan's Pride?* "Ermengarde injected.

"Yes. This will help me out too along with clearing Jimmy Castro's name." Suddenly the dispatcher on the radio interrupted the conversation.

"All units! All Units! Report to the Bay Marina! Civil disturbance in progress! Handle code 2!"

"Remind me Ken of the case. It's been awhile." Ermengarde sat back and relaxed in the back seat.

"You got time Agent Ermengarde? It's a long story," warned the officer.

"Yeah, my target isn't going anywhere for two more days. I got time," Ermengarde said looking out the window at pedestrian traffic.

"I'm going to pull down this side street and then I will tell you," Dillon promised cranking the air conditioning to its maximum setting.

In a No Parking Anytime zone on the side street, Officer Dillon maneuvered his cruiser to face the highway as if on duty checking for speed violators. He turned his attention to the avenging agent in back, resting his arm on the back of his seat.

"It was in 1982. I was working with the force in early fall that year. We had some problems with the local youths around here especially with a greaser gang. One of these guys, Ricky Salvano, a regular hood with a penchant for confrontation was involved in a fight at Terry's Burger Shack. As usual, he and his gang would pick on some guy with his date and usually the two would be intimidated enough to leave. But this one time the guy was a member of the high school football team and managed to throw two punks through a plate glass window on the side. Well, Ricky pulled a switchblade and knifed the football player in the side. I was on break and coming in to get something to eat. I rushed in when I heard all the commotion. When I came through the door, the football guy's date was screaming over her boyfriend who was bleeding badly on the floor. Salvano was still there with one of his other punks. He looked as though he was high on something because his eyes were so wild. I pulled my revolver and told him to drop the knife. His buddy took off running through the back. That is when Salvano lunged towards me with the knife. I couldn't believe it! I had handled this Salvano before with no confrontation, but he came at me. My instinct took over and I shot him in the chest, killing him instantly. It was clear cut self-defense. And that's the way it was portrayed until I found out that Salvano was the nephew of a local real estate developer."

"His name was William 'Big Bill' Danko and he was responsible for most if not all of Seaside's present and future building projects. He wanted me charged for murder and he was not going to accept my account of what happened. In an attempt to get me charged for the crime he then blackmailed the Mayor of that time, Stanley Craddock with a threat of going public of bribe payments to the Mayor in the granting of building contracts for his company, a charge the Mayor was guilty along with conspiracy in denying rival companies from getting the lucrative contracts."

"Mayor Craddock in turn leaned on the Chief of Police to dismiss my report and have me arrested. I still don't know how he managed to do this, but I believe he too was blackmailed. The Chief was my closest ally until he suddenly without reason went the other way. Terry Gleason, the burger guy had a suspicious fatal car accident. The football player left town and transferred to an out of state team. His girlfriend testified that she did not witness the shooting since she was attending her boyfriend on the floor. My defense attorney, Michael Donovan, hammered away at her testimony and got her to admit she did hear me say 'drop the knife.' Michael Donovan was the owner of the *Donovan's Pride* if you didn't know."

"You know about that incident. He was about to present the definitive evidence to prove my innocence when his boat went missing. There was a fry cook who saw the whole incident and then hid in a cooler in the back. He was working here as an illegal alien and feared deportation if he got involved with the police. Donovan assured his safety and had him in protective hiding and was going to produce him as a surprise witness, but that would never occur."

"After an understandable court delay after Donovan's disappearance, I hired another lawyer; but one who was incompetent and intimidated by his opposition funded by Danko and controlled by Craddock. Our surprise witness managed *to flee* suspiciously from his hiding place and return to Honduras. They even tried to link the sinking of the *Donovan's Pride* due to shoddy maintenance performed by Jimmy Castro to divert any claims that Danko sabotaged the boat. But, without Donovan there would be no case."

"Jimmy still carries that burden with him and the State made a feckless attempt to have his license revoked blaming his deformed hand for improperly installing a new exhaust line. Jimmy can't weld so he was reluctantly cleared because his signature appeared on the repair order. Jimmy maintained that somebody had forged his signature on the order."

" So, I was railroaded and did time for involuntary manslaughter before succumbing to as irony would have it a knife wound at Jessup State Prison, perpetrated by someone with a link to someone who had a personal vendetta against me, Bill Danko; who is now doing time for racketeering and conspiracy in Lewiston, Pennsylvania. Once the Feds started to interrogate about Big Bill's past in Seaside, Mayor Craddock under stress had made arrangements to talk with them and reveal everything, but not before Danko's henchmen got to him first."

"They beat him to death in his office and left a Seaside police badge pinned to his tongue. My badge! This took place after I was killed and some grave digger paid by a Danko associate liberated it from my uniform at the cemetery after the graveside services were concluded. That sent a message to everyone involved in the conspiracy that even though "Big Bill" was under investigation at that time, anyone who aided the Feds in the investigation will still be dealt with harshly, especially our *beloved* Police Chief, Carl Davenport."

"That is why the town is so paranoid in talking about anything relating to the corrupt past. To this day, the threat is real. And by the way, it was Danko's experiences *after* Seaside that landed him in prison. Now, you know the rest of the story, Agent Ermengarde."

"Thank you, Paul Harvey." She teased referring to the syndicated news commentator. "So, you're mission is to get this conspiracy out in the open?" Ermengarde inquired patiently.

"Yes. And when they raise *The Donovan's Pride* all the pieces will fall in place. Of course I have to steer and motivate Milton Craddock to do some of the leg work. I'm sure he will being doing some research about his father's interest in *railroading.* But, when all is said and done, my name will be cleared and then I can rest in peace. I'll be retired forever." Dillon exhaled.

"That's great, Ken. I envy you that you will be at peace soon. I still have a long way to go but I like my work," she admitted. "I need you to go to a vacant lot down the highway. We need to pick up Mr. Fleming."

CHAPTER 16

Exhausted from the encounters of the day, Ted Minnis and Octavia Bledsoe exited the Coast Guard Station. Speechless, they focused their attention at the site of the grounded yacht, bathed in floodlights from all sides. The cacophony of various rescue agencies coupled with the booming of the distant fireworks display combined to render any conversations useless. Still, not enough to quell the outbursts of Richard Evergreen whose impression at the Station office, all but drowned out the noise outside. The two sauntered down to a park bench near a sidewalk to collect their thoughts and to silently commiserate. The bench overlooked the scene in the channel, and was previously used by rescuers drinking coffee and soda as evidenced by the scattered debris of Styrofoam cups and aluminum cans. Rescue vehicles were departing the scene as were the barge and tugs. *The All In* was being readied to return to the marina. A shuffling of somebody approaching from behind caused the pair to look back. It was Jimmy Castro.

Placing his hands on the backs of Minnis and his guest as if to convey his support, Jimmy too peered out into the channel.

"Rough day for everyone, guys." The two shook their heads in agreement. "Did you both give the coordinates to the CG?"

Minnis turned halfway back to respond not making eye contact. "The CG rejected our report. They think it's a joke. Jimmy, I know what I saw dammit! So does Tavia," Minnis insisted.

"I believe you. Did you give them the location at least? It is very important, "Castro iterated.

"No. But there is a reporter in there from the local paper who was interested. I gave her the coordinates because she was truly intrigued. I can't believe that the Coast Guard would not hear us out," Minnis said kicking an empty Sprite can towards the edge of the sidewalk.

"The reporter, was it Gwen Blasingame? Is she here?" Jimmy clamored.

"Yes. How did you know?" both inquired in unison.

"Hey I got to run. You guys behave yourselves and stay out of trouble!" Jimmy joyously announced, running back towards the station.

Jimmy raced up the slope to the Coast Guard Station. As he approached the double doors, he could hear an ever increasing commotion outside the building. At a public phone, Richard Evergreen in full profanity was exhibiting the outrage of a teen-aged girl who couldn't hang out at the mall on a school night. Once again Captain Mueller abided by an authority other than his boss.

Seaside Fire and Rescue was demanding that the *All In* return to port at once since it was righted and able to maneuver. The channel had to be cleared and it was imperative for Mueller to comply instantly. Evergreen insisted that Mueller wait for him before he steamed back to the marina but, Mueller under repeated warnings had to proceed without Evergreen. Evergreen was incensed that his captain had once again failed him and with his wife in transit back to the condo, Evergreen was stranded. Jimmy would have to pass this man on the sidewalk leading up to the station, bowing his head from making eye contact.

"AND, D'ONT THINK I FORGOT ABOUT YOU, FIDEL! YOU'LL BE HEARING FROM ME!" Evergreen cried out as Castro passed by.

"That's great, Dick. I get lonely sometimes, so I will be hanging by the phone when you call! Have your girl call my girl, we'll do lunch!" teased Castro turning his back and walking up the steps to the building. Jimmy knew how to push the appropriate button and relished in the reaction. A guy like Evergreen was child's play. He couldn't hear the response from the angry business tycoon, but was positive it was laced with some quality obscenities that would make a stevedore blush. Jimmy pulled the glass door open and noticed the lobby was empty. Gwen Blasingame had left. He turned around and felt for the radio holstered on his belt and panicked. It was missing. "I must have left it at Colletti's," he figured.

He sprinted out of the building as his heart raced hoping that nobody took the radio. Coleman not only would reprimand him but insist on Castro to buy a replacement. It was critical for Jimmy to get to Colletti's. Gwen Blasingame would have to wait. As he ran down the sidewalk, he noticed that a severed cable was dangling from the public phone where Evergreen had been moments before. The phone receiver had found its way into passing traffic cracking the windshield of an angry Asian man who was busy *discussing* the issue with Mr. Evergreen in the middle of the street. To resolve the matter before the police got involved, Evergreen reached into his pocket and slammed three one hundred dollar bills on the hood of the astonished man's Volvo. Jimmy could not have appreciated it more and continued his jaunt to Colletti's.

The fireworks display concluded, a small mob pressed at the entrance of the bar. Jimmy made his way around the back through an open door left open by the dishwashing crew who were removing trash. Dodging a slightly wondering waitress, he exited the kitchen to the bar trying to locate somebody who could help him. The bar owner, Frank Colletti, in the midst of confusion behind the bar, reached down and pulled up the object of Jimmy's search, the radio.

"Damned thing's been goin' crazy, Jimmy. I bet you're in hot water!" grinned Colletti, handing it over to the panting jack-of-all-trades. "Couldn't help to overhear, but

it seems like they are going to torch the marina office. Let
me know if you see any of them with pitchforks."

"Thanks, will do Frank. See you!" With radio in hand,
Jimmy raced out the back as he had entered earlier.
Running down the planks of the dock, he arrived at the
skiff. There he contacted Donna.

"Donna! Donna! Over."

"Jimmy, where the hell are you? We need you back here
immediately! The place is going nuts! Over." Donna
sounded stressed and Jimmy knew he was needed.

"I'm on the way. Leaving the CG now. Over." He
grabbed the mooring line and tossed it on the dock which
splashed in the remnants of a small pool of rainwater.
Tugging on the cord took the usual 5-6 pulls to start.
Slowly, Jimmy proceeded to reverse and once clearing the
dock, opened up full throttle. The trip would take a
minimum of ten minutes to the marina office. Jimmy
employed whatever warp speed the small skiff could
muster, and skimmed the rough choppy water
hazardously. Meanwhile, the *All In* now free from the mud
that had entrapped it for the past few hours was
maneuvering to return to the marina with a relieved
Captain Mueller at the helm. Evergreen was still on shore!

On his right flank, Jimmy noticed the familiar red and
blue flashing lights of police cruisers rapidly responding to
the situation at the marina. A deep concern for the safety
of Donna and Oscar now descended on him. In the
distance he could see the Marina office, illuminated by the
headlights and high beams of cars.

"Jimmy? How close are you? Over." Donna pleaded.

"Two more minutes, Donna. Over"

"Be careful pulling up! I recommend you dock away
from the office. We're surrounded by drunks and lunatics.
Over." she alerted.

"Roger. Full moon crowd. Over."

As Jimmy neared the office, he could see an officer
trying to placate the mob as if a town sheriff dissuading a
lynch mob in the old West. To sneak in to the office, Jimmy
shut down the motor drifting the skiff silently towards an
open area to dock. As he closed in, he could hear a familiar
authoritative voice over the mob. It was Corporal

D'Antuano, Donna's ex-husband trying to reason with the crowd. In the background a chant emerged, "WE WANT OUT! WE WANT OUT! Using a bullhorn from his cruiser, Corporal D'Antuano pleaded with the mob to disperse or face incarceration. He couldn't understand why these people were demanding to leave the marina. The fireworks were over, it was dark, they were drunk, and there would be boats returning with drunks. Ah, the wonders of alcohol had worked its magic to a small group wishing to demonstrate their first amendment privileges on the day we celebrate our independence. D'Antuano reckoned to make sense of the scene but duty was duty.

"THIS IS AN ILLEGAL ASSEMBLY! IF YOU DO NOT DISPERSE .YOU WILL BE ARRESTED!"

Oscar and Donna peered from the upper windows. For a brief moment, Donna admired her ex for his valiant attempt to stave off the horde from invading the office. Oscar Coleman too, felt comforted, knowing the cavalry was on its way. That was until the notorious front man of the mob, Bobby Willloughby, chucked a beer can at the bull horn as Corporal D'Antuano attempted to remind the crowd to disperse.

His voice choked on the half-drunk Budweiser as it seeped through the horn to his throat. Angered, Corporal D'Antuano veered towards the beer bellied trouble maker, throwing down the bull horn in disdain. Willloughby braced for the charge catching the officer as he tried to tackle him at waist level. With all his strength he swung the policeman to the ground and dove on top to pin him down, reaching for his service revolver.

That was all Donna needed as she swung open the door and raced down the steps to aide her ex-husband. Her adrenaline surging, she administered the first of several round house kicks a la Chuck Norris sending the obese drunk backwards, reeling. Trying to realize that he just got his manhood handed to him by a woman, he rushed her in full anger. Donna prepared and delivered a precisely driven kick to the groin of the indignant dipsomaniac sending him clutching himself in reverse and plummeting off the bulkhead into the murky green of the marina water, creating an ideal cannonball effect. The accelerated sounds of engines and sirens of police cruisers sent the crowd in all directions like a scene out of *West Side Story*. The impending riot imploded.

Brushing off his uniform, Corporal D'Antuano walked towards his wife as the scene inundated with arriving fellow officers. Oscar Coleman and Jimmy Castro stood at the bottom step of the office surveying the situation. Two officers attempted to fish out Willoughby, having to use a pole to drag him to the side of the dock. Once on the dock with the advice from Corporal D'Antuano they charged him with assaulting a police officer, public intoxication (his usual weekend charge) and inciting a riot. He was handcuffed and escorted passed Donna to an awaiting police car.

"Thanks, Donna. Who knows how that would have ended?" Her ex confided.

"I've been wanting to do that for two years, Vinny. But *you* were the target in my fantasies when it came to administering an act of justice. God, that felt good!"

"I bet you do. But why did you do it for me?" Vinny asked brushing himself off more.

"I don't know right now. Instinct I guess. I'll have to talk with my therapist about it," she said shrugging her shoulders.

"Well, when you find out, call me." Vinny turned to walk back to his cruiser to proceed with his duties. Donna sighed as he walked away. She grinned at Oscar and Jimmy and walked back towards them.

"I'm here now Donna. What was the emergency?" Jimmy quipped.

"What timing." Oscar declared looking out towards the channel. The *All In*, in view of the three, was making its way into port. The incident was finally over.

CHAPTER 17

Gwen Blasingame drove up into the concrete driveway of her modest beach home in West Seaside Village outside of town. From her car, she could see her husband of thirty four years, Calvin, entrenched in front of the television watching the local news. He had torn away his attention to notice the headlights of the '84 Plymouth Reliant K Car illuminate the living room. Seeming annoyed he emerged from his recliner in his blue wrinkled boxer shorts and faded white undershirt to close the curtains. What a compelling image to present yourself to your neighbors who might be walking by! Of course it would be more sensible to perform this task when you are decently attired. But, Calvin not honoring the etiquette required from such mundane functions, lived his life in simple ways. One would hope he would have the wherewithal to change his underwear on a regular basis.

"You never cease to amaze me, Calvin." Gwen announced as she entered the house.

"I'm not putting my pants on just to close the curtains! How many times do we have to have this talk? "Calvin complained sitting himself back down.

Gwen placed her purse and carry-all bag down on the kitchen table, noticing a half opened pizza box with one remaining cold piece inside. Anchovies, onions, and pepperoni! Oh it's going to be a memorable mélange of malodor tonight, she thought.

"Hey, I saved you some pizza from Paulie's. Help yourself. Might be a little cold though," he offered from his perch in the living room.

"You're so thoughtful Cal. As inviting as this *one* piece appears, I might have to fight the urge to wolf it down. Thanks anyway though. I had a hamburger for dinner," she commented knowing her husband was engrossed in deep thought over the concept of a medicated shampoo commercial.

"OK. Suit yourself. Hey, they said there was some sort of problem in the bay today. You know anything about it?" he hollered from his chair.

"Yeah. It was my assignment. Some jerk thought he could cruise his yacht out of the bay in low tide. Got grounded. Tied up everything. Big mess!" she related in a UPI ticker tape like manner. "Cal, do you know if the banks are open tomorrow, I mean Monday?"

"Wait a minute, Gwen. Orioles highlights!"

Gwen did not expect her husband to respond because of his short attention span. It was the same every night; news and Carson and bed. On this night since it was Saturday, and after the news concluded, Calvin dedicated himself to watching an Alfred Hitchcock Presents rerun as the mournful theme of *The Funeral March of a Marionette* enraptured its casual viewers. The music could have been Calvin's own theme song by the way he moved so Hitchcockesque.

As inviting as her husband appeared, Gwen had managed to tear herself away from her personal *Adonis*. She figured that since the Fourth of July had fallen on a Saturday this year, then the day of observance would be Monday. Hence, the banks would be closed. She would have to wait until Tuesday which derailed her impulse to resurrect her story about the ghost ship sighting of the *Donovan's Pride*. She jotted down a list regarding contacts and made four copies of the coordinates given to her by Ted Minnis. Her notes of the boat's disappearance were stored in a safety deposit box at the bank.

Her editor was under the impression that all notes were destroyed by Mrs. Blasingame as she set fire to them in the newspaper office in a metal waste basket under his supervision and Mayor Stanley Craddock. She indeed had set fire to the originals but her journalistic instincts propelled her to duplicate her notes on a copier at the County library. She sensed the magnitude of the story after her interviews with Benjamin Jacoby, the man who was institutionalized.

He had revealed to her in detail the description of the *Donovan's Pride*. Her editor demanded that she drop the story claiming Jacoby had plenty of time to study newspaper pictures of the missing boat. But when witnesses to the Dillon trial coincidentally died or relocated or recanted their accounts of that fateful night Gwen knew she had the makings of a conspiracy laden story worthy of Watergate. To maintain her personal safety and job security, she feigned indifference and honored her boss's request to drop the story. When questioned by her boss later about a fact of the story, she would simply act forgetful which satisfied her boss. She would show preoccupation with a current assignment such as a story about a middle aged blind Lebanese woman who produces art masterpieces from conch shells. (a story highlighted on the local TV show, Seaside Citizens Magazine). But on the inside she was gathering information as discretely as possible.

Calvin entered the kitchen scratching his stomach. He opened the refrigerator door pulling out a cold can of Fanta grape soda. Looking over at his wife while she jotted down notes, he remembered a phone call he received about an hour ago.

"Some guy by the name of Castro called. He wants you to call him back tomorrow. His number is on the pizza box. Anything I should know about?" Calvin mentioned as he struggled opening the pop top on the can.

"Yes Calvin. He's my lover. We're hopping aboard a chartered jet and heading off to Rio tomorrow. He can't live without me! I've struggled with living my life with such a dynamo as you are or settling for the instant gratification of a weekend jaunt with a man who just figured out how to use an electric razor," she retorted dryly.

"OK Gwen. We're almost out of toilet paper. Get some before you take off."

Gwen shrugged her head in amazement, smiling knowing that this was just Calvin being Calvin. She gazed at the phone number on the pizza box. She knew Jimmy was aware of the information she now possessed; the exact location of the *Donovan's Pride.*

CHAPTER 18

The man stood alone in an empty deserted unmaintained parking lot rife with pot holes, puddles, trash, glass, and weeds which burst through the asphalt to re-establish its natural claim to the Earth. The light poles supported swaying and dangling fixtures devoid of the heat of electricity for five years. An occasional flash of nearby traffic illuminated him briefly as he stood motionless in the dimness of the vacant lot. A nearby ice cream parlor, now busy from the fireworks finale bustled with cars and a rushing crowd as patrons moshed at the doors of the small store. Every once in a while courageous passer bys would venture through the lot including a mother with a small boy. As they hurried passed the lone figure, the mother dragging her child by the hand, just realizing they were being watched, quickened their pace. The boy glanced back at the man in wonder.

"Mom, that man is scary looking!"

"It's not polite to stare, Joey! Come on, now!" The mother ushered her son rapidly by the lone figure.

A police cruiser pulled into the lot to the delight of the mother and son. Its tires crunched over the rusty chain long since used as an effective deterrent. The cruiser proceeded cautiously over to the suspicious figure as the mother and child stopped and looked back to witness the confrontation. The man did not move as the cruiser pulled up to his side. With the din of traffic drowning out any probability of eavesdropping, the mother and child proceeded to the ice cream store. Officer Dillon permitted the rear passenger window to lower so Agent Ermengarde could introduce herself to the man.

"Mr. Fleming, I am Agent Ermengarde. I sent for you. Please get in."

The lone figure complied hesitantly and entered the police car. A small golden beam of light radiated from a hole just above his right ear. The hole was about the size that a .22 caliber pistol would create if there was a crime scene specialist on the scene, but in this case one would not be needed because the origin of the wound was already known. Officer Dillon's uniform concealed his numerous illuminated wounds from his multiple stabbings in his thorax. Agent Ermengarde concealed her wounds by wearing a sheer scarf around her throat. Officer Dillon adjusted the rear view mirror to take note of Fleming's bewildered face.

"What is this all about, Agent Ermengarde? I was experiencing real peace until I got pulled down to who knows where."

"Mr. Fleming, are you aware of the sacred observance and obligations of the Blood Moon?"

"Yes, but not entirely. It has something to do with the dead seeking revenge, right?" he assumed.

"In short, that's it. It only applies to those whose own life was curtailed before meeting their ultimate predestined goals, set forth by God. And, to those who were wrongly dispatched by the acts of evil men before the attainment of those predestined goals. You are here because you meet the parameters of the obligations and you are required to perform this *task* under my guidance. Now, can you think of any one person responsible for you not meeting your predestined goals?" she enticed.

"Absolutely! Richard Evergreen, Esquire. That dirty scum.....," his voice rising in crescendo.

"I understand your resentment, Mr. Fleming. There is no need for vulgarity. I have been looking over your dossier, but it only states the cold facts and not the reason on what led you to taking your own life," Ermengarde inquired pouring through the report.

"Is he going to listen in?" Mr. Fleming pointed to Officer Dillon who sat monitoring the activity on his police radio.

"Officer Dillon and I are working together on your case. You have nothing to worry about since we are wholly obligated to the Supreme Council. Any deviation in our duties will be harshly dealt with, so you can be confident that you are in good hands. All I need is a brief synopsis of the events which led up to your demise," she stated pulling a cap off a Bic pen with her teeth.

"Okay. I was an associate in the law firm of Evergreen, Goldberg, and Carlson. I was busting my ass in meeting the outrageous demands of my billable hours quota. The stress was unbelievable! Even on my vacations with my family, I had to check in with the firm on a regular basis to be kept informed on current issues and to maintain my work responsibilities. It took a toll on my family who relied on me to share my good side with them. But, that wasn't to be. They never saw my good side. I was one miserable s.o.b."

"Anyhow, there was this case I was assigned to by his majesty, Evergreen. It was with a small up and coming ad agency that was being sued for an ad campaign by a larger ad agency for *creative plagiarism* of their client. Evergreen figured it wasn't a big suit and appeared disinterested since the rewards were not huge. The small company had no chance and so it would be dissolved. They were already behind in their retainer fees with us. I chose to fight the larger company relentlessly since this was my big chance for recognition by the firm. I always took the side of the underdog in any dispute especially in matters of David versus Goliath. It was right up my alley. Despite the lack of support from *his highness* in our regular meetings, I proceeded to launch an effective plan to derail the larger firm's attack on the smaller firm. The jury saw it my way and the case was dismissed. I then, filed a countersuit for damages from libel and slander on behalf of my client to the amount of one million dollars. We won. Was I congratulated? Was I rewarded with promotion? No! My achievement was given a very cold reception by the partners."

"At our annual company function recognizing the achievements of employees of Evergreen, Goldberg, and Carlson, by the way there is no Carlson, I was misled to believe I would be recognized for my victory of the past year. I was in a way recognized, but not the way you would think. As Evergreen addressed the audience of 500 employees, friends and relatives, including my wife, he made a 15 minute part of his 30 minute speech dedicated to me, On How *NOT* To Win A Case! He singled me out using terms as greedy, immature, naive, irresponsible, unprofessional, and dim-witted. He chastised me for putting *my selfish interests* above the firm's interests. I was totally embarrassed at my table with my wife by my side and some co-workers. It was the longest 15 minutes of my life!"

"And the harshness reverberated for the rest of my life. I never recovered from this public execution. After the speech as he left the dais in sporadic applause, he came to my table with a wireless microphone. He extended his hand for me to shake. I couldn't believe it! I stood and shook it out of courtesy, hoping that he would reveal to me that this was some cruel joke that he and everyone in attendance was in on. And then, he fired me in front of everyone! He laughed! And over the loud speaker he told me, 'Well I hoped you and your wife enjoyed the meal. Consider this as a farewell gesture. It is your last and your presence in our firm is hereby terminated. You two are to leave here immediately so the rest of us can enjoy the more deserving of our firm's accomplishments.' The hotel sent two uniformed security guards to our table to escort us out like we were criminals! I was totally humiliated. My wife, Deborah, was in tears, both of us in shock. Not making eye contact as we left, we could feel the blatant stares of those who felt we got what we deserved."

"Later, I found out from a secretary who was loyal to me, that I *rocked the boat*. My handling of the case caused some of Evergreen's lucrative clientele to abandon our firm citing conflict of interest in our prime directive. The firm lost more money than we received from the law suit. We were supposed to lose this case to discourage newer client's access to the vast ad market dominated by the established elite; a point which was implied but never stressed to me."

"Being that I was employed at Evergreen for the past 6 years, I was black-balled from getting a job reference. I could not find work anywhere and went into a dark depression which led to me placing an old .22 caliber pistol I had around for protection and blowing my brains out in my car on a scenic overlook along the Palisades Parkway. I was out of options. Evergreen even threatened termination of any employees who attended my viewing and funeral in a videotaped message to all employees! I found out from a coworker who died from cancer. That's just my story!"

"He once berated a man who had taken time off to be with his dying mother. After a few days, he called him at home and practically asked him *'why she hadn't died yet?'* In other words, tell her to hurry up and croak already, it's costing me business! So when she did pass, he did inform his secretary that he would require time off to grieve her loss and that he was not to be disturbed. This incensed Evergreen and when he did return to work *Mr. Sensitivity* went into a tirade in front of the entire office scolding the poor guy. The man just lost his mother for crying out loud and was terminated on top of that! And then there was the time he called out this secretary who suffered the longing effects of diabetes which caused one leg to be shorter than the other one. She misinterpreted a memo and faced this guy's wrath in front of everyone too. Her obvious affliction was included in his rant. She was crushed beyond repair! I could see it in her face! It seems no matter where this guy goes he leaves a path of destruction of souls. And the sickening fact is that he gets delight from these attacks."

Agent Ermengarde shook her head in disgust. Officer Dillon clenched his teeth at the outright evil that a man like Evergreen could induce. If Fleming couldn't muster the motivation to avenge himself, Dillon would gladly step in to administer the coup de grace.

"Mr. Fleming. I have prior experience in handling guys like Evergreen. Just say the word, and I can do a job on him you would appreciate," offered Dillon.

"Ken? This isn't your mission. You are only to transport us and by the way you have your own mission. We don't need you to get carried away!" advised Agent Ermengarde. "You better control that temper or you will regret it."

"You don't have to concern yourselves with my vengeance. I am capable and I won't let you two down. Evergreen is going to get what he deserves as prescribed. Pure Hell on Earth and pure hell in Hell!" Fleming avowed broiling in his recount of the maliciousness of Evergreen.

CHAPTER 19

Jimmy's first moments with the naval psychologist, Dr. Bennett Quarles, did not reveal anything. The office quiet and comfortable equipped with the usual sofa and leather chairs, did nothing to ease Castro from relating his nightly revisits to the hangar deck in flames, and now other symptoms were emerging. His right hand would shake uncontrollably and he would utter inane phrases under his breath as his mind wandered aimlessly in his travails eventually leading him into a flashback. Sometimes in mid sleep he would wake himself up by screaming. Jimmy would describe the emotion as his speech as being 'suffocated' and that the eventual release was the result of his intense feelings being bottled up. Sunny would awaken too, wondering what was he dreaming about and why would he repeat the same phrase over and over. What did it mean, "I want to go home!" You are at home! Does it mean Brownsville?" Jimmy would say to Sunny it was something that triggered him inside, something horrible, the fire.

Dr. Quarles sat in his chair stroking his graying goateed chin and waited for Jimmy to initiate the conversation. The clock on the wall ticked loudly as the lone two faced each other in silence. The session dragged.

Jimmy stared at the floor as Dr. Quarles, hands clenched
in his lap, feigning disinterest. "What a job this guy has!
He calls people to his office to stare at them for $100 per
hour. What a gig! Fortunately my VA benefits pay for this."
Finally, the showdown of silence was broken when Jimmy
figured it was he who should initiate the conversation.

Jimmy leaned forward in his chair clasping his hands
together to commence the session. Dr. Quarles swiveled his
chair to the side to indicate he was ready to listen to
Castro's problem.

"Doc, I don't know what has been said to you regarding
my situation, so I'll just tell you about my recent lack of
sleep; although, for the past two nights I've been able to
sleep. I guess it's like taking your car in for repair because
it makes a bad noise and when you arrive at the mechanic
the noise stops."

The psychologist chuckled in acknowledgment of the
analogy. "Why do you think you've managed to sleep the
past two nights?"

Jimmy embarrassed to admitting about his torrid
intimate relations with his wife struggled with the question
before the inevitable response a guilty grade schooler
would reply, "I don't know."

"Have there been any changes in your life over the last
two days? Quarles sat back in his chair making eye contact
with his squirming patient.

"Well, I kinda got released from my job," Castro
admitted weakly.

"Well, it was probably your *own* fault, right? You hate
your work, your boss. You believe the world owes you
something!" Quarles insinuated to a startled Castro.

Instantly, Jimmy got irate over the Doctor's assertion.
How could he know the situation at work? How dare he
accuse him for his lack of integrity! Castro felt his blood
rise and his heart thump.

"You, insensitive asshole! You don't know a damned
thing about me or the hell I experience every night!' Jimmy
stood from his seat pointing to the uncaring and
unimpressed psychologist who was toying with a rubber
band between his fingers. Dr. Quarles was ready to push
the next button to elicit the root of Castro's problem.

"What makes your case so special? I've seen a lot of guys in your *so called* condition."

"So *called* condition? Have they seen their buddies burn up in front of them or trapped in their quarters screaming for help? Have they been burned like me?" Castro exhibited his hands and pulled the hair up above his damaged ear, "Have they seen bodies in flames diving into the sea? Do you know what burning flesh and steel smells like, you cold-hearted bastard?" Jimmy braced himself on the edge of Dr. Quarles's desk staring wildly awaiting the doctor's response.

The alarm on Doctor Quarles's desk announced the end of the session with Castro in the heat of the exchange. Dr. Quarles jotted down some notes as Castro related his experiences. While Jimmy was in mid-rant inquiring about his Doctor's experience at sea, the psychologist handed his irritated patient two pieces of paper. One was for a prescription of Prozac to ease his depression and stress. The other was for the next scheduled appointment.

"Mr. Castro. I advise you to pick up where we left off for the next session. You're admission to what happened will be beneficial in our future sessions. Only you can help you. I'm just the guide. The prescription will help you manage better in your daily routines." The tall African-American psychologist stood and extended his hand. "Good day to you, sir."

Jimmy hesitant about shaking the hand of such a cold indifferent professional reeled back from his anger in confusion and politely shook the doctor's hand. He exited the office past the receptionist who had seen the *lost look* on Dr. Quarles's new patients numerous times before. Jimmy spent the rest of the day contemplating the session and whether or not he would attend the next session before he prepared himself to go to night school. On his way to the school, he stopped by the base pharmacy to get his prescription filled. Not knowing if the prescription helped, he slept every night without incident before his next appointment one week later. His nights of sleeping on the sofa were over to his wife's delight.

CHAPTER 20

Milton Craddock still perplexed from his encounter with Officer Ken Dillon, had written off the intention to drive to Seaside Emergency Hospital to initiate contact with one of the *All In* victims. Instead he focused on the sudden disappearance of Officer Dillon from their brief exchange on the highway. He turned into the police station hoping to resolve this mysterious encounter with the lawman. Perhaps he was at the station. It was now 10:30 PM. as he strolled through the entrance which was now a bee hive of activity. Sergeant Donald Quigley Yeager who went by the sobriquette "Dairy Queen," because of his initials, was his usual cheerful complacent self in on summer weekend evenings when it came to rounding up the usual violators. D. Q. was one of those guys who never had a stressful day in his life and viewed life from the perimeter, always offering his unsolicited opinions to the disinterested. The rotund Sergeant spied Craddock maneuvering past the mob to get to the front of the counter.

"Hey Counselor. Lots of folks here requesting your talents in getting them out, especially your main client, Bobby Willoughby. We just brought him in not too long ago. I don't even think he's made the phone call yet. You must be psychic," the desk sergeant grinned and announced.

Craddock reached into his pocket for the citation which was now compressed into a fragile wrinkled yellow ball of a carbonized document. The lawyer placed the ticket on the counter and smoothed it out in front of the curious sergeant. Craddock strained his thin voice to rise above the escalating detestations inside the station.

"I got ticketed about an hour ago by Officer Dillon. Is he here now D. Q.?"

"Hmmm, I don't recall an Officer Dillon. Must be one of the on loan cops we hired for tonight. Let me check on it." The desk sergeant scanned the duty roster on his computer.

"Nope. Don't see anyone by that name. Is that the citation?" he wondered.

The sergeant looked at the citation and furled his brow. The citation itself had been out of use for years and had been replaced by a more modern detailed one. Yeager studied both sides of the carbon ticket in wonder. Licking his index finger, he placed it on Craddock's signature. It smudged proving the freshness of issuance.

"Is there a problem, Sergeant Yeager?" Craddock again had to yell above the noise of the crowd and the incessant ringing of telephones. Yeager turned briefly to see if the phones were being answered. The desk sergeant motioned for Craddock to follow him around the counter to a vacant office down the hall so the two could converse in private. Yeager didn't want the possibility of a police imposter to be broadcast in front of the mob in front and since Officer Dillon was not on the roster for the night nor was he a current member of the Seaside PD.

"Can you describe this officer to me, Mr. Craddock?" insisted the now concerned sergeant.

"That's the problem. I couldn't see his face with the bright lights from his car and all. I was hoping he was here so I could talk to him. He made some off the wall comment about my father that got me wondering. I didn't take notice at first but now it's festering and nagging the hell out of me!" the counselor complained in vain.

"How about the cruiser, Mr. Craddock? Did you get a good look at it?" Headlights from outdoors scanned the darkness of the office illuminating Yeager's quizzical face.

"Like I said before, the lights were so bright, I couldn't see and then he left with no trace. He friggin disappeared, D. Q.! I'm not making this up!" Craddock stressed to the sergeant not wanting to sound crazy.

"No trace?" Yeager repeated raising his eyebrows in disbelief. "Have you been drinking tonight, Mr. Craddock?" A plain clothes cop brushed by the two in the entrance to his office flipping on the light switch. His interest was obvious to the discussion as he made his way to his desk flinging off his nylon windbreaker onto an empty chair by his desk. His tall frame collapsed into the squeaky swivel of his ancient looking cushioned chair. He exhaled loudly to elicit an explanation from the desk sergeant who should be out front at his post attending to the mob.

"Dave," the sergeant addressed the plain clothes cop," Mr. Craddock got cited by what I think is a man posing as a Seaside Police Officer. You know anything about any cases like this, today? I just came on duty an hour ago," Sergeant Yeager asked inferiorly knowing he was going to be reminded to return to the front desk in any second by the detective.

"No D. Q. What do we have?" he asked dismissively sliding his fingers through his black hair.

"Look at this citation, Dave!" Yeagher cried out in his usual annoying high pitched voice snatching the ticket from the surprised lawyer.

Immediately the elder cop scanned the citation noticing the out of print style. Again both sides were examined and then the plain clothes cop froze glaring at the officer's signature at the bottom. Without notice, he leapt from his chair and hurried to the file room hoping that the records were not locked. Just as he thought, all personnel records were secured and could not be accessed until morning when Officer Marge Lowe came on duty. He would have to fill out a request form and have it approved by the Chief to access the file of Officer Kenneth Dillon, a man who he was acquainted and worked with him in the past.

His sole quest was to compare signatures from records against the citation to see if they matched. But, what if they matched? Is Dillon actually alive? It has been almost eight years since his murder in prison. To reopen this case again would have to be handled in a subtle and discrete way without placing his safety in jeopardy. Lieutenant Dave Nichols returned to the entrance of the bustling counter area, signaling Sergeant Yeager to come over for a private conference.

"Sergeant Yeager, you are not to talk with anyone regarding this citation. I am going to investigate it and if you say anything to anyone at the station or outside of work, you will be reprimanded. Is that understood?" he demanded peering intensity into the sergeant's soul.

Nichol's rugged granite face was intimidating. His darting blue eyes stressed obedience and nobody questioned his motives, not even the Chief. Nichols took pride in honing his senses and kept a strict self-discipline in maintaining them to keep them razor sharp. He never dallied with any vices that would weaken his fierce determination. He could wear a tweed sports coat on a hot afternoon in July and not break a sweat. With his five foot eleven frame, gray and black peppered hair and sturdy muscular build, one would assume he had a military background, but his no nonsense charisma indicated a special talent with intimidation. A session with Nichol's interrogative methods could melt the iciest of suspects to confess their crime. Try to bullshit him on any subject and you would get a lengthy, factual, detailed lecture of his worldly knowledge compliments of Tufts University and his short lived career in the Central Intelligence Agency. He would diminish those who thought themselves astute on the matter of the discussion to a quivering mass of mumbles when Nichol's confronted them with follow-up questions. He once called out a subordinate to meet him after roll call when the officer feigned boredom during the morning meeting. A reprimand from Nichols was not a pleasant experience and the officer's fellow patrolmen immediately garnered the lieutenant's message by sitting up in their seats.

"Okay Lieutenant. Does that include the Chief?" the sergeant blubbered.

"Especially the Chief! This is something that happened before you started here. So you are in no position to discuss this with anyone. What you don't know is to your benefit and safety. So keep your mouth shut on this! Tell Mr. Craddock we will investigate this. We are holding on to the citation as evidence and he doesn't have to pay the fine. In other words we are treating this as an imposter issue. Tell him this is a department issue and not to talk to the press or anyone!"

The sergeant did as his superior requested. Craddock nodded his head and nervously smiled when D. Q. informed him of Lt. Nichol's demand. However, he was not satisfied with the explanation. There was more to this then he could imagine. He left the station without addressing the legal needs of his rowdy, ranting, intoxicated clients in the downstairs cell area. In the morning, he would drop by to visit his mother and ask her about his father's interest in railroads.

CHAPTER 21

A restored 1963 Ford Fairlane taxi cab belching exhaust fumes whisked an infuriated Richard Evergreen into the driveway apron of the Coastal Charm Condominium complex. The ruffled driver accelerated a short distance and then slammed on his brakes as the cab pulled off from the highway, causing his fare to lurch into the back of the front seat. After being subjected to Evergreen's belittling for three miles, the driver wanted to give his fare the Dan Rather treatment of driving him around recklessly until he begged for mercy to stop. But the driver, an ex-convict did not want to risk incarceration again and so he felt satisfied with his handling of Evergreen. The corporate big wheel exited the cab slamming the door in disgust. He dared the cabbie to follow him and demand the fare for which he was entitled.

"Hey! You owe me 11 bucks and change!" the driver yelled as he ran from the cab leaving his door open.

Ignoring the driver and feeling that he might be accosted, Evergreen motioned for a condo security guard to the front gate. Of all the owners in the Coastal Charm, there was one who was known to all the guards, Richard Evergreen. Feeling he was about to be harmed, guard Sammy Travis rushed down to open the gate. The twenty-two year old guard pushed the green button allowing the gate to swing inside as Evergreen squeezed his six foot one frame through the narrow opening. Once inside safely, Travis pushed the close button as the driver reached the gate trying in vain to grab Evergreen. The lawyer turned back towards the cussing cabbie. Feeling attention from the Coastal security staff, he held up his index finger to the angry cabbie and whispered to Travis his rescuer.

"Sam. You got twelve dollars on you? All I have is twenties and I know this guy is not going to give me any change," he condescended. "I'll make it worth your while if you pay him."

Travis buying into the sincerity from Evergreen reached into his back pocket for his wallet. He had seventeen dollars total; three fives and two ones. Reluctantly, he pulled the bills from his wallet and handed them to Evergreen.

"No, Sam. Pay him!" he commanded, "I don't want to deal with this scum! He drives like a maniac!" The cab driver expecting his money ripped the bills from Travis's timid hands through the decorative wrought iron bars of the gate.

"Hey thanks for the tip you cheap bastard!" Evergreen expecting that comment as in all his dealings with the proletariat turned away from the gate and walked towards the entrance to his condo building. Travis stood motionless and victimized like a dim witted audience participant in a magic act. Evergreen didn't even thank him. He was left with an uncertainty.

"Just how and when was he going *to make it worth my while* when he just walked away with at least twenty dollars in his pocket?"

The Coastal Charm consisted of three five story high rises which catered to the wealthy elite. Security at the complex was the best money could buy and an elaborate background check of all employees was mandatory considering the valuable possessions and lives they were entrusted with guarding. The complex was envisioned by a retired Department of State official who adapted his knowledge of U.S. foreign embassy security to the Coastal. Residents had a unique bar code label attached to their vehicles so when they passed through the gate, the car was scanned and thus passed the secondary phase of security was ensured. No one could pass without the bar code. Only local police and emergency vehicles could clear security and only after security had been notified by residents of an emergency. The beach front of the complex instituted the latest in identification detection utilizing an intricate network of sensors and cameras imbedded in the dune grasses to check residents in and out of the protected beach area. The complex maintained a buffer zone of half a mile flanking the beach area with roving security on ATVs to deter trespassing. In short the place was impregnable.

As Evergreen trudged towards the door of his building, he caught eye of the security chief, Bill Alexander who was exiting the lobby.

"Bill. I assume Mrs. Evergreen is home?" he queried as Alexander held open the door for him.

"Yes, sir. We brought her home about an hour ago. Everything went well." Alexander assured Evergreen even though there was a miscommunication between his wife and security.

Without an expression of appreciation, Evergreen turned and marched to the elevator banks where he punched the buttons vehemently. Mrs. Evergreen had taken advantage of another of the coastal's amenities which included transport to and from the Coastal Charm. She was left stranded at the site of the grounding and was advised by her husband to contact them to pick them up near Colletti's. When her husband didn't show up for the ride, she had assumed he was going back to the marina on the yacht. From the marina, he would drive his Mercedes back to the condo she postulated.

But her husband had found himself immersed into a bidding war over the cost of the windshield with the owner of the Volvo who demanded one thousand dollars. With every counter bid made by Evergreen, the Asian man refused with a threat of calling the police using the disconnected pay phone receiver as a prop. Evergreen caved and paid the man his money as a police cruiser rounded the curve towards the impromptu windshield repair negotiation in the middle of the street.

Evergreen sighed in disgust as he waited for the elevator to descend from four floors. He looked at his watch and shook his head in regards to a wasted and costly evening fraught with inconveniences and undue stress caused by incompetent subordinates performing their menial mindless tasks. The doors parted and Evergreen brushed by a couple on the way out, not noticing their reaction to his rudeness of not waiting for them to clear the car. He poked the penthouse button several times before the doors closed unacceptably in 6 seconds. The trip to the fifth floor took about 40 seconds. The doors opened and Evergreen reached inside his pants pocket to once again retrieve his security card to open the glass doors shielding the hallway to his penthouse front door. Cameras positioned at either side of the doors followed his progress to his ultimate destination, his penthouse. At the front door, he suddenly remembered he had left the key to his front door on the key ring with the car keys which were on the yacht. He cussed in silence and banged on the door, hoping Pamela was not sound asleep. She peered through the peep hole and had only opened the door partially when Evergreen stormed through knocking her back to the wall.

"Richard, I hate when you do that! I am not some doorman you ignore in Manhattan!" she scolded.

"Ignore? Ignore? How about you ignoring me when you didn't wait for me downtown, Pam? I had to flag a cab down and ride back here choking on exhaust fumes. It cost me twelve bucks and since I only had twenties, the driver took the remaining eight dollars as a tip and sped off!" the millionaire explained to out duel his supermodel looking wife.

Evergreen ambled to the bar clinking the tumbler glasses in the cupboard behind the bar. He slammed a glass on the oaken surface while plunking ice cubes carelessly into the glass. Again he turned behind the bar to find the object of his thirst. Mixed among the various liquors and liqueurs, the Chivas Regal was proudly displayed for easy access. He decanted the bottle to the brim of his glass, sipping its robustness and emitting a sigh of relief from the evening's turmoil.

Pamela knew to leave him alone for a few minutes as he enjoyed his drink. She would reveal to him the important messages on the answering machines. Some of the messages would require more Chivas, perhaps to the point of sleep inducement. Hopefully, she thought he could wait until the morning to listen to the messages and when he sat on a bar stool and picked up the phone, she knew it was time for bed. He dialed pressing the keypad ferociously and waited as the answering machine finished its greeting.

"Kaz? I need you to do a job for me. His name is Alan Mueller. Captain Alan Mueller. I want to destroy him, along with two locals here in Seaside. One is named Jimmy Castro and the other is Oscar Coleman. Make this a priority. Ruin their reputations and everything they hold dear. Slander their asses! I want them to suffer badly for their actions tonight. I'm talking a memorable and irrevocable impact on their lives that when they contemplate when their lives went bad, they will recall this moment. Ruin them, Kaz! Ruin them for life! Turn them into zombies like everyone else who has gone up against me! I'll expect a report from you by noon tomorrow." Evergreen hung the phone up beaming. "They'll pay. They'll pay like the rest of those sorry sons of bitches! Nobody humiliates me and gets away with it. Nobody!" he boasted swigging his scotch.

***

Officer Dillon and company cruised by the entrance of the Coastal Charm Condominiums accepting the intense security of the premises. Abiding by Agent Ermangarde' instructions he turned down a side street several blocks down to discuss the plan. He found a vacant space out of sight of any traffic including police and turned off the engine. Ermengarde briefed her recruit.

"Mr. Fleming, you have been chosen to be the surprise speaker at a banquet honoring Mr. Richard Evergreen, Esquire. He has responded to the invitation to the event and he will be accompanied by his wife. The event will take place Monday July 6th in the ballroom of the Clayton Hotel in mid-town. This is your speech and you can not deviate

from the copy. Everything is in place and timing is crucial.
We have planned the vengeance which will occur at the
end of the festivities. Your role will allow you to personally
direct the wrath of God to your tormentor. You may not
exhibit any exhilaration once the deed is done. I stress this
point emphatically! It is not and I repeat not *your* will but
that of the Almighty that is to be satisfied. Do you
understand?" she directed sternly.

"It's going to be hard Agent Ermengarde but I guess I
can control my feelings," Fleming confided in a not so sure
commitment.

"You MUST control your feelings or your own fate will
be at issue with dire consequences," Ermengarde insisted
in a supervisory tone striking the cushioned car seat.

"Okay, you have my word," Fleming acknowledged.
"Keep this in mind Monday night. Now, Officer Dillon you
know your role, right?"

"I will be driving the limo to take the Evergreens to the
banquet. The limo is parked in a safe lot near the Clayton
Hotel. The Evergreens do not have to contact the limo
service because it was included on the invitation along with
the time. All I have to do is remind the Evergreens prior to
me picking them up so they can alert security at the gate.
After dropping them off, I will meet you at the rear of the
ballroom. We will act as security for the occasion," Dillon
replied distinctly.

"How do you know Evergreen has not contacted the
Chamber of Commerce to thank them for this 'honor'?"
asked Fleming.

"The invitation he received clearly states that HE is the
surprise honoree and that the surprise is for the audience
who are NOT to be contacted or the event will be ruined.
This is how he would expect an evening like this to be, the
audience kowtowing to his Mussolini-like ego. We are
positive that this ploy will work and he would not even
consider revealing to anyone of his presence. We also,
implied in the invitation that the keynote speaker is
someone very special and deserving of utmost secrecy, so
this is playing on his mind. He might be under the
impression that The President of the United States will be
the speaker. We are worried about his wife opening her

gossipy mouth, but we are sure Evergreen has a tight grasp on her blabbing, due to the fact that he *is deserving* of a Presidential pronouncement and he would not risk cancellation of an event in his honor due to a security leak. After all Washington D.C. is about 3 hours from here and every effort is being made to imply the President is coming here."

"Sounds kind of sketchy, Agent Ermengarde," Fleming injected, "What about the guests?"

"Our guests like you Mr. Fleming all have one thing in common. They lost their souls to Richard Evergreen. And now the Moon is red and full from the blood of the innocent. It is time for divine vengeance to descend upon the likes of Evergreen and others who delight in the dismemberment of souls. For those who felt as though they were superior on Earth, the Blood Moon will render them as beggars for mercy in Hell," Ermengarde stated factually to her captivated acquaintances in the police car.

CHAPTER 22

Gwen Blasingame awoke the next morning to the incessant shrill of the telephone. Calvin did not stir from his deep sleep, even as the phone next to his wife's side of the bed pulsated in rings of urgency. Gwen knew it had to be Jimmy Castro. It was a wonder she could hear the phone. Her ears were plugged to drown out the jack hammering snoring effect of her apneic husband. She grasped for the receiver still lying prone forgetting about the foam ear plugs she routinely jammed into her ears nightly. Baffled as to why she could not hear the caller, she removed the waxy ear plugs placing them daintily on the mattress by her side. Calvin undisturbed by his wife's activity continued his usual attempt at gasping at air that hovered just above his open yap. Gwen likened this appearance as a frog in a pond snatching a clueless fly out of the sky.

"Gwen? Jimmy Castro. I'm sorry to bother you this morning. Wow! What's that noise?" he asked anxiously.

"It's my husband's imitation of an urban renewal project. What do you think?" Gwen replied sarcastically trying to evoke sympathy from her caller.

"Can you go to another room? I really need to talk to you." Jimmy had been awake most of the night anticipating how Gwen Blasingame was going to handle the news she had culled from Ted Minnis on the location of the *Donovan's Pride*. His anxiety made him short on manners and hopefully he wished Gwen would forgive him for his rudeness, realizing how important this information was to his plight.

"Give me a few minutes, Jimmy. I'm going to the kitchen and then I have to come back and hang up the phone next to the saw mill," she said swinging her night gown draped legs out of the king sized bed.

Jimmy heard Gwen pick up the phone in the kitchen and her plodding back to the bedroom on the hardwood floor in her flat bare feet to silence the phone there. Not hearing the actual click, he realized she had either hung up the bedroom phone or smothered her husband with a pillow silencing the loud ruckus. " How could anyone endure a night's sleep like that," he wondered, " If I snored like that, I'd be required to alert the National Geologic Survey to regard my snoring as a non-seismic threatening event!"

"Jimmy, sorry about that. I figured you would call, again. Listen, I plan to get a hold of a diving crew today just for an acknowledgement that the boat is actually there. It's going to be a major deal to raise the boat and it's going to attract a lot of attention." she explained groggily interrupted by yawns and pushing her graying brown disheveled hair out of her face.

"I considered that too Gwen. But, if the boat is there, maybe you could get the divers to examine it. See what actually caused the boat to sink and take pictures, gather evidence. That shouldn't take too long and if the evidence supports sabotage, then the boat can be raised at a later date with a court order or something," Jimmy had rehearsed all the possibilities to present to the reporter during his restless night. His urge for vindication was evident.

"Jimmy, if they do find evidence of sabotage and it leaks out, well you'll know what happens to us," a certain air of discretion took hold of Gwen realizing that her phone may be tapped, "We'll just concentrate on finding the boat for now," she hoped Jimmy would get the implication.

"We can get the Feds involved, Gwen! I have a connection. Just contact me when you get a hold of the divers. I would like to go. Maybe we should both go. Do you think the divers will be available today? I mean it is Sunday," Jimmy had ignored her cautious tone and was hyped up on his multiple cups of coffee to have her accept his ideas.

"I'm hoping my nephew Petey has no plans. He's the one who does diving and salvage for a living," Gwen indicated still trying to quell Castro's enthusiasm.

"The weather is supposed to be clear today. I hope that yesterday's storm won't be an issue with the dive," Jimmy wondered aloud.

"Jimmy, I will call you with all the information when everything is organized. It's too early to speculate. Give me a few hours and I'll let you know," Gwen arose from the hard wooden kitchen dinette chair stretching her back and hung up the phone abruptly. Now wide awake she tended to cleaning off the kitchen table beginning with removing the pizza box from the night before. An official brown envelope dropped from the greasy bottom of the pizza box. It was addressed to her and marked CONFIDENTIAL. It was sent by a special courier from a M. L. Polanco. Calvin signed for it and neglected to tell Gwen because of his preoccupation with his hectic world of retired living via the wonders of cable television.

"Thanks, Gwen." Jimmy sensing Gwen's early morning grumpiness, hung up the phone out of respect not realizing she had already done so an instant before. Gwen Blasingame was Jimmy's main ally in clearing his name and now instrumental in locating the *Donovan's Pride*. Jimmy contemplated the effects of finding the boat would have on the community. How would Danko react?

Sunny entered the living room and approached her husband giving him the customary hug. It had been 21 years since they had left the quiet serene paradise of O'ahu. In 1969, they welcomed their son, Daniel Gilberto Castro into the world. Sunny's surfing days had long ended since the move east when she accepted a transfer to the Bethesda Naval Hospital in Maryland in 1972. Both she and Jimmy regretted the move, but it was an opportunity

with a promotion she could not afford to decline. They
found a home in Wheaton, Maryland, a community formed
from the benefits of the GI Bill. It was rare that a
neighborhood here did not consist of any veterans from
World War II or the Korean War. Jimmy would be one of
the first Viet Nam veterans to own a home here.

On Fridays after work, Jimmy made his weekly
pilgrimage to the local Veterans of Foreign Wars post. He
found great comfort there. There was the usual congenial
combative conflict among the armed services. A GI and a
Marine in conflict over which branch had the most
accurate mortar firing team after they had witnessed a ball
game where tee shirts were launched into the crowd. There
was "The Gunny," a one armed nine ball shooting marvel,
welcoming all comers and spouting kind insults to swabs
and grunts while downing bottles of Miller High Life.
Jimmy hooked up with "The Chief," a Chief Petty Officer
from *The USS Forrestal*. Both found it therapeutic to relate
their experiences on flat tops. Both had seen death on their
respective carriers from fire. They didn't delve into the
horrors of the past. Instead, they silently shared the bond
of camaraderie and respected each other from not recalling
the traumatic images of the past due to the possibility of
reliving the hell as they slept. Their discussions centered
on events usually humorous aboard their ships, sports,
and current events. Jimmy also was in the company that
shared mental and physical damage from wars past.
Nobody dared express their obvious wounds. It was
unwritten but understood. Despite the verbal sparring
from members, it was a mutual acceptance of one's
sacrifice of the best years of their lives. Afterwards, Jimmy
driving a 1968 Mustang would drive "Kung Fu James"
home.

Kung Fu James was a silent regular of the VFW. He
pulled three tours in Nam specializing in infiltration of
North Vietnamese Army tunnel complexes. Outside of the
VFW he was known as James. He never caused problems,
but his struggle with PTSD was going uncontrolled since
he had no faith in what he regarded as "the quackery" at
Walter Reed Army Medical Center which was trying to heal

his disorder. On occasions James would help out agreeably in the kitchen of the VFW to pay off his bar tab.

James was an averaged sized guy with an Oklahoman drawl, brown hair and had the upper body strength of Superman and considered a genius. According to friends, he once took his television apart during a get together at his apartment out of wondering how a television works. When he invited the gang to come back the following night, the television not only was re-assembled, it worked better than before.

There were also art supplies, paints, an easel, and canvasses strewn in the living room. Beautiful paintings of Southeast Asian women, and rain forest scenes adorned the walls of his apartment. On close inspection of the rain forest images, James mixed a dark magenta color dripping from some of the leaves of the lower flora and added menacing Asian eyes peering through the bush. And then there was the testimony of his strength.

According to a young kitchen worker, James once pulled out a 20 pound plastic tub of breaded fish lengthwise which measured 2 feet long by 20 inches wide and 6 inches deep. He held it by the pan handle on one end with his fingers curled under the lip of the pan extending straight out without losing his grip for one minute! The veins in his bicep bulged to the point of throbbing from the skin bearing testament to his endurance. He informed the amazed youngster that he would show him how to do this one day. That was James's good side.

But, if he felt wronged or endured undue stress, he would become a raging bull, and that was exhibited in a restaurant cocktail lounge when James took on a rival suitor for a woman at the bar. The fight escalated with two bartenders, the restaurant manager and another customer trying to break up the fight. Each participant received a memento of the bull's fierceness causing them to retreat from the squabble. James held his own until the police arrived and then it took four police officers to finally subdue him. Usually, you just respected "Kung Fu" James for his silence and thousand yard stare because there was a dangerous aura that surrounded him that a blind man could sense. You knew not to incense him. On Friday nights, Castro would drive him home from the VFW which was appreciated by all because of "Kung Fu's" short fuse.

The ride to his home in the District of Columbia would be a mostly one-sided affair with Jimmy carrying the burden of conversation along the way interspersed by the static scratching of the AM car radio in its evening broadcasting mode. Numerous times exiting Castro's car, a shot glass *compliments* of the VFW, would find its way out of his GI olive drab trench coat and tumble into the gutter. James would always appreciate his fellow vet's company with the usual gracious gratitude, *"Thanks you fuckin' swab!"* Castro would in turn reply, *"See ya around you fuckin' grunt!"*

James's condition worsened over the next two years. He became withdrawn and eventually dropped from his social circle at the VFW. Friends were dismayed to find that he was evicted from his apartment and his whereabouts were unknown. There were sightings of him around the National Mall downtown rummaging from garbage can to garbage can and sleeping on park benches huddled under mounds of blankets and garments even on hot summer days. It was a day at the National Zoo that someone had noticed him.

He stood motionless in the midst of tourists staring towards a horizon that was shielded by parklands and high rises. His tattered olive drab clothing and matted long hair and unkempt beard infested with flies and gnats screamed attention as visitors to the zoo passed him by treating him as an odd silent attraction. It was a security officer that came to his side and notified the Metropolitan Police to have him removed. The guard, a veteran himself, made it a point to the police to handle this man with great care and dignity. James was later institutionalized and forgotten by his friends at the VFW. The war had claimed yet another casualty.

Jimmy's PTSD had abated somewhat, and he would attend therapy at Bethesda Naval to alleviate his chronic problems. The sessions in Honolulu with Dr. Quarles proved to be beneficial. Referring to an innovative and unproven study, Quarles was able to link Castro's disorder with his work at the shipyard. When it was revealed that the nightmares had ceased somewhat after his work at the shipyard, Dr. Quarles was able to deduce that the trauma was triggered by something at the shipyard. Castro's last weeks at the shipyard consisted of welding steel. Dr. Quarles then researched what was known as the "Proustian Phenomenon" a reference to the famed French author Marcel Proust.

In his novel of *Remembrance of Things Past* a character's memory was jarred by an odor from a past experience that had all been forgotten in his memory until the character was exposed once again to that particular smell in a different facet in his life. In Castro's case the smell of burning steel which he was welding coupled with the docking of Naval ships nearby were causing him to relive the fire aboard *The USS Oriskany*. The episode on the altar during his wedding was triggered by the welded steel crucifix which hung over him. However, the episodes decreased, only to surface in times of stress. Dr. Quarles study was helpful in diagnosing Castro's case, but other applications weren't as successful in treating most other cases. When the Castros relocated to the East, Dr. Quarles sent the case file to the Naval Med Center. Jimmy would never touch a welding torch again.

CHAPTER 23

Milton Craddock awoke the next morning unsatisfied but still curious over the handling of the citation by Yeager and Nichols at police headquarters. Maybe, his mother could shed some light on his father's interest in railroads which continually gnawed at him. The way Officer Dillon inflected his voice to stress the point must have meant something, he thought. He replayed the conversation over and over. To resolve the issue, he would drive to the assisted living home in nearby Dawes where his mother was residing comfortably recovering from a stroke. The radio news lead-in blared as he started his car.

"To repeat if you haven't heard former Seaside developer Bill Danko was found dead in his cell in Lewiston Federal Penitentiary last night. Authorities have not released the exact cause of death. Early indications are that he died of natural causes. We will keep you informed on this developing story and now we return to our normal programming."

Gwen Blasingame heard the same broadcast on her kitchen radio. She had just finished reading the confidential letter from M.L. Polanco, a discrete code for Maria Louise Craddock, Stanley Craddock's widow. Mrs. Craddock realized she could deflect any attention to herself in any correspondence to The Seaside Daily News reporter by using her maiden name considering the constant threat by Danko and his thugs on the outside. The coincidence of reading the letter and the news of Danko's death sent shivers through Gwen's flabby body.

The letter was a revelation of events surrounding the Ricky Salvano case. In the four page letter, Mrs. Craddock enlightened Blasingame of the behind the scenes scheme of murder, payoffs, intimidation, threats, sabotage, and blackmail that were employed to win the case and sending Officer Dillon to prison. Her husband was an instrumental part in the execution of the plan; a point not lost on Gwen Blasingame when she burned the files of her reporting in front of her editor and the Mayor. Gwen now had the smoking gun in her possession to give her suspicions and her collected data credence.

The Ricky Salvano case led to at least six murders indirectly at the hands of Mayor Craddock. Mrs. Craddock, in failing health and driven by her guilt of silence of ten years past, had revealed everything. Now, Gwen had some phone calls to make; one to her nephew, one to Jimmy Castro, and the other to The Baltimore Sun. She went to her home office and closed the door.

Warden Grant Morrison strutted to Bill Danko's cell where the Pennsylvania State Forensics team was collecting evidence. Guards on duty that night and nearby inmates were interrogated and all reported hearing loud screams by "Big Bill" pleading with somebody to keep away from him in his lone cell. And then one of the guards admitted to hearing a dog bark and children screaming. "A Dog?" Children?" The investigators were astonished when the guards account corresponded with the inmates' account.

The Warden peered at the stiffened corpse on the cot. Dankos's contorted face was frozen in fear; an image as frightening as "Big Bill's" last vision on Earth; his eyes wide to the point of being thrust from its sockets; his mouth frozen agape from his last wail of torment; and the last confounding image, his right cheek ripped violently from his face and spat neglectfully on the cell floor resembling a whiskered freshly carved slice of turkey breast with blackened blood adhering the underside to the cement floor. Danko's molars and mandible could be viewed by the sizable gaping hole on the right side of his face. Above his cot the word "VIM" was emblazoned on the wall in red. It must have been too terrifying to withstand judging by the man's final pose. Meanwhile, a thin wiry man in a suit collected fluid samples from the cell floor and plucked some hair samples from Danko's torn pant leg. He sniffed the sample in the vial.

"What is it, Cooley? Urine?" a fellow evidence collector deduced.

"Nope. Smells like *sea water*," he stated in confusion. "I'll have to rush this to the lab," he stated holding the vial up to the fluorescent light.

The fellow technician peered at the illuminated cloudy contents of the vial and looked at Danko's body on the cot. "You know what this guy's body position reminds me of? The way rigor froze him on his back with his arms reaching upwards?"

"Kafka's Metamorphosis? Gregor Samsa, the cockroach?" Cooley mentioned pedantically while examining more elements of the scene.

"No Cooley," his aide protested unimpressed at Cooley's reference. "Gregor who? Look at the way his arms are frozen upwards trying to force something off of him and the way his face is frozen in absolute fear. It reminds me of a tale from a pre-med professor I once had about premature burial in the 1800s and how body snatchers would find fresh corpses in this exact position when they dug them up!" the young aid exclaimed. "I forgot the term he used to describe premature burial, though."

"Vivisepulture," he responded, distracted and annoyed by his assistant's non sequitur discovery. Cooley did not agree with his co-worker's implication and rolled his eyes. "Your professor's name, was it FRONKensteen?" referring to the movie, "Young Frankenstein." He then turned to the dismay of his assistant locating the Warden with his finding as he fixated on Danko's contorted corpse.

"Warden?" he asked suspiciously. "Which one of your guards had access to a dog last night?"

"I will find out!" the Warden confirmed noticing the paw prints which had tracked through Danko's blood on the cell floor while a photographer snapped photos of the tile. I'll get to the bottom of this! I guarantee it!" Morrison asserted to deflect any personal involvement or conspiracy that the investigators might consider him to be a suspect including Federal Prison authorities.

Weeks later, a report of the crime scene was issued. Briefly, it stated that the vial contained sea water consistent with the Atlantic Ocean! The hair sample at first thought to be human was actually a fur sample; fur from the coat of a dog, an Irish Setter! The paw prints in blood cemented the proof that there was an Irish Setter in the cell with Danko. The evidence led to the conclusion that Bill Danko died from a massive heart attack and it was agreed by all involved due to the unexplainable nature of the evidence to bury the details of the report until a rational conclusion could be derived in the future. To this date the report remains unchanged despite the constant clamoring from conspiracy theorists.

"Big Bill's" cell once declared a crime scene would now be readied for future guests of the state. On certain hot and humid summer nights when the Moon is full and red on the horizon, the walls of the cell dampen with the salty scent of the sea and a faint tune ,only audible to the occupant, descends from the ceiling, playing persistently through the night on a tinny piano, Tura-Tura-Lural, interrupted by the tortured muffled screams of Bill Danko from beyond. Many a toughened convict has begged for mercy to be relocated from this hellish haunted cell to the point of a babbling atonement for their criminal act that landed them here.

Responding to legal pressure, Warden Morrison invited both Priests and psychics to investigate the cell. All have avoided entering the cell sensing a dominating demonic-like presence. Technicians were brought in to inspect for hidden microphones and video projection equipment in the cell that may have been part of a prison conspiracy. None were discovered. Inmates were instructed to remove the word "VIM" from the wall above the cot. No matter what combination of chemicals were applied to the area, the word returned; resistant of the various attempts at removal including sand blasting. One guard volunteered to sleep the night in the cell on a dare. He was awakened by a dark shadowy figure staring at him. He lost the bet as he begged for his fellow guards to free him. Inmates next door to the cell, dreading the proximity to the ultimate portal to Hell, demanded relocation. Conspiracy theorists declined invitation to spend the night in Danko's cell upon hearing of the horror of those who dared to do so. As time went by, the theories ceased due to lack of proof and intestinal fortitude to proceed.

The notorious reputation of the haunted cell grew as new inmates experienced the same occurrences that befell prison inmate 679345, Bill Danko. Thus, the three cells were never to be used to house inmates again. When given the option of solitary or the haunted cells, punished inmates chose solitary confinement because *they felt safer!* Eventually citing lack of use the cells were walled up, never to be occupied again. The relevance of the Irish tune and its link to Danko was never connected; a secret only the Donovan's can explain. It's an Irish lullaby!

CHAPTER 24

Life in Wheaton, Maryland for the Castros was happy. Sunny and Jimmy devoted their lives to their son, Danny. Weekends would find Jimmy and his son fishing from a row boat in a nearby river as he grew in age. A basketball court was erected in the backyard for Danny to enjoy with his neighbors, all of whom were about the same age. Birthday parties, PTA meetings, Boy Scouts, baseball teams, all became a part of the Castro home. Visiting neighbors adored the Castro living room, replete with Hawaiian mementos, wedding pictures, and framed pictures of Sunny surfing in Waikiki, the North Shore, and South Padre Island along with her prized possession, her autographed poster of Duke Kahanamoku.

Above a roll top desk in the corner of the room, hung an ink sketched drawing of the *Oriskany*, a framed letter of accommodation noting Jaime Alonzo Castro's heroic action 26 October 1966 endorsed by President Lyndon B. Johnson, and a mahogany framed, velvet background display of Jimmy's Purple Heart. Atop his desk were framed pictures of his family at a petting zoo and one picture of his parents beaming their pride at him from their home in Brownsville.

Sunny wanted to add her longboard to the living room, but with young Danny running wild with his friends around the house, it was considered a falling hazard. It later served as a makeshift bar in the basement when the Castros entertained. Jimmy added a bamboo façade with cabinets, bar stools, and a sink to complete an island bar effect. The surfboard served as the counter top. All that was missing was a piano with Don Ho singing *Tiny Bubbles.*

Jimmy Castro's line of work was in maintenance for the Montgomery County Public School system. Utilizing the skills he culled from the trade school in Hawaii he was able to find work immediately in his new environment. The scars on his face had healed to the point of acceptance by all who he came in contact and now were just a minor reminder until he shaved in the morning. To cover his scarred hand, he fashioned a golf glove to avoid the inevitable curiosity of his peers.

His supervisor and coworkers loved his good nature and found him fun to be around. Serving several schools, Jimmy had a rock star following when he had to repair, replace or recommend major repair work at a particular school, but when it came to a situation regarding items like repairing a loose stair railing, Jimmy made the recommendation for welding. Jimmy could do the rest as long as he wasn't near when the welding was active.

He was confident in his role of jack-of all trades. Castro kidded with the students and if he spotted a student secretly sneaking a smoke in the bathroom, he would admonish them despite the hypocrisy of his own nicotine habit. The students considered Jimmy a strong fatherly source of security.

Sunny reunited with Candice Middleton who was living in Silver Spring, Maryland. Candice still had that worry free face. It was the kind of face you would notice from a generic prodigious all girl college prep school yearbook. She would be the one pictured in numerous school clubs standing front and center emitting that smug confident smile that detracted attention from the others in the group photo. Candice owed her demeanor to good genes, good jeans, and family wealth. Her classmates noted that 'Candice has an *heir* about her'. And no image of Miss Middleton would be complete without videos of her horseback riding in the Middleburg, Virginia countryside attired in her English riding breeches, leather jodhpurs, topped off by the requisite black show coat and helmet. Coincidentally, she served as Candice's maid of honor in her wedding and Sunny had her hands full in keeping Candice out of the photographer's lens on her special day.

Candice met her fiancé at a campaign rally for Senator George McGovern in 1971. Gregory Harding an FBI agent was assigned to the event to search for student radicals who were under investigation by the Bureau at the time. Candice and Greg would bump into each other regularly since Candice's work with the Democratic National Campaign and Harding's assignment crossed paths.

The Castros and the Hardings became good friends and would see each other regularly. Going to movies, having dinners, or just a backyard barbeque were regular events. Sunny and Candice picked up where they left off in Hawaii while Jimmy and Greg hit it off immediately discussing football, fishing, or just shooting targets at Quantico. What made the friendship sturdy was the departure of shop talk in any conversation by all four and politics was strictly verboten. They even vacationed together in nearby Seaside, Maryland. Jimmy and Sunny were so enamored of Seaside, they bought a lot in Seaside Village, where they could build their vacation home and eventually retire there. The Harding family grew by three over the next five and a half years. Candice too wanted a place at the beach but understood the demands of the Bureau. Greg could be relocated in an instant and in 1980 he was transferred to the Los Angeles field office along with his young family. Candice and Sunny vowed to keep in contact despite the distance and they did with birthday cards Christmas cards and occasional visits to the West Coast.

The Castro's dream house in Seaside Village became a reality in 1977 when construction of their home was completed. Sunny had informed her husband of her plans to retire and settle into Seaside where she would occupy her time volunteering in school functions where Danny was enrolled and finding work on a part time basis. It would be great to have Sunny at home to tend to Danny and not worry about child care in the afternoon when he came home from school. Jimmy made sure he had access to the canal which ran through the development. A new boat purchase was inevitable to complement the shaded one story custom abode with 3 bedrooms and 2 bathrooms. He still had his row boat for fishing, but he desired one with horsepower.

His deck overlooked the canal and it was here that all would share their time together with nightly cookouts, crab feasts, and various Mexican seafood dishes courtesy of Rosa Castro when she and Gilberto visited. Gilberto loved angling with his son and they would start out in the early morning usually bringing home sea bass, flounder and blue fish. Jimmy's dad, proud of his son and daughter-in-law for purchasing the beach home, never seemed so content.

To him his visits, though short and limited each summer with his son and his family, had to be memorable and fun. It seemed Gilberto knew something about his future and every moment had to be treasured. He had lived a hard and wasteful life viewing it from a barstool inside the stale beer infused confines of dive bars and saloons. Only now he realized what true life actually was as it materialized in the joy of his son's family. He observed the happiness in his son, opening his own eyes to what was wasted when Jimmy was young. Gilberto showed more devotion to Rosa, surprising her with flowers, or attending to home repairs that Rosa thought would never be finished, but most of all his self-imposed prohibition of drinking. But, the damages of hard drinking, tobacco chewing, and rodeo life had already taken its toll. Gilberto was aging rapidly before his time.

The summer of 1981 would be his last. He died in Brownsville with Rosa at his side in January 1982. His last thoughts consisted of a reminder to Rosa.

"Let Jimmy know we are coming to Seaside this summer."

The news hit Jimmy hard. Why did it have to be this way? We were finally bonding as a father and a son after all these years. The image of his father with him fishing together in Seaside was perhaps the best moments of his life. His heart cold and empty reduced him to breaking down sobbing in random moments of reflection. Sunny understood and consoled him silently by hugging him. Jimmy could see his dad laughing as his son reeled in a horseshoe crab thinking it was a prized tuna last summer in the bay.

"Jimmy, that is the ugliest tuna, I've ever seen. Your Mom's gonna have a helluva time filleting that damned thing! Do Maryland tunas have legs? I've heard of Chicken of the Sea. That thing looks like it's Sickened of the Sea!" Gilberto would tease.

Rosa of course was experiencing shock. After forty one years of marriage, Gilberto the love of her life was gone. She reminisced about the first time she met him after a rodeo. She admired his machismo in riding bulls.

"It was almost as if the bulls were frightened of him to ride them. He showed no fear when he was young. Oh he got bounced a lot but Gil would just brush himself off and find another one. One time the clown got chased and Gil ran after the bull to rescue the clown. Gil got gored and thrown back in the stands. He broke his ribs and his wrist and had a concussion. The doctors nearly had to tie him down to the stretcher when they put him in the back of the ambulance. He wanted to finish his rides! He was the bravest man I ever knew. You got a lot of him in you, Jimmy. More than you think," she revealed to her son dabbing her eyes.

Jimmy stayed in Brownsville for the next two months helping Rosa to sell the family home and move in with an older sister in San Benito, Texas just up the road. The offer to come to Seaside was still open for his mom to the point of spending the entire summer with her son and his family. Rosa accepted knowing it would have been insisted by Gilberto in his dying request. Sunny understood and without blinking an eye welcomed her mother-in-law to stay in Seaside for a while to transition her life away from the pains of grief. Jimmy would have done the same for Sunny's folks if one of them had passed.

In July of 1982, Jimmy finally found a permanent job working for the Bay Marina Maintenance Department where he could utilize his jack-of-all trades skills. His main responsibilities were to maintain rental properties located around the marina and fill in at the boatyard if needed. His previous five years of employment in Seaside consisted of short term seasonal work which he never received the salary that his abilities commanded. The Bay Marina selected him immediately when he applied for the job opening dismissing his written comment on the back of the application, I *don't weld!*

CHAPTER 25

O fficer Marge Lowe entered the station with her usual collection of bags and boxes, containing lunch, snacks, and minor home projects to keep her busy if the workload didn't. After all it was Sunday and the populace was either heading out of town this day or sleeping off hangovers. It was 8:10 AM and her usual 10 minute tardiness kept Lieutenant Nichols anxious for her arrival. His shift had ended at seven and he wanted to pounce on her before the Chief arrived.

"Hey, did you all hear Danko died?" she declared bubbly as she strolled through the doors fumbling with the bulky items in her chubby arms.

The staff all nodded in bored unison that they too had learned of the news on their way into work. The station house was rather serene compared to the night before when the lobby filled with lawbreakers and lawyers. Lieutenant Nichols approached her with a welcoming smile and his offer of helping her carry her articles to her already cluttered desk.

"Wow, Dave. How do I rate this respect this morning? You're out of here by the time I come in on Sunday," she said dropping her things on the floor.

Nichols scanned the area for anyone who could hear him. Once he felt safe and to Marge's astonishment, he whispered in a low voice. "Marge, I need you to do something for me. It's urgent."

"Dave, I didn't think I was your type! Hey let me get settled and let me know what you need," she kidded removing her purse from her shoulder.

"Marge. The Chief will be here shortly. I need something out of the personnel files. It will take five minutes. I need to compare a signature. That's all! I know he'll deny me access," Nichols begged knowing of Lowe's dedication to her job.

"Whoa, Dave! You know what will happen to me if I violate procedure. The Chief will have my ass!" she stated with her hands on her hips.

"I guarantee I'll take full responsibility. If we are caught, I'll tell him I forced you to open the cabinet. It will be my ass on the line, not yours! Come on, we're wasting time! Five minutes at the most! Please Marge!" a pause ensued keeping Nichol's unshaven face frozen with his mouth agape and his hands outstretched as if to catch a watermelon.

Marge hesitated and rolled her eyes then capitulated. She waved to Nichols to follow her to the records room jingling the keys to the file cabinet.

"Okay. Last name?" she sniped.

"Dillon."

"Ken Dillon? Whatever you're looking for is going to take more than five minutes, Lieutenant! That's an awful thick folder," Marge indicated her familiarity with the folder.

"I only need to compare a signature from an old citation to see if it is actually his. We may have an imposter posing as a cop out there," Nichols insisted but Lowe didn't believe his reason because the Chief would have allowed the search.

Marge relented with the explanation shaking her head in disapproval of the excuse. She located the D's in the cabinet and retrieved Dillon's folder handing it to the lieutenant who eagerly and hastily snatched the folder form her chubby hands. He dropped the folder on the top of the file cabinet as Officer Lowe stood at the door watching out for the Chief. Ravaging through the folder and pulling out the wrinkled copy in his sports coat, he managed to find a document that Dillon had scribbled his signature in haste as he had done on the citation. After scanning the third document, he finally found the match that he was looking for. It was a perfect match. He shoved both the citation and the corroborative document in his pocket.

"Chief's coming through the front doors! Leave, I'll put everything back," she yelled in a loud whisper. "Go out and stall him!"

"Marge. I owe you one!" Nichols smiled and left the records room satisfied as Marge hurried to put the file back and lock the cabinet. The Chief greeted his Sunday staff with a look of genuine relief, a departure from his usual preoccupied worried self. His grinning countenance caught his staff off guard. They were not use to such a display of happiness. Maybe the Chief got laid last night they conjectured humorously. The Chief's gleeful face turned to concern when he spotted Lieutenant Nichols.

"Dave, why are you still here? Something happened last night that I should be informed about?"

Knowing he needed to stall the Chief's progress to his office and passing the records room, he blocked his way down the hall. "Nothing Chief. I was just finishing up my reports from last night. Hey, you look great today!" slapping his hand on the Chief's left shoulder, "Looks like you got some good news or something. Listen, Chief I had a busy night. I'm going now. See you tomorrow!" and under his breath, "You gutless slob!"

The Chief's gleeful mood had diminished as Nichols exited the station. Something was afoot by the way Nichols acted. The Chief had suspicions about his star detective ever since Ken Dillon was convicted. Dillon and Nichols were close friends and there was an air of an unspoken distrust that existed between the Chief and Nichols over the years. Nichols could never understand how the Chief stabbed his friend in the back by not backing him up after the Ricky Salvano incident.

Somehow, the Chief was influenced and it was obvious to Nichols that a conspiracy had included his boss. Nichols had to find the link to Danko and the Chief, but now he was elated with the news that his buddy was alive with the indisputable comparisons of the signatures. Somewhere in Seaside, Dillon was patrolling around in police cruiser number 583. Though tired from the night's work, Nichols set out searching the town while monitoring his police radio hoping to hear Dillon's voice. How did he escape? What was Dillon up to? Where has he been hiding?

CHAPTER 26

G wen Blasingame had managed to track her nephew down. Feeling her home phone was being tapped, she drove to a nearby Shell gas station to use the pay phone. Petey had returned home from eating breakfast at a popular diner. On Sunday mornings the diner was packed to the rafters with the after Church crowds and regulars. The wait to even get a seat at the counter sometimes would take half an hour. Her nephew Petey, had spent the evening out carousing with his cohorts and craved breakfast consisting of countless cups of coffee and creamed chipped beef to absorb the creative collection of cocktails careening uncontrollably through his circulatory system. The refreshed twenty-five year old lad returned to his home just in time to answer Aunt Gwen's call. After the usual comfortable chit chat, Gwen got to the point.

"Petey, I need you to do an extremely important thing for me this afternoon," she stressed.

"This afternoon, Aunt Gwen?" he protested, "Me and the guys were going to go out and do some recreational diving."

"Perfect, Petey that's what I wanted to hear. I have a place in mind for you to dive. It's extremely important. Did you ever hear of the missing boat, the *Donovan's Pride?*" the aunt quizzed her befuddled nephew.

"Yeah. I think so. Hey that's the ghost ship, right? Somebody found it?" he jumped in excitement.

"Well yes and no. I need you to go to the coordinates that were given to me and dive down to see if it is actually there. I need some kind of proof," she stated while watching a maroon El Dorado pull up to the pumps facing the phone booth. The passenger got out and proceeded to the back of the car to fill the gas tank while the driver sat.

"Are you going there with us, Aunt Gwen?" the nephew asked hoping the answer would be no. He didn't want to have his sixty seven year old aunt scolding him for his language or his appearance in front of his diving companions.

"No, but I have a man who is very interested who will go with you. His name is Jimmy Castro," she said apprehensively as she felt herself being watched by the driver of the El Dorado.

"You mean the dude from the marina?" Petey like everyone else in the area who docked at the Bay Marina knew of Jimmy.

"Yes exactly. He won't dive but he needs confirmation that the boat is actually there. It has to be kept quiet with your friends. Can you do this for me? I'll buy you all dinner tonight," his aunt promised trying not to sound worried.

"Ok. I'm sure my friends won't mind the change of plans when they hear we are diving to locate the ghost ship. I need the coordinates now to compare with my charts. If it's over nine fathoms, we can't do it," Petey pulled a dull pencil from the kitchen drawer under the phone.

"I understand, Petey. Got a pencil and paper? They are 38 degrees, 27 minutes, 11 seconds lat. And 74 degrees 50 minutes, 25 seconds long." She repeated the information for confirmation turning her back to the vehicle at the pump.

"Got it," he said scribbling down the data on the wall by the phone. "Let's see it's eleven now. I got to get the guys up and get our gear ready. I'll pick the dude up near the CG station in my boat around two. I'll call if there is any change in plans Aunt Gwen," her nephew offered.

"I'll call the dude um Mr. Castro and let him know," she chuckled, "I don't think this will be a problem with him. He wants to go as soon as possible. He's been waiting for this for nearly ten years. Thanks again, Petey." She hung up the phone stuffing the pad of paper back in her purse. A sense of relief fell over her as two more cars entered the station for gas while the mysterious El Dorado continued being filled. The reporter scurried to her faded blue Reliant and fled the Shell station hoping to find a secluded public phone so she could contact Jimmy Castro with the plans. Her intuition guided her to a privately owned gas station where she would feel safe being that she knew the proprietor. If the El Dorado was stalking her, she would know for sure if it pulled up to pump more gas having done so at the previous site.

The public phone was in sight of the cashier located on the outside wall near a Coke machine. She pulled out the pad of paper and dialed Jimmy's number. She scanned the road to see if she was followed while waiting for Jimmy to answer. Fortunately this particular station was located off the main highway and required three turns. The phone rang half a tone when Jimmy picked up the receiver. Gwen spoke for less than a minute to relay the plan to Jimmy and told him she was in a hurry. Jimmy excited slammed down the phone. He told Sunny of the afternoon's plans. Jimmy and Sunny had also gleaned the news of the day from the radio that Bill Danko was dead. A great burden of stress had been lifted in the Castro home.

Throughout the stress laden ordeal of the trial, Castro again went without sleep, re-experiencing the horrors of the fire. Now anyone effected by the conspiracy and threat could breathe a sigh of relief. Justice had been served finally after nine long years. Jimmy exalted and felt that he could finally clear his name completely from being linked to the sinking of the *Donovan's Pride* even though he was reluctantly cleared at the trial due to inconclusive evidence.

The proof now lay in the actual cause which Jimmy believed was sabotage all along. His belief was based on two new employees at the marina who were assigned to working on the *Donovan's Pride* that day to work on the exhaust system. He was pulled off the job and reassigned to another less demanding chore when the welding of the exhaust pipes was initiated. Jimmy never saw those employees again after the boat was released to Mr. Donovan. Jimmy's supervisor resigned that same day claiming he had hit the lottery jackpot and was leaving Seaside forever. The supervisor and the two employees never appeared at the trial.

CHAPTER 27

Milton Craddock pulled into the parking lot of the Sunshine Assisted Living Home. The building was majestic compared to the drab surroundings of vacant lots, faded billboards, rusted Coca-Cola signs, and decaying forestland. The Seaside Drive-In Movie Theater adjacent to the home once a popular venue on summer nights had almost disappeared from sight. The generic marquee sign was all that remained and was camouflaged by the rapidly encroaching unmaintained forest curling around and crushing its aluminum façade.

The assisted living center was actually a pre-fabricated home brilliantly painted in white and yellow. One would have to wear sunglasses when exiting their cars to enter the home due to the brightness of the Sun reflecting from the siding of the home. It was a sparkling diamond in a rough of overgrowth and ironic abandonment. Milton's mother had been residing here for nearly a year and enjoyed the carefree environment and amicability of both the staff and her neighbors. Milton proceeded to the front counter to sign the Visitors registry as he engaged in polite banter with the cute receptionist.

"I'll let her know that you are here, Mr. Craddock," she smiled.

After the routine phone call, she gave Craddock the approval to proceed to his mother's room. He passed numerous rooms all with doors open containing seniors glued to the usual mundane television programs like The Lawrence Welk Show on the Home's closed circuit TV system. There was an odor of cleaning and sterilizing products in the air. The tiled floors gleamed from routine waxings and no effort was made to remove the blackness of rubber trails from wheel chairs.

Mrs. Craddock using a cane for support craned her neck from the door of her room and motioned her son as if he had never visited before. She smiled that he had taken time to visit her. Her room resembled a simple bedroom with a bathroom. The once houseful of collectibles and furnishings was greatly reduced to some framed family pictures, writing materials, a few books, and perfumes. There was a small desk with a chair which Milton sat in to address his mother who sat in a decorative wing chair across from him. After the usual pleasantries were exchanged, Milton segued into his concern regarding his father.

"Mom, I ran into somebody last night who knew Dad. It was a strange conversation with this man, a police officer, stressing to me that Dad had an interest in railroads. Do you recall anything about railroads?"

Mrs. Craddock hesitated. The stroke had taken its toll on her reaction time to questions. One had to be patient and her son realized by the confused expression on her face that she was formulating the answer. After moments of reflection, she responded.

"Who was this man who asked you about your father?"

"Like I said, Mom, it was a policeman. His name was Dillon."

"Ken Dillon?" she asked weakly.

"Yes, Mom," Milton was curiously happy that she knew Dillon's first name.

A long delay ensued with Mrs. Craddock aka Mrs. Polanco contemplating how she could answer her son's question. Torn between her limited communication and her obligation to informing her son of the harsh details of his father's corruption, was overbearing. She pointed her index finger as time elapsed, meaning for her son not to rush her in her response. The longer she paused, Milton knew there would be a lot of information. She motioned for him to close the door.

"Milton, promise me you won't get angry. What I am about to tell you," she coughed dryly causing Milton to act. He rushed to the bathroom sink and drew a glass of water for her. Sipping on the glass and thanking him, she continued. "You were away at school at the time so you did not know what was happening here at that time. There was a policeman who shot a young hood at Terry's Burger Shack in self-defense. Do you recall that?" Milton's mother took another sip of water.

"I think I remember it in a letter you wrote to me."

"The policeman's name was Ken Dillon. Your father was receiving bribes from a developer. I didn't know about it, I swear. The developer, Danko, threatened your father if he didn't get the policeman indicted for murder. You see, the developer was the hood's uncle. So, your father had to do some dishonest things to protect himself or risk imprisonment for receiving illegal payments. By the way, your UCLA education was partially funded by the bribes as well as our vacations, cars, and jewelry, and that was before the shooting. I was naïve at first but figured your father was being bribed," she said picking up the glass of water.

Her son's face fell and he slumped in his chair from the shock. He could not envision his father participating in anything illegal. But when the gruesome account of his father's death came to light around the time of the funeral, he knew that this was no random act of violence. Local police acquaintances had assured Milton that they would track down his father's killer.

His father was an upstanding citizen and a successful lawyer who became a three term mayor. Milton's world collapsed from the revelation from his mother. Until now, he was in denial that his father was mixed up in illegal activity. Hearing the facts of his father's suspicious death was harder to accept than his initial shock of hearing the news of his death. But now all the pieces were falling in place making sense.

"Shall I continue, son? I know this is difficult for you," his mother consoled patting her son's knee.

"Yes, Mom," he reluctantly murmured, "continue."

"Your father was under a lot of stress. He had to do what Danko instructed or he would end up ruined or in prison or dead. I noticed a change in your father. He was not his usual joyful self during this time of the trial. He was always nervous and looking over his shoulder. He didn't eat or sleep regularly. He lost a lot of weight," she handed the empty glass to Milton who refilled the container.

"Mom, did you hear Danko died last night?" he asked pouring the cold water.

His mother's eyes widened. A small smile broke the grimness of her face. "Is that true, Milton? I hope that murderer got what he deserved!"

"It was on the news this morning. He died from natural causes. What about Dillon? I told you I saw him last night," her son placed the filled glass on a nearby table for her to reach.

"Dillon was sentenced for manslaughter and murdered in prison. I don't know who you talked with last night, but I can assure you it wasn't Dillon. I remember the day we got the news. I was very sad. That kid he shot was bad, very bad. Everyone knew the kid around town. Terry Gleason used to hate it when that kid came in his place. It was always trouble. The man you talked to was someone to scare you. Ken Dillon is dead," she asserted.

"Now, the railroad thing makes sense to me. Dad railroaded Officer Dillon to protect himself, right Mom?"

"Yes," she slowly admitted, "Now, Milton there is something else you should know. As you know, <cough>my days are getting shorter. I can't die without letting this injustice go on. There are a lot of innocent people who have died<cough> and suffered from this. I blame myself for not exposing it before it got out of hand, so I gave in written details the actual facts of what happened with my expressed concern and validation that you were in no way<cough> involved," his mother took another sip of water to combat the dryness of her throat.

"In a way, I was involved, Mom. You said it yourself that my education was funded by dirty money," he sighed acknowledging the repercussions to his local law concern founded by his father. There goes my life here, he thought.

"I omitted that detail from the report. It was sent with the warning that I will recant everything if they publish<cough> the report with you as the scapegoat for their misplaced anger. I even stressed the point that you are innocent. You must be strong and denounce your father's illegal actions. This will put you back in good standing with the locals. Just remember the good times<cough> we had before your father became Mayor."

"Where is this report now?" her son questioned.

"I will not tell you because you will try to stop its publication."

"You know, Mom. You're getting out of this easy. I'm going to suffer the consequences for years. I might have to move from here!" Milton complained in a panic.

"Milton, I love you. I'm doing this for all who suffered. It's my duty. Most of the community<cough> has figured this thing out about your father. It shouldn't be a shock to them. I can't go into the hereafter with this guilt on my conscience. All things must pass and this will pass in time. You'll have to be strong. Thank God, you don't have a wife and children. I only hope that the good Lord forgives me."

With that, Milton stood and walked to his ailing mother. He hugged her and kissed her on her head. Mrs. Craddock patted his hand. "Mom, I just realized what you have done. I will support you because it will show some sort of righteousness in the face of those affected. I will make a trident effort in dissolving the past and promoting the future by being a better man than I am now. I will prove to everyone, I am not the son of a corrupt man but I am the positive force in the community. They will forget about Stanley Craddock and remember Milton Craddock with pride!"

CHAPTER 28

Ted Minnis emerged from his bed aboard *The Rough Rider* and sat on the edge, rubbing his head. The sunlight pierced through the side of a drawn shade. Octavia was still huddled under the covers sound asleep. A calmness and short silent breathing indicated she was dreaming peacefully. The harshness of yesterday's events played on Minnis's mind. The screams of a family in distress at sea, still reverberated in his brain. He did not sleep well as he recoiled constantly from images of the *Donovan's Pride* infiltrating his dreams. Getting up and slipping on shorts, shirt and sandals, he went over to a chest of drawers and removed an envelope and a pencil and jotted a note for his friend.

"Tavia. I went to get some coffee over at the Marina Restaurant. I'll bring you one back. Ted"

Ted climbed from his boat onto the pier already sweating from another hot humid day in Seaside. As he shuffled towards the restaurant, squinting into the morning sun a familiar horn beckoned his attention. A red Ford pick-up pulled along the side of him interrupting his trek to the restaurant.

"Minus! What are you up to?"

"Just getting some coffee for me and Tavia, Jimmy."

"Hop in. I'm going there too." The door creaked open causing a half drunk Snapple bottle to roll out. Minnis in his tired state picked it up and tossed on the floor of the cab as Jimmy swiped his empty cigarette packs and papers on to the floor to make room for his guest. Minnis wiped his hand on the seat where the fruit drink had leaked on his hand.

"Maids day off, Jim?" Minnis supposed.

The truck proceeded to the Marina Restaurant. Jimmy found a parking spot after several passes. The lot was full of Sunday morning breakfast regulars from the marina. A line formed outside with the main topic of discussion focused on the previous night's events climaxing in Donna D'Antuano's kicking of Bobby Willoughby off the bulkhead. The inconvenience of being penned up all night in the marina had all been forgotten as boats now were heading in and out of the channel regularly. The crowd delighted in the ass kicking of Bobby Willoughby, their once fearless spokesman.

"Yeah. I heard it this way. When Bobby went into the water, he created a tsunami that dislodged the yacht from the sandbar! I hear they have issued tsunami warnings as far away as Portugal!"

Jimmy grinned as he overheard the exaggerated accounts. Minnis and him squeezed by the line hopefully to get seats at the counter which were usually open to single patrons. And as luck would have it, out of the eight seats at the counter, six were occupied. Jimmy imposed on a regular who was enjoying his blueberry pancakes and grits sitting in between two empty seats.

"Hiya, Mr. Foster. How ya doing today?' Jimmy greeted the white bearded weather-worn old man clad in the usual attire of the marina: tee shirt, shorts, sandals and an old orange Orioles floppy hat.

While chewing with his mouth open, the old man extended his syrupy sticky hand to Jimmy.

"Hey Mr. Foster. Me and my friend would like to sit together to talk. You mind moving over one?" Jimmy pleaded as he shook his sticky hand. Without hesitation or complaint and not missing one bite, Mr. Foster complied by sweeping his breakfast order to the vacant area to his left.

"Thanks, Mr. Foster. You're a gentleman." On the word "gentleman" Mr. Foster emitted a loud belch to signify his standing in society and in the restaurant. It was his trademark which elicited frowns from newcomers and laughter in the kitchen.

"So, Ted. I am going out to the site where you saw the *Donovan's Pride* yesterday. "Hey, Linda can we get two coffees here? Thanks."

"Jimmy, I've thought of nothing else since I saw it yesterday. It really shook me up. I can still here those poor people screaming for help," Minnis admitted sincerely looking straight ahead at the bustling of the grill cooks.

"Minus, uh Ted, did you notice anything about the boat. I mean were there holes in the hull or anything that you could notice that would make the boat sink?" Castro persisted hoping to hear the response he wanted to hear.

Minnis appreciated the address of Ted instead of the usual Minus by Castro." No Jimmy. I stood on the deck and searched from bow to stern and below. Nobody on board. The boat was in perfect shape. It didn't move. The anchor wasn't deployed. It just stood there still during the storm! Creepy as hell! And then when I got back on my boat, Tavia called me to tell me 'it disappeared!' Ted's recalling was cut short as Linda set the two coffees down in front of her customers. Jimmy dispatched her when he conveyed that coffee was all they needed." Have you ever heard of such a thing? I mean Gwen Blasingame told me about some guy who ended up in an institution over the same thing."

Jimmy sipped his black coffee. "You don't concern yourself with that. You had the position plotted not like Ben Jacoby."

"Hmm Ben Jacoby. He was one crazy son of a bitch!" Mr. Foster interjected.

Jimmy smirked at the old man indicating he didn't need validation from him. Foster returned to slurping his watery grits. In a hushed voice, Jimmy leaned to Minnis. "I'm going out there in a couple of hours with some divers. I want to know are you sure about this? Is there anything you saw on the boat that can prove you were on deck? This whole thing is very important to me and others in the community. It's not too late to say you imagined this."

Minnis looked around for eavesdroppers and waited for the next slurp from Mr. Foster. "Jimmy, I'm telling you the God's honest truth. I swear everything I told you is true. But if you need proof, I saw a life preserver mounted on the wall outside of the cabin. It was wooden and painted like the Irish flag colors and had the name of the boat painted on it."

Jimmy took another swig from his coffee and hesitated. "Ok. Mr. Minnis. I believe you."

"Jimmy? If the boat is down there, you got to tell me," Minnis stated staring into Castro's face, "I'll be driving home tonight with Octavia. My home number is on my business card. One thing, do not leave any messages on my answering machine. Talk to me directly. You understand, right?" He slid the embossed card on the counter as if passing classified information to a spy.

"I understand, Minus. You don't want your wife to find out about your weekend fling with Octavia," Jimmy smiled.

"Thanks, Jimmy. I'm glad you understand," Minnis sighed sipping his coffee.

"I do and I don't. It's none of my business. But I would never do such a thing to my wife, buddy. She's been by my side since the beginning! There's a lot to be said for loyalty for a woman that cares for you!" Jimmy finished his coffee looking at his watch. "Hey, I got to head up to the Marina office and then head over to the Coast Guard station. See you later, Ted. I'll call you."

Minnis sighed feeling relief that Jimmy would resolve the boat sighting. "Hey, I'll pay the bill you cheap bastard!" he swiveled turning to Jimmy who waved his acknowledgement. Minnis then hung on Jimmy's obvious jab in the gut comment about loyalty.

"Heh, heh, he got you too! That Jimmy Castro is as slick as WD40 on a eel!"

"Just eat your grits, old man!" Minnis muttered still obsessing with the guilt that Jimmy had just laid on him.

CHAPTER 29

Milton Craddock still had clients waiting for him at the Seaside Police station from the previous evening's encounters with the law. It was the same thing every year with some exceptions. There was always that *unique* incident where alcohol stimulated a creative thinking individual to rise above the mundane acts of his fellow boozers in the matter of establishing a new trend of defiance to society. Craddock looked forward to these cases and would have him researching rarely cited precedents to defend his client. He pulled into the parking lot and found a space open next to a maroon 1988 Cadillac El Dorado. In front a janitor was actively engaged in hosing down the sidewalk and ridding it of the stench of involuntary human expulsions from the night before.

The thin balding counselor sauntered by the janitor holding both his brief case and his breath sidestepping the wet pavement. He entered the station overhearing one of two GQ looking gentlemen commanding the officer at the front desk in a stringent voice,

"Make sure the Chief gets this and reads it immediately! It's important!" He then slid a sealed 9x11 manila envelope on the counter to the puzzled young female officer. She froze from the glaring intensity of the man's stern visage acknowledging his directive with a nod. The two spun away unsmiling from the counter simultaneously colliding with Craddock as he entered. The shorter of the two peered into the lawyers face with a bewildered stare. Craddock paused feeling a cold sense of familiarity with the sinister looking man. The taller man pushed his companion's shoulder to prod him along to the exit door. Craddock shook off the awkward moment and announced his intentions to visit his clients in the cells downstairs to the now receptive smile of the front desk officer holding the manila envelope in her right hand.

CHAPTER 30

Sunday July 5th 1992 would be a very active day for Jimmy Castro. Shortly after his phone conversation with Gwen Blasingame had concluded the phone rang. Greg Harding was calling from Los Angeles responding to the news of Bill Danko's death and the newly revealed link to the corruption in Seaside. Though never substantiated from the FBI investigations prior to his death, there was now a growing amount of calls to the local FBI offices of Danko's control of Seaside from sources that now felt safe to open up. Harding was interested in his friend's personal account of the developments. It could not have come at a better time for Castro who was more than eager to expose the corruption along with the possible finding of the *Donovan's Pride.*

Inspector Harding was skeptical and even laughed aloud when his friend relayed the portion of the details of *the ghost ship.* Harding knew of Jimmy's penchant for humor from the earlier days back in Montgomery County, Maryland. But when his friend relayed the coordinates of the location of the missing boat, Harding took note. Castro's tone was serious and stressed. The inspector then informed his buddy of the penalty for making a false report to the FBI and requested to talk to Sunny to update her with news about Candice and the family, which was a ploy to see if Sunny would provide information regarding her husband's mental state. After flagging her down in the house, Jimmy gave his wife the phone.

"It's Greg Harding. He wants to know if I'm sane," Jimmy deduced holding his hand over the phone speaker. Sunny grinned disbelief.

After the usual pleasantries, Sunny responded with yesses and nos to the inspector/friend's interrogation about her husband's current condition for the next five minutes with a random response about Danny and the secret ingredient to her chicken salad recipe to throw Jimmy off as he sat nearby. Sunny smiled with a request to Candice that she wished her well. She returned the phone to her husband.

"Okay Jimmy. I am going to contact our dive team that is located near you. The Bureau will handle the investigation of the missing boat and you are to inform your dive team to call off their dive. We have jurisdiction now and they risk imprisonment if they compromise the crime scene. Do you understand?" Harding stated officially. "I will call you back in an hour to let you know the details."

Castro acknowledged the inspector's request worried that he may have jeopardized their friendship.

"One more thing Mr. Castro, are you an American citizen?" Harding asked knowing how Castro hated this question in dealing with officials.

"I'm a veteran and Purple Heart recipient. Does that answer your question, gringo?" Castro proudly responded with his regular lighthearted stab at Harding.

"I'll be in contact with you Jimmy. Stay by the phone!" the conversation concluded abruptly. Sunny catching the last words by her husband was intrigued.

"What was that last remark about?" she asked curiously with a smile.

"Greg wanted to know how I rate *HAVANA* cigars versus Tiparillos." This was the usual reaction Jimmy would give his wife when his name was called into question when somebody assumed he was Cuban. Sunny too would hear the same assumptions through the years and would reply derisively, "I wear a fruit basket on my head while doing the samba around the house in the nude singing Day-O," to astonished inquisitors about her ethnicity. Her retort was better than her husband's because of the reaction it would evoke.

Sunny would leave her inquisitors with their mouths agape and stunned as she happily strolled away. At PTA meetings she could see wives whispering to their husbands on the current new gossip regarding her "Carmen Miranda" performances, directing their husbands focus by eye contact towards Sunny. This would usually pique the husband's curiosity with the inevitable mouthing of the word "Really?" and the complimentary ogling of Jimmy Castro's shapely wife. Male participation increased at the PTA meetings while Danny attended school there, thanks to Sunny. At a bake sale function, one husband volunteered his Harry Belafonte record as background music for the event while another husband brought along a waxed fruit basket. Sunny was amused, the husbands disappointed, their wives miffed.

Gwen Blasingame was also busy after talking to Castro that morning. She contacted the Baltimore Sun. Being a long holiday weekend, the regular staff at the Baltimore Sun had taken off except the assistant editor, Willis W. Watkins and some intern. She mused at the irony of his name. In Journalism 101, you are taught the five W's and one H. (Who What When Where Why and How) Here is a man whose name contains three Ws. The first syllable of his last name is *Wat* for Pete's sake! One wonders if this was the man's destiny in life to be involved in reporting the news. She knew Watkins from his days as a feature reporter at The Baltimore Sun. He would regularly contact Gwen on the yearly *Summer In Review* edition on the activities scheduled in Seaside for that particular summer. They had an enjoyable relationship for many years.

After the initial cordial exchange, Gwen revealed her story from the letter from Mrs. Craddock. With an intern typing verbatim on an extension phone, Watkins was impressed to hearing the entire story before bombarding her with questions. This was not the usual tale of a man landing a record size flounder in Seaside! What a news day for Sunday! Danko's death and now a story that links him to a murder conspiracy in Seaside! For Watkins and his skeleton staff this would be no idle Sunday. As she concluded the story, a short pause ensued. Watkins sighed at the enormity of the conspiracy in the resort town.

"I suppose your editor is in on the conspiracy. That's why you have to report it to me, Gwen," Watkins inferred.

"No Willis. His involvement is a matter of conflict of interest. Danko advertised heavily in the newspaper and his legitimate real estate firms still do. Without that regular revenue the paper would just about break even. Anything Danko-related like the trial we either had to *embellish* our reporting or as you just learned, burn them."

"Chief Davenport our police chief is mixed up in it some way too. We still don't know what the connection was between Danko and him," she paused briefly to add, "I do have other information stowed away in a safe place, but I can't get to it until Tuesday."

"Okay, Gwen. I'll be alerting my boss. We'll be sending our best reporter there on Tuesday or Wednesday to meet with you. His name is Rob MacElvoy perhaps you've heard of him? If you can, fax me that letter! We are going to hold on your story until everything is confirmed. Keep in touch and stay safe, Gwen!" The newspaper office now was a rush of interns, ringing phones, and the buzzing of fax and teletype machines .Watkins notified his boss, the Sun's editor. The story was on the verge of going national.

CHAPTER 31

As prearranged with Agent Ermengarde, Sunday July 5th was scheduled for Officer Ken Dillon to *reunite* with his surviving family. He could only visit in spirit form. Officer Dillon awoke at eight and got himself prepared wearing shorts and an orange tank top. He wore faded white deck shoes with no socks. To accent his looks he fished out a pair of bronze sunglasses from a gym bag and concealed a special object around his neck and under his shirt. It was a silver chain with a miniature duplication of his shield. He eagerly anticipated being with his family for the first time since his funeral and looked forward to seeing Marla and their two sons, Ken Jr. and little Andy.

His family usually would be enjoying the morning sun of the beach at about this time every Sunday. He exited the Clayton Hotel towards the parking lot and halted, frozen in his tracks. Someone in a shirt and tie was examining his police cruiser. It was Dave Nichols. In a one hour search Nichols had located Cruiser #583. To entertain himself, Dillon approached the furtive detective who now was sitting in his own car about to contact the station on his locating the impostor's car. Officer Dillon materialized in the back seat positioned so that his face appeared in the rear view mirror of Nichol's car.

"Take me to your worthless leader, Nick!" he announced.

The detective froze in a sudden paralysis holding the mic in his right hand and adjusting his rear view mirror to reveal the familiar voice from the back of his car.

"Dillon? Dillon? I can't believe it! I knew you weren't dead!" Nichols elated and turned back to view his old buddy in the back seat who wasn't there.

"You have to look at me in the mirror, Nick. It's one of the symptoms associated with a condition called terminal death. You may have read about it in *The New England Journal of Medicine,*" his brother cop kidded as his confused friend turned towards the front and readjusted the mirror.

Nichols slapped himself in the face owing the moment as a hallucination from the lack of sleep. He again looked back in the mirror for reassurance hearing a hearty laugh.

"Let me know if you need any help, detective."

"You're a stinkin' ghost?" Nichols cried.

"Wow! I'm amazed Nick. Now I know how you passed the detective exams with that keen ability of yours. I'm impressed, so stop showing off," Dillon persisted. "I'm here to tend to a matter. It will all make sense to you soon, Nick."

"You know about Danko?" the detective asked while looking around to see if anyone noticed him speaking to himself.

"Yes. I can't go into detail about my purpose here, Nick. I saw you and wanted to say hello. Watch your back and be careful! Also, check the front end alignment on that cruiser! It vibrates like hell over sixty. And don't say a word about this meeting!" with that Dillon's benign face vanished in the mirror leaving his friend to murmur,

"If I say anything about this they'll stick me in a padded cell with ole Ben Jacoby!"

Dillon found himself huddled amongst a small group awaiting an approaching northbound city bus. As the doors open he filed in with the crowd and found a seat in the middle of the bus while the others tended to the dollar fare in front. His destination was about two miles from the Clayton Hotel and his anticipation of seeing his family was building. To ensure that nobody would make the assumption that his seat and the seat next to him were vacant, Dillon emitted a ghastly offensive odor.

"Whew!" two teenage girls cried in unison. "It smells like death in here!" the blond pony tailed girl exclaimed placing her hand over her mouth and rushing to the rear. Dillon mused about the dead on ironic comment. The bus continued its herky-jerky journey down the highway. The odor of diesel exhaust combined with the feckless bus air conditioning, sent nauseated passengers scurrying for the next stop after riding for only five minutes. Being a ghost does have its privileges Dillon thought smugly. The place had not changed much since Ken's death. He braced for the next stop where a fiberglass brown and yellow Cyclops welcomed young golfers to the miniature golf course. It was 89th Street. The beach was already packed. He hopped off the bus as others merged to get on brushing by him and experiencing Dillon's coldness.

"They must have the air conditioning cranked. Did you feel that air?"

Though it was nine thirty AM the beach was a considerable mass of basting bodies simmering in various scented sun block and sun tanning lotions. Turn a cannibal loose and he wouldn't know where to begin this beachside buffet. And that is what perplexed Ken Dillon. The Sun suspended about 20-30 degrees above the horizon blinded anyone who ventured to the beach to stake their small claim of sand. It would be a task to locate his family. The main problem that presented itself was to recognize his sons. It had been six years since his death. Ken Jr. would be 15 years old by now and Andy 11. Marla's red hair and fair skin was always an issue for her at the beach even though she loved being here. She should be under an umbrella with a big floppy straw hat lounging back reading a book. The boys should be either in the water or tossing a Frisbee or a football behind the throng of sun worshippers. So, Ken stopped and surveyed the scene noticing two kids about his son's age tossing a football with two others. The football would be thrown into the breeze for ten yards, hang in midair and fly back 5 yards. But the boys seemed to enjoy the fun of frustration catching the ball and tackling the recipient.

"Come on Andy, you got to put some muscle behind that throw!"

"Hey, Kenny you're a little older and stronger than me. Get off my back!"

A smile ran across the face of the ghost. He felt proud that his sons were strong, clean cut, and playing football like he did as a boy. Like a misplaced Nordic nomad in mukluks he schussed through the hot sands towards his sons and their friends enjoying the vision as he neared them. Ken Jr. was ripped and could heave a pigskin. It reminded him of his days at Collier High School when he was the star quarterback. God, he thought, maybe Ken Jr. has my football skills. Not wanting to scare the kids due to his unfamiliar face, he sat on an elevated sand dune and admired his boys at play. He sat satisfied. Dillon's insides were torn between happiness and depression. He sat and soaked up as much to take back with him. And, then he got angry. His mind raced and darkened with how unfair his life had turned and why he was missing these precious moments with his family. Chief Davenport is going to pay for this! Suddenly, a familiar voice beckoned Andy. It was Marla his wife whom he affectionately called her "Red."

"Andy. You're burning. Better come back to the umbrella and I'll put some more sun block on your back."

Ken gazed at his wife. Still, the doting mother as she attended to her youngest. She looked as if she had lost at most 30 pounds since his last days on Earth. It must be hard on her to raise their sons without a man in the family and then he heard a confident voice.

"Yeah, Andy you're back is red. Better let Mom take care of that. We'll wait for you," his older son took the words out of his dad's mouth.

Ken Jr. impressed his father with his commanding voice. It was obvious there was a man in the family, Ken Dillon Junior. It was just the same way he used to address the boys. Even the manner in which he instructed young Andy was indicative of his fatherly style. His stature and facial expressions reminded him of himself. Out of the chaotic world he departed, his oldest had assumed the reins of leadership. The ghost smiled as the football landed near his feet. His oldest ran towards him to retrieve the errant throw.

He was close enough to touch him, smell him, hear him, and hug him, but to no avail. It would have to suffice for now. His frustration turned into depression noting what he was missing in the joy of love for his family and how he truly missed them. Separation from his family at the zenith of parenthood was unfair. Experiencing it from a distance so close but a dimension away was just cruel. Again the recurring question about Chief Davenport entered his mind.

"Why did he betray me?"

Down near the beach, Marla sat in a chaise lounge shaded by a beach umbrella with an opened book in her lap admiring the ocean. Her visions drifted past the horizon. Her countenance showed signs of longing. The pain of loneliness was still apparent after six years. Compared to the familial joy that encompassed her at the beach, there was a silent and overt void shrouding her. It ate at her every time she came to the beach. Memories roared at her from the breaking of the waves and she used those images to drown out the joy that others were enjoying around her. Images provoked some fond times with her husband and young family. It was those images that provoked a smile that rinsed her soul of hurt and tears. Suddenly the hissing of sand announcing an approaching figure was nearing her. She turned and shielded her eyes, but there was nobody; only a sudden chill that briefly comforted her swelter in the mid-morning heat of the sun.

"Marla, I wish you could hear me. I miss you all and wish I was here. From what I see, you are holding up well with the kids. One day we'll all be together and hopefully there's a beach like this where we can all enjoy a life of being a family. I was robbed of my life, Red. And you were robbed of a husband and the kids robbed of a father. I will wait for you and we will pick up where we left off. I love you, Red." He rubbed her shoulders as Marla leaned forward in her chair holding her weeping face in her hands. After a moment, she turned wiping away her tears and scanned the area behind her. There was only the void in her soul suffocating from the weight of the callous unyielding of time.

CHAPTER 32

anny Castro entered the house with a Santa sized sack of soiled laundry, his usual monthly load. As he opened the squeaky screen door "Chicken" the peach faced love bird announced his entry with the routine *Hey you* whistle from its cage. The sound of the screen door slamming sent his mother rushing from the back bedroom where she was cleaning and greeted him with a smile. His dad busy on the phone at his desk raised his hand to acknowledge his entry. Danny sensing something dire was occurring lowered his voice hugging his mother. Danny would bring a month's worth of laundry to the Castro home from his house that he shared with three other bachelors. The washer and dryer at his house had been long out of order.

"This has to do with Danko," he surmised in a whisper to his mom.

"Yes, Danny. They may have found the *Donovan's Pride!* Your dad is in the process of coordinating a search of the area," she explained for Jimmy's preoccupation with the phone.

Jimmy found himself in a dilemma. He had to stop Gwen's nephew from diving to the location of the boat for fear he may risk contaminating the FBI's crime scene investigation. On the other hand, he sensed that his friend

Greg Harding wouldn't be able to dispatch his team out there as soon as he had desired. There existed briefly a selfish urge for Jimmy to have an immediate resolve in regards to the findings of the missing boat's sinking. Logic prevailed and Jimmy realized that his fate would have to be placed on the back burner for a while until the FBI could conduct a thorough and scientific study of the evidence if the *Donovan's Pride* was located at the coordinates that Ted Minnis had recorded. Castro did not want to rile Inspector Harding or risk their friendship. Confident in his decision he dialed Gwen Blasingame to have her alert her nephew to cease his preparation for the dive to the ghost ship. Quickly he flipped through the notepad where he had jotted down Gwen's phone number. Finding it he punched the keypad furiously. The phone rang twice before Gwen picked up. In the background he could hear Gwen telling Calvin that the syrup is in the pantry.

"Gwen? Gwen? This is Jimmy. Call your nephew now and tell him he has to cancel the dive."

"What happened, Jimmy? No, It's on the shelf right in front of you, you old goat! If it was a snake it would have bit you in the nose! Sorry, Jim we got an issue here with Mrs. Butterworth," Gwen explained.

"S'ok, Gwen. I wish my problems were that *demanding!* Anyway, the FBI is getting involved so we can't go out to the boat. It has something to do with Federal Jurisdiction Laws. If your nephew goes there, he's going to be arrested! You must tell him and call me back. They will be here soon!" Jimmy declared falsely giving the reporter motivation to call off the dive by her nephew.

"Good thing you reached me now. I just got home. Don't worry! I'll call him now, Jimmy, and then I will let you know if I got a hold of him before he left," Gwen assured the flustered Castro who placed the phone back on the cradle and sighed. Sunny stared concernedly at her husband's confused and deep in thought state.

"There's one thing I don't understand, amigo. Danko is dead. What possible good can it do to find evidence against him now?" Danny stood next to her supporting her question with a nod.

"The investigation will prove that the Donovans died from sabotage and not from sinking in a storm the way the Coast Guard had concluded. In other words the file will be changed to read homicide, and the case will be closed. It's a matter of record and the public will be informed. That's where Gwen is going to be valuable. We've been in contact a lot since the trial. I think once this is finally resolved, this town can breathe again. I know I will! The momentum is changing. I can feel it." Once again the phone rang.

"Jimmy? Gwen. I managed to stop Petey before he headed out and he knows the consequences if he proceeds. He's not going out there. He gave me his word. His friends all have hangovers and were in no shape to dive anyway," Gwen admitted happily.

"That's great, Gwen. How is your involvement with the story going?"

"It's really a hectic Sunday. I've called the Baltimore Sun and they are sending reporters here Tuesday or Wednesday. I'm getting everything organized before they come. This is going to be huge! It might even go national!" she exclaimed heartily.

"I don't want any part of the spotlight, Gwen. I just want to live my life in peace," Jimmy indicated to make sure the reporter got the gist of his meaning.

"Jim. Make sure you get me the news about *The Donovan's Pride*. You know, if they found it or not. You're going out there, right?" she prodded.

"As far as I know. The FBI guy is a close friend of mine. I'll let you know the findings if I'm permitted." Castro wished his accomplice well and turned his attention to his son and the mountain of soiled garments on his living room floor.

***

Danny now twenty two years old resembled his dad in many ways. The dark hair, brown eyes, and moustache reminded him of his youth. His son's mannerisms including his stride were even identical to his own. Danny had found work as a commercial fisherman in Seaside and shared a house with three friends that he knew from school. The house he rented though affordable was truly remarkable. It was to be considered as an historic landmark with its roots tracing back to the later years of the Visigoths and their establishing in Seaside as a respite from their tireless raping, looting, and pillaging in Europe.

Sunny once offered to clean up the two story townhouse for fear that her son could come down with a rare strain of disease associated with the slob-like livings of bachelors. On approach to the house it looked normal except for the multi-colored unused condoms that were strung along a string in the kitchen window. This was somebody's idea for a creative Christmas ornament which now became a permanent fixture due to its ice breaking conversational effects and the elicitation of critiques from female guests. The living room itself was nondescript except for the random dispersal of strategically placed lager vessels and containers which conjured up a notion that every beer ever produced on the planet had been sampled to some degree of approval gauging by the remaining level of hops and malt.

The kitchen off to the left of the living room had the *requisite* Nike sneaker prominently displayed in a frying pan on the stove with grease stained tube socks draped on the oven door handle hopefully serving as oven mitts. The refrigerator a once magnificent and impressive structure defied the laws of gravity straddling a widening trench below it caused by the constant leaking of a water pipe in the back. A quarter inch to the left or right and the refrigerator would be listing like the *All In*. Inside the barely cooling appliance one could find the inviting smells associated with expired, unidentifiable multi-hued food products which were dampened by the continual dripping of condensation caused by a weak door seal.

Upstairs one would find fine, stately, and monthly works of art on display everywhere including the attic access door in the ceiling. Playboy centerfolds galore were proudly plastered to every inch of wallboard giving the appearance of a continual flow of well-endowed double-dee wall paper. Scotch tape had to be a regular purchase at the grocery store judging by the infinite amount of mountings. Curators at Le Louvre would be moved by the sensitive and tender way certain demonstrations of the art would leave its appreciators in awe and open to speculation of the photographer's intent. Sunny wasn't one of them and she left the house swearing never to return until she had a tetanus booster shot. Jimmy had two words for his son's abode when it came to house cleaning, "wrecking ball." But, Danny had revealed to his folks that he was in the process of finding a new place for himself and that the *camaraderie* he once shared with his friends had run its course. Danny was ashamed of how his parents perceived his lifestyle. He admitted that his roomies were slobs and he echoed a famous proverb that he augmented.

"Familiarity not only breeds contempt, but it breeds germs, too!"

✱✱✱

Meanwhile, Ken Dillon sat on the bus returning to the Clayton Hotel. His thoughts were dark and cold considering the emptiness of the brief exchange with his surviving family members on the beach and how he was robbed from these experiences. He wanted so badly to be back with them, but as fate and the Supreme Council would have it, these tender moments would have to suffice for now. His family would be reunited with him someday, but when? His attention turned to the target of his mission, Chief Carl Davenport. How can somebody enjoy life knowing that his actions or in this case his inaction led to the soulful killing of a man's family? Ken could sense the impact of his absence from his family. There was an obvious gash in their spirits concealed by the thinnest of gauze. The deeper his concerns for his family ran, the hotter his emotions stoked the furnace of vengeance. Tonight's the night. Chief Davenport will pay dearly for his indifference to the deaths which he allowed to happen. The last person he encounters on Earth, will be me!

Dillon touched the tab to alert the bus driver of his intentions to exit at the next stop. He jumped alone from the bottom step and gazed at the sun lit pinkness of the Clayton Hotel. Inside, Agent Ermengarde would be coaching Mr. Fleming on his speech and his duties at the banquet. Outside the police cruiser had been removed from the lot. In its vacant space, Dillon noticed the familiar dust remnants and tape from fingerprinting. Nichols might have had the prints lifted as a matter of procedure or to satisfy his own curiosity that Dillon was actually alive. The ghost smiled and passed the trashy scene on his way to the ornate lobby of the Clayton Hotel shaking his head. The elevator doors parted and Dillon stepped in behind a small group. He maneuvered to the back of the elevator causing a few of the others to flinch from an intense cold that had brushed by them.

The doors slid open and he emerged frantically to get to Agent Ermengarde. His stride now evolved into a trot; the urgency of his mission controlling him. He wanted to act now against his adversary in light of the morning's sadness. He arrived at her door and knocked frantically causing the chamber maid to wonder where the knocking was coming from. As Agent Ermengarde opened the door, Dillon rushed inside shouting.

"I need your permission to execute my mission now, Agent Ermengarde!" he spoke facing the sliding glass doors to the ocean overlook. He expected the usual reprimand from his boss, but became puzzled when silence permeated the room. There was something wrong.

"Our mission has been scrubbed by the Supreme Council in regards to Mr. Evergreen and the honorary dinner tomorrow night. They have decided that they will handle this case directly due to a new development in the case. It seems our friend has directed his ire towards three souls for destruction. The SC is stepping in to the recent development before he can activate his devious plan. The Commissioner is deploying me, Mr. Fleming, and other affected souls to a site shortly to deal with Evergreen. I was told to inform you that your case too may be affected and is pending review. I should know something in a few hours. So with that in mind, your request is denied." Ermengarde prepared for the outcome of making the unpopular decision to Dillon. By rehearsing her frank speech, she readied herself for the ultimate result and permitted Dillon to register his protest.

Dillon balked. "They can't do this to me! My family is suffering and the person responsible is enjoying life as if nothing happened. He can go on vacations with his family. Share a child's achievement. Watch his son round the bases after hitting a home run. Admire his daughter at a dance recital. It's not right!"

"I understand your situation, Ken. I am sure they will rule in your favor. It's only because of the change in status of the Evergreen case that has led to this delay. Be patient!" She assured. Dillon slumped on the end of the bed his head cradled in his hands,

"Death is so unfair!"

CHAPTER 33

The fax machine convulsed violently on a weak Ikea
stand that Pamela Evergreen had purchased for
the home office at the Coastal Charm. The whole
stand vibrated as the fax machine dispensed its
usual documents for Richard and Pamela
Evergreen's endeavors. Evergreen reacted and
rolled joyously from his bed as he heard the
machine reeling off pages continually. He couldn't wait to
hear what Kaz had in store for Mueller, Castro, and
Coleman. He didn't sleep well the previous night and
entertained the options for his ever unfulfilled quest for
vengeance and hatefulness which now was becoming
compulsive and crippling.

Pamela could see it in full bloom as she lay in bed next
to her husband who curled into a tense ball cussing and
cursing those that would dare confront him. Her efforts to
placate him with comforting words and embraces had
waned. She had warned him that the possibility of
suffering a stroke was imminent if he didn't get help soon.
He ignored her because she was a woman and didn't
understand a man's world. Only he and he alone knew how
to deal with the declining human condition. He would
make the world "Evergreen" and die trying if he had to. The
Evergreen brain had to be imparted in all who came in
contact with him. If you agreed with him you had the

luxury of his company, but to disagree you would experience a traumatic event that could only be linked to his sinister and twisted mind where one would come to the inevitable conclusion that is was Evergreen inspired. His mouth salivated as he reached the fax machine and pored over the documents until he found the one he desired.

"I, John Kasimir do hereby resign my position of Consultant to the firm of Evergreen, Goldberg and Carlson effective immediately, July the Fifth 1992. I request that you do not contact me ever again or I will be forced to use any or all legal and law enforcement services at my disposal. Kaz."

Evergreen focused on the message reading it several times for proof of what had occurred. "Why? He thought. Kaz was always rewarded for his deviousness and treachery. Was this a matter of more money? Is he ill? Did I call him at a bad time? He has always responded to my needs with fervor. What has changed?" Evergreen slumped in a nearby chair and contemplated the possibilities clutching the resignation in his hand dangling over the arm of the chair. The confusion of the matter didn't last long. The Evergreen temper took hold. He gritted his teeth and slammed his fist down on the arm of the chair.

Pamela entered the room and turned back noting her husband's heated mood change. She knew better to inquire what was causing her husband to react for he would take it out on her. "It was *her* fault he was angry!" She could hear him angrily cussing the world with every profane word in the swear word dictionary. He kicked a footstool sending it into a wall. The family cat cowered under a bed in the guest room. He shoved open the balcony door with a force slamming the glass encased door against the jamb.

The resignation letter was balled up and thrown off the penthouse balcony landing in the swimming pool below to the wonderment of sun bathers, swimmers, and the lifeguard shielding their eyes looking skyward. This was not the first time an object sailed from the penthouse balcony to the pool below. There was a time that the Evergreens were engaged in a heated argument that sent Richard storming out towards the balcony. Not realizing the screen door was closed, he burst toward the balcony launching the spring loaded door off its track skyward catapulting it into the night sky and surreally splashing into the water below. The next morning the maintenance crew enjoyed a hearty laugh at the sight of the screen door as it stood upright bobbing in the eight foot section of the pool.

***

As customary on Sunday mornings the Evergreens would drive to their favorite French bistro, L'Alsace for Sunday brunch. After Evergreen had cooled down momentarily on the balcony, he looked at the clock inside the living room. It was now 9:30. He walked back inside his anger subsided and softly called for Pamela to get ready to go out. Pamela was seated at her vanity shaping her brown eyebrows with an eye pencil, a loosely draped silk robe barely concealed her freshly-showered nude body. Startled by the entrance of her *master,* she cinched her robe, denying him of a lustful peek. Whether she would attend brunch with him was open for discussion basing it on his current emotion. In most cases she felt the worst was over and besides she loved the cuisine at L'Alsace and she adored the attention lavished on them by the owner and other patrons. Every once in a while she would be asked to be photographed by a lone paparazzi reflecting back on her days as a supermodel. She would put her true feelings aside and not aggravate her husband even more.

While his wife was in the shower, Evergreen called down to the security office for them to have his Mercedes at the front door in an hour. After some tense moments of confusion in the office as to the whereabouts of Evergreen's car, Sam Travis remembered that Evergreen arrived in a cab the evening before. He also included that he paid the fare out of his own pocket in a disgusted tone. With the information provided the officer relayed the incident to a waiting on the verge of impatience Evergreen who just remembered that his Mercedes was still parked at the marina.

"Have the courtesy limo meet us in front in an hour!" Evergreen demanded directing the blame for his forgetfulness on the security officer and hanging up. With that, the security officer announced that the new guy be given the honor to drive the Evergreens to their desired destination since nobody else wanted the unenviable task. Of course just like any other job, the FNG is always assigned the point. However in this case, the new guy seized at the opportunity with zeal.

At 10:30 precisely, the chauffeur pulled up front to Evergreen's building entrance. He stood outside the vehicle allowing it to run with air conditioning cooling the dark limousine. He wore the standard chauffeur uniform complete with cap pulling it down to his eyebrows. Standing like a military honor guardsman befitting the image that would please Evergreen, he waited his guests with pride and opened the door as they emerged from the building lobby. He went unnoticed as the Evergreens ducked into the limo engaging in conversation with each other regarding their afternoon plans. With the Evergreens inside, the driver swung the limousine towards the front gate where Sam Travis was stationed. As they passed he waved, but was not sure they had noticed due to the tinted glass windows. Travis smiled closing the gate and wishing Mr. Evergreen an untimely death under his breath.

After a short six block ride to L'Alsace, the driver stopped at the front and opened the rear door. Evergreen helped his wife from the back seat and turned to the driver who was positioned himself with the sun at his back causing Evergreen to shield his eyes to address his servant. The driver complied and drove the limo to a secluded part of the parking lot.

"I need you to wait here for us. After we're finished I need you to drive us to the marina." The driver smiled and acknowledged with a professional yes sir. Evergreen took two steps and paused experiencing a familiarity with the voice. But he shook off the notion as coincidental since he never shared time with mundane professionals. The driver acknowledged Evergreen's instructions and drove the limousine to a secluded part of the parking lot.

The outing didn't go without the usual Evergreen flair for excitement though. Mr. Evergreen was not pleased with the location of his seating by the maître d', Henri

Broussard. In this rant he had complained about having his table facing a table with a man and wife and the man's mother in a wheelchair. She was suffering from Parkinson's syndrome. Mr. Evergreen made it clear to everyone in earshot distance of his displeasure with his seating assignment, including the man's mother in the wheelchair. If he wanted to see this much trembling, he would hold a board meeting. Pamela sat embarrassed and registered her dissatisfaction at her husband's cold comment.

Of course, Monsieur Broussard faced his wrath and was inclined to move the Evergreens to a more suitable location in the restaurant away from the object of his scorn. The maître d' fought off the urge to guide them to the restroom, the appropriate place for Mr. Evergreen but not his caring wife. As they stood to be moved to another table both were scorned by every face in the bistro for Richard's obvious and hurtful rudeness. The word 'jerk' reverberated through the restaurant under hushed breaths.

Mrs. Evergreen felt the ire of the diners and walked with her head down as if to deflect the bombs of hate being hurled towards them. Richard Evergreen did not react. To him it was comparable to Hail Caesar! He dined unaffected by the dissension he created in the bistro. Pamela ashamed of her husband just listened to his conceit and poked at her food not feeling the urge to eat. Pamela had participated with pride in many charitable causes over the years. One of them was for Parkinson's research funding. She never felt that humiliated in her life and now was contemplating divorce after her husband's scene in the bistro. He paid the bill and left no gratuity; the cherry on top of the sundae of harshness. In Evergreen's twisted mind, it was *he* who should be thanked for gracing the restaurant with *his* presence especially on a weekend where *he* was being honored for his *charity, sacrifice, and goodwill*, compliments of loopholes of the US tax code.

"Oh, I'm going to use the same speech I made at the dedication of my statue last year in New York. These podunks won't know."

As they passed the maître d' podium in front, Evergreen continued his delusional ramblings of self-importance to his disinterested wife. Broussard stared his hatred at Evergreen as Pamela looked hopeless in his direction trying to win some dignity points but to no avail. There were no words like, "Please come back to see us soon." The stare indicated "rot in hell!"

The Evergreens stood on the top step looking towards the limo in the back of the lot. Richard waved for the driver who showed no signs of moving. After frantically waving and whistling for five minutes, Evergreen started jingling the change in his pocket. He told Pam to wait because it was not going to be pretty on what he was going to say to the driver. He stormed off the steps and marched madly to the limo which was parked about two hundred feet away. Within ten feet of the limo he launched into a diatribe of insults for the driver to hear. The chauffeur opened his door and the door to the rear of the vehicle without retort.

"Are you done playing with yourself you moron?" Evergreen growled ducking to get into the back seat. He then noticed the driver was not alone. There was a blonde in the passenger seat. "Now I see what the delay was. I'm going to report you to your boss. What's your name?" Evergreen leaned forward to the sliding glass partition behind the driver.

"My name is Edward Fleming!" he declared removing his cap and adjusting the rear view mirror for Evergreen to recognize him. The blonde turned to Evergreen. She had no face. "There's been a change in plans for where I am to drive you next." Suddenly the ground below the limousine rocked sending geysers of sand, dirt and steam into the air surrounding the vehicle. Sensing danger, Evergreen struggled with the door handle but it was locked. He tried opening the window. It too was locked. Propping himself back on the seat he kicked wildly at the sun roof. He pounded at the glass watching Pamela fade from view as the sand immersed the car and now it was sinking. The driver and the blonde in the front simply vanished.

The parking lot below the car was rapidly disintegrating and now darkness consumed the vehicle. Then the car plummeted into the abyss that was created when the walls of the massive hole expanded. The expansion pulled everything in along with it; concrete curb bumpers, light posts, and two hundred square feet of parking lot. The limo crash landed into the bottom ground of the pit causing the wheels to explode from the chassis. Evergreen vaguely conscious felt a talon-like hand on his arm, then another on his leg and another grabbing his hair from behind the back seat and still more hands grasping at him from the darkness until they all dragged him forcibly in all directions from the various portals of the vehicle apportioning him into writhing sinewy pieces. His terror laced screams for help were drowned out by the continued deafening roar of the unsettled earth.

Pamela stood on the top step of the restaurant trying to reconcile conflicting emotions; one of shock and one of relief. Other patrons and employees including the maître d' exited in panic thinking an earthquake had just occurred. When Monsieur Broussard inquired about what had just happened to Pamela, she shrugged resignedly and softly uttered, "Fate."

CHAPTER 34

Soon after Gwen Blasingame's phone calls were made in the morning, she received an urgent assignment from her boss at the Seaside Daily News. He wanted a feature piece written about Bill Danko's civic achievements in Seaside. There would be no mention of his imprisonment or his alleged crimes. It would be a fluff piece honoring the late sponsor of their newspaper.

Danko's real estate offices still advertised regularly in The Seaside Daily and were responsible for its growth and eventual profits. It was an obvious ploy by the editor to portray the newspaper as sympathetic to its raison d'etre and would be appreciated only by Danko's doppelgangers. The majority of Seaside residents knew the real story and would see through the farce. However, Gwen Blasingame reported enthusiastically to the offices to retrieve the background information and write the feature according to her editor's guidelines.

She would enjoy this project and embellish the story to the point of outright transparency without her editor seeing the irony. It would be written with the determination of receiving the ultimate praise from her corrupted-save-my-ass boss, but all readers would see the hilarity of the piece's intention. As she drove to the offices she had envisioned the topic line of the first paragraph...

"Bill Danko was born in a log cabin in Kentucky. His parents Jedediah and Hildegard supplemented their living by making moonshine from an old country recipe handed down to them from the first pioneers. When "Big Bill" was three, he kilt a bar up in the tree with a stale - hard as a stone vanilla wafer - slung from a slingshot and thus begins one of America's true success stories."

Of course that would be too obvious as she entertained the notion of laughter in the streets of Seaside reacting to the obvious farce. The story had to be written factually with some interspersing of sarcasm that could be appreciated by those who shared inside information about Danko's dealings. The majority of Seaside residents would expect such a story of ridicule about a man who held the town hostage for nine years with the threat of harm and death looming over the community during that tense period.

***

Calvin Blasingame now wide awake cranked up his antique restored 1951 kelly green Mercury sedan and attended to his Sunday obligations; his weekly pilgrimage to Big Bubba's Beer and Wine. On Sunday Calvin went through the trouble of showering and shaving to make a favorable impression in his rare public appearance. He combed his receding gray crew cut and slapped on some Aqua Velva to entice any woman-folk he would encounter on his outing. To add to this manly image he wore a clean white undershirt with faded blue khaki trousers which draped over his worn black work boots. The initials "CB" adorned his right tricep below the hem of his undershirt. Look out you Seaside women, here comes Calvin Blasingame!

Calvin's mission was to restock his beer supply. He was down to his last two cases of Miller High Life and the storage space in the kitchen indicated it was time to restock. The space on the wall where the beer was stacked was never painted to keep up with the current choice of color. Therefore, when the cases got low it would present an eyesore. Calvin had painted the area around the beer stack an egg shell white while the wall behind the beer

stack was a pastel green. The color of the Miller High Life
beer cans was almost a perfect match. So instead of using
the time to paint the wall in this area to match the current
color, Calvin resorted to stacking more beer to block the
contrast of wall color! Twelve cases would do the trick.
That should last me three weeks he ruminated. A stock
clerk at Big Bubba's readied a hand truck as Calvin
entered the store.

"Hey, Mr. Blasingame! How many this time, sir?"

"Make it twelve of the usual, kid." The twenty year old
eagerly escorted the hand truck to the back. Calvin could
hear the clanging stacking of cases of 24 twelve ounce cans
commence as Bubba the owner approached the front of the
store.

"I see you're here for your monthly supply, Cal.
Retirement must be going good for you. Your refusal to
paint that wall keeps me in business! Gwen must surely
love you!" Bubba whispered to his new naive female
cashier. "Make sure you check this guy's ID! He may look
over sixty but he is actually over sexy! You'll have to fight
that womanly urge to follow him out to his car and that's
how I lose all my cashiers." Brandy the young cashier
blushed as Calvin chuckled.

The "kid" carted Mr. Blasingame's purchase to the front
as Brandy counted them. The old cash NCR cash register
chimed the total $117.26. Reaching in his pocket, Calvin
produced a wad of twenty dollar bills and handed six over
to Brandy. After receiving his change he bade farewell to
Bubba and motioned for the young stock clerk to follow
him to the Mercury. The trunk of the car was roomy and
the twelve cases of beer were not a problem in comparison
with modern compact cars. The "kid" loaded the vehicle
receiving the two dollars and change as a tip.

Gwen Blasingame now occupied with the file and dossier
on Bill Danko, perused through the material and developed
an outline on how she would portray this generous and
gregarious man to her readers. Among the items were
various pictures of Danko dedicating new building projects

and his acceptance of awards for his civic involvement. As Gwen studied the pictures, she noticed two men in the background who appeared to always shy away from the photographer's focus. But, there was one picture at an awards banquet that caught the men unaware of the picture being taken because they were in the background. She pondered who these men were and deducted that they had to be bodyguards for Danko because of their regular attendance and proximity to Danko at the social functions. Pulling out a magnifying lens she studied the mysterious looking men and concluded that they were the same men in every picture.

In the front of the newspaper office lobby, she could hear a man inquiring about permission from her editor to speak with her. She stood from her desk and peeked out beyond the cubicle. It was Milton Craddock. Seeing that his reporter had already noticed the man, he reluctantly led him to her office. Gwen's boss didn't want anything to interfere with her attending to her urgent assignment.

"Gwen, this is Milton Craddock. Mayor Craddock's son. He wanted to talk with you. Don't be long, I want to have your first draft by four."

"Well that kind of depends on what Mr. Craddock wants to talk about doesn't it, sir? I mean this could be newsworthy which could take priority," Gwen replied snidely.

The editor turned and left the office shaking his head in anger in response. "Don't worry about that, Mr. Craddock. How may I help you?" Gwen welcomed her guest with a welcoming smile.

"Call me, Milt. My mother wanted me to speak with you to verify the facts of my father's involvement with corruption and the facts about his death. She says you have all the information. Is that correct?" Gwen took out a legal pad and scribbled testing out an old pen.

"Keep your voice low. I don't want my boss to hear you. Your mother sent me a letter with all the details and her revelations support my suspicions of the facts surrounding the corruption that took place," she said looking around her office cubicle for her paranoid editor.

As Gwen stood and scanned the neighboring cubicles, Craddock saw the photographs on her desk. He craned his head to examine them. There he could see his father presenting an award to Danko in one of the press photos and then something even more grabbed his attention; the photo with the two men in full view near Danko.

"Do you mind if I look at this photograph?" he asked politely. The intensity of his stare was noteworthy as Gwen noticed his curious reaction which involved moments of studying the photo.

"Milt? Milt? What is it?" She moved her chair closer to her guest intrigued by his interest which she hoped would satisfy her curiosity of the two men's identity in the photo.

In a hushed voice he clamored, "I saw these guys today at the police station! They were dropping something off for the Chief. They didn't appear normal." Gwen was awestruck. In an instant she knew, that the Chief was probably being *reminded* to keep his mouth shut even though Danko was dead or the two were extorting money from the crooked cop. The story was adding another chapter. "I can smell Pulitzer Prize," she thought.

CHAPTER 35

A few hours had passed since Jimmy had spoken with his Federal friend, Inspector Greg Harding. He accepted the fact that it would take Harding time to coordinate a search off the Seaside, Maryland coast from his house in Los Angeles, California. The nearest FBI field office to Seaside was in Washington D.C. and Castro sensed that his buddy was having a difficult time locating a dive team and above all communicating with fellow agents and Federal authorities about the sketchy thin probability that the *Donovan's Pride* was located at the coordinates that Castro had given. One thing for sure, Harding believed his friend and Castro realized Harding was sticking his neck out for him. The point that Harding was suggesting to his cohorts in D.C. was that Danko was still a federal case and the file remained open on all issues that were now coming to light. They had to investigate the mystery surrounding the disappearance of the *Donovan's Pride*.

Jimmy felt trapped in his home waiting for the phone call from Harding. While his wife tended to the mountain of laundry presented to her by Danny, he turned the stereo on to ease the tension. Danny regaled his father with his adventures at sea and his bout with a bull shark trying in vain to alleviate the obvious worry in his dad's face. A traffic report on the oldies station broke in with the news of a massive sinkhole that may have claimed the lives of two people at the restaurant L'Alsace. Danny sat up on the sofa wondering if his father heard the report and looked back at him slumped in his chair deep in thought. The phone rang sending Jimmy to his desk. It was Greg Harding; the call he anticipated.

Harding updated his friend with the status of the search prompting Castro to scribble wildly the details on a pad of note paper with his deformed right hand. A smile now appeared on his face. Sunny entered the room with Danny motioning for her to be silent with his finger in front of his lips. He mouthed the word "Greg" to quell her curiosity to who was calling. Her husband was bubbling with excitement.

"Userts? What are userts?" Castro interjected halting his friend's explanation of details of the plan.

"USERT is the acronym for the Bureau's dive team. It stands for Underwater Search and Evidence Recovery Team. These guys can find a BB in three inches of ocean floor mud! If the boat is where you say it is, they'll find out how it sunk," Harding proclaimed proudly. "We have a team that just wrapped up an investigation in the Delaware Bay on Friday that can be in Seaside first thing tomorrow. The bad news is you can't go with them to the site."

Jimmy paused with the disappointing news and was not going to beg his friend for special permission. "How will I know if the boat is there?"

"I will call you after the evidence is collected and the site is rendered open. It might be a few days and I urge you and whoever else knows not to go there. Before I forget, I will need information about this Minnis character and his female guest. Our Baltimore office will need to interview them," Harding demanded.

"Okay Greg, I understand," he replied dejectedly. "I have Minnis's business card in my wallet. I'll call you back with that information, but I don't know anything about his guest who happens to be his mistress. You guys are going to have to be careful with this because I don't want to get him in trouble with his wife."

Harding snarled. Hyper-vigilance fueled by heightened national security threats emanating from the Gulf War had finally taken its toll on the dedicated government servant. "He has a *mistress*! He saw *a ghost ship* that disappeared! Jimmy you know how this makes me look if that boat isn't there? And you want *us* to be careful? Either way Minnis is going to be contacted if the boat is or isn't there regardless of his infidelity! I'm only doing this for you because I believe you need to be exonerated for something you didn't do and I surely hope for your sake that the boat is there!" Jimmy recoiled never seeing this side of his friend in an official role and slouched back in his chair. He tried to gather a thought to ease the uncomfortable tension.

"I understand everything Greg and I appreciate your efforts in clearing my name. If I struck a nerve with you, I apologize."

Harding's past experiences with witnesses' demands had emerged. He was not in the habit of being dictated by civilians when it came to the Bureau's investigation of subjects. During his service with the Department of Justice he had encountered too many of these type of situations which riled him internally to lashing out at a witness. This time it happened to be his friend Castro. Sometime later when he was alone and reflected back on his behavior, he would regret his action. In his professional stance, he would not admit fault for his rudeness even to his friend.

"Jimmy call me with the info on Minnis as soon as possible. Tell Sunny and Danny, I said hi."

Sunny noticed her husband's demeanor had changed as he hung the phone up gently.

"I think I just ruined our friendship with the Hardings," he somberly admitted. "Am I crazy to try and clear my name, Sunny? Greg's having a hard time believing me."

"You're scaring me, amigo. Does the name Ben Jacoby ring any bells?" Sunny warned. "I just think Greg like me and everyone else will be glad when that boat is finally found. When are they coming to search?" she asked rubbing his neck.

"First thing tomorrow."

"That's great, Dad!" Danny added to lift up his father's spirits. Jimmy stood and walked slowly back to the bedroom to retrieve his wallet. He returned to his desk.

"Hey, I got to call the guy who gave me the information to tell him to expect a call from the FBI in Baltimore." Castro picked up the phone again and dialed getting Minnis's answering machine. Recalling his instructions, Jimmy hung up with the notion to call again later. He then called Harding with the desired information noting not to include any mention of personal instructions.

CHAPTER 36

The 1988 Cadillac El Dorado parked around the corner from the Blasingame home. As Calvin headed out to attend to his Sunday errand in his '51 Mercury, the maroon El Dorado pulled up near the Blasingame home. The two occupants, Gianni Sebastiani and Pauley Molinaro, carefully surveyed the surroundings for passer bys and exited the car and advanced the ranch style home. Sebastiani picked the front door lock in seconds and entered while Pauley continued to look out. From under his sports coat Pauley produced a black construction strength garbage bag and proceeded to the side of the house where the trash cans were placed.

The actions did not go unnoticed though. Cheryl Ashford while straightening her daughter's bedroom saw the two strangers walking by her house from the window. They weren't the usual Mormon's on bicycles or Jehovah's Witnesses soliciting membership to their religious communities. It was the way they had their heads on a constant swivel culminating with their easy access to the Blasingame home without knocking on the front door. Also noticeable were the nylon gloves they were wearing on a sultry July summer day. Immediately as agreed with any member of this close knit neighborhood, she dialed the police.

Still smarting from his scrape with Bobby Willoughby the night before, Vincenzo D'Antuano prowled his normal beat in his patrol car. After a restful night sleep with the help of a few Motrin, he commenced his shift willingly at two PM. Sundays were always serene in this coastal community. All the hell raising had climaxed last night. The troublemakers were either heading out of town or sleeping off hangovers. He didn't mind working on Sunday. It was the one day where his renal glands could take a break and he could still get paid. That was until Sheila Kerr his dispatcher contacted him about a possible breaking and entering in his area. D'Antuano floored the Ford Crown Victoria to the scene which was about half a mile away.

Molinaro opened the Rubbermaid containers pulling out the white trash bags that had been deposited over the last three days. He carefully and quietly inserted them into the larger bag, dangling it in his left gloved hand. Sebastiani was ransacking Gwen's home office for information. He too had a bag and swept documents, computer discs, and random objects into the plastic sack. Satisfied of his collection in the short time allotted, he headed for the front door and exited in haste towards the El Dorado. Molinaro struggled with the awkwardness of his bag and dropped it to get a better grip. Near the end of the driveway where the neighbor's hedge had concealed the gangster, Molinaro heard the familiar racing of a police motor responding to the scene.

It was D'Antuano who screeched to a stop twenty feet away seeing the flight of the two burglars. Jumping from his cruiser and using the door as a shield, D'Antuano hollered his command to halt the suspect closest to him, Molinaro. Molinaro drew out his army issue 1911 ACP .45 and opened fire as Sebastiani raced towards the El Dorado. One round thumped into the door of the cruiser causing the officer to duck behind the open door. Out of consideration for his own neck if he shot a cop and was captured, the thug fired off two more shots striking the front of the cruiser; one flattening a front tire and one puncturing the radiator.

Sebastiani seeing that the road was now blocked by
D'Antuano's cruiser veered the El Dorado in a mid-street
U-turn striking some parked cars on the passenger side.
He reversed the car rapidly so his partner could escape
with him. As he was maneuvering, Molinaro provided cover
for his partner, peppering the cruiser more with his
shooting. D'Antuano, pinned down by the fury of the gun
battle, was now engulfed in smoke and steam from his car
engine, being cautious to return fire from his .357
magnum fearing he may strike a civilian. It was the first
time D'Antuano had ever had to fire his weapon and the
adrenaline surged through his body causing him to shake.

Molinaro struggled with the passenger door being
dented and pushed in by the collision with the parked
cars. He tossed the garbage bag into the rear seat and dove
through the open passenger window as Sebastiani
accelerated away from the scene in a stagnant veil of gray
gun smoke and burnt rubber turning left at the next
intersecting street. Neighbors once crouched behind their
picture windows now stood to see what was occurring
outside their homes.

"Shots Fired! Shots Fired! This is D'Antuano! Suspects
are two white males driving a late model maroon El
Dorado! Pennsylvania plates! Suspects are armed and are
driving south on Nicholson and probably headed out of
town on Route 30.Over," the shaken officer frantically
shouted the situation into his shoulder mic.

Calvin Blasingame turned right onto his street enjoying
his tape deck of instrumental music consisting of big band
music of the 40s and songs of the 50s. His windows rolled
down, he could hear kids still lighting off firecrackers that
still remained from last night's festivities. Completing his
turn, he came to an abrupt stop to see the aftermath of
battlefield of his neighborhood. Neighbors streamed from
their homes to console Corporal D'Antuano and his
smoking vehicle while others angrily shouted their dismay
of the hit and run nature to their damaged vehicles. Taking
advantage of the location of Calvin's Mercury, D'Antuano
broke through the crowd of concerned citizens and ran
towards the confounded Calvin.

"Sir. I need to commandeer your vehicle immediately. I'm in pursuit of dangerous felons!"

Calvin hesitated but not before Jerry Ashford his neighbor convinced him.

"Hey Calvin. There were two guys who broke into your house! They were shooting at the officer."

Calvin looked to see if his wife's car was in the driveway and grimaced with anger. Confident she was not at home he opened the passenger door. "Get in Officer. I'll drive!"

Using his radio attached to his shirt, D'Antuano updated the dispatcher. "This is D'Antuano. I am now in pursuit of two armed suspects. A citizen has volunteered to drive after them. We are in a green, what year is this vehicle?" He asked Calvin who was turning down the volume on his tape deck. Calvin used to this type of interrogation at car shows replied with the primary information along with other features and specifications which were not vital at this time. D'Antuano cut his partner's details short only announcing the necessary data to the dispatcher.

"We are in a green 1951 Mercury heading west on Sunrise. Alert all units!"

✳ ✳ ✳

Back at the Seaside Daily News, a police scanner broadcast the intensity of the incident. The editor rushed into Gwen's office interrupting the meeting between Milton Craddock and the reporter.

"Gwen. Are you listening to this? Drop this assignment and get out there now! Follow the progress with this portable scanner and finish the feature at home. Gwen? What's wrong?" Her editor handed her the portable scanner used to follow police and fire emergencies in the city. He noticed a frozen trance from his star reporter who was not flinching.

"The report says the officer is following the suspect's car in a green '51 Mercury on Sunrise. We live on Sunrise and my husband Calvin has a '51 Mercury," she replied worriedly. Milton Craddock showed his concern for the reporter with sympathetic eyes.

"That's great, Gwen! We can get a first person slant on the story!" her opportunistic heartless boss proclaimed. Gwen gathered her files and photographs together and placed them in a brown paper shopping bag by her desk, while listening to the urgings of her boss.

"If he survives." She stood and grabbed her purse, paper bag, and scanner, slowly exiting her office.

"Gwen. I'd like to go with you." Craddock offered. "I'll drive. You are in no condition."

"Thank you, Milt. Let's go.

✱✱✱

Meanwhile, Calvin and Vincenzo had caught up to the fleeing pair who were ahead of them by five car lengths as they weaved in and out of slow traffic and running red lights. Calvin hadn't experienced this much excitement since his days in the Navy aboard a submarine tender. It didn't take long for Sebastiani to realize he was being tailed. The 1951 Mercury sedan did attract attention even if it wasn't duplicating the hazardous veering and weaving of the El Dorado.

The chase was approaching the open lanes of the intrastate without any traffic controls for miles. Dispatchers from the State police were now involved and committed to action to bring this chase to a halt. Noting the closeness of the Mercury, Molinaro leaned out the passenger window and fired back at the antique auto. Motivated by his love of NASCAR, Calvin swerved and screeched to avoid the shots to the delight of Corporal D'Antuano who was aiming his chrome barreled .357 out the passenger window. Large blasted holes in the trunk of the El Dorado proved that D'Antuano was quite adept at pistol marksmanship. Calvin maneuvered his car to stay to the left when Molinaro returned fire.

Up ahead a State Police cruiser was inching out of its camouflage hiding place where it was stationed to flag down speed violators. Punching the accelerator as the El Dorado passed, the State Trooper swung out from the grassy roadside sending dirt and gravel back towards the median. Calvin in consideration let up on the gas to allow the Trooper to pursue then with the local police in his rear view mirror slowed his rate of pursuit at the urging of Corporal D'Antuano, concerned for the safety of his volunteer driver. Besides, it was only a matter of moments before the whole thing ended. A State helicopter was now employed in the chase and up ahead flashing lights indicated the presence of a roadblock. Among those poised behind the barricade was Lieutenant Nichols coolly aiming his Beretta nine millimeter at the speeding vehicle. Nichols was at the State Police barracks on police business when the alert was transmitted.

In the El Dorado, Sebastiani had decided silently and unilaterally to run the road block. Molinaro tightened his seatbelt and braced for the encroaching impact. Clouds of smoke obscured the roadblock and the El Dorado careened off the road on the right side of the highway flattening a makeshift memorial to a young traffic fatality and crashing front end first into a muddy field. It came to rest at the base of a billboard advertising the law services of Lawson and Kramer after bullets and shotgun pellets smashed into the front of the fleeing vehicle. The chase was over.

Molinaro lay motionless pressed into the deployment of the blood soaked air bag in the passenger seat while Sebastiani's lifeless corpse was squeezed out of the broken driver's side window diagonally, his arms stuck to his sides as if he was launched partially out of the car from the immense impact resembling a cherry flavored push-pop ice cream treat, a nine millimeter hole in the middle of his forehead complements of the expert marksmanship of Nichols. Behind the scene of the crash, Calvin Blasingame rolled the '51 Mercury along the shoulder and stopped as the fleet of cruisers blocked the highway. Corporal D' Antuano cautiously emerged from the car with his pistol drawn as other law officers did the same. Calvin exited his car trembling and leaned back on the hot hood to observe the rapid gathering of lawmen descend on the scene surrounding the vehicle. The helicopter hovered noisily over the crash site.

Knowing he would be in the way, Calvin inspected his entire car for damages. The engine had never been pushed so hard since the restoration was completed, but it

performed flawlessly. Not one of Molinaro's shots struck
the car. Calvin out of relief opened the trunk and pulled a
Miller from its plastic ring holder. He returned to the
drivers seat to quell his nerves in private listening to Patti
Page sing the Tennessee Waltz on his tape deck. Calvin's
mind now reminisced the past as the activity increased at
the crash site. He had removed himself back to the world of
his happiest times in the 1950s and how his life could have
ended this day. A tapping on his driver's side window
brought him out of his sereneness. He turned to see an
anxious face. It was Gwen.

"Calvin! Who do you think you are, Steve McQueen?
You had me worried to death!"

"No, I was thinking more of Cale Yarborough. How did
you get here, Gwen?"

Gwen explained to her husband the details of her
hearing about the chase while introducing him to Milton
Craddock who had driven her to the site. Calvin opened the
door and shook hands with Craddock and then gave his
wife a synopsis of the chase. She stared down the culvert
where the El Dorado had crashed noting that somebody
had placed a blanket over the body that was protruding
awkwardly from the driver's door.

Chief Carl Davenport was the last to arrive at the crash
site. Blowing his horn he parted the blocking police
cruisers on the highway and inched his way to the scene.
Yellow crime tape sealed the area where the El Dorado left
the road. Paramedic units flashed on the muddy field near
the billboard. Two firemen were slicing into the driver's
side of the El Dorado to extricate the body of Gianni
Sebastiani; his legs wedged tightly between the door, the
firewall and the front seat. Crime photographers snapped
away at the crash scene, including the audacious image of
the El Dorado resting at the base of the billboard which
enticed passing motorists with a loud yellow slogan "NEED
A LAWYER?" The Chief was anxious to see the victims of
the crash. Something about a maroon El Dorado and its
occupants interested him.

Inside the Toyota, Craddock took the liberty of
examining the photographs that Gwen had shown to him.
The brown bag had tipped over when Gwen left his car in

haste to check on Calvin and the photos spilled out onto the passenger side floor mat. It was Craddock's instinct to be nosy and he collected a handful of the glossy photographs. He knew Gwen wouldn't mind. He looked around to make sure there was nobody on foot passing by his car. He then noticed Chief Davenport cautiously navigating his car through the jumbled traffic of emergency vehicles.

As he examined them he was intrigued by the sheer audacity of the magnanimity exhibited by Danko at social functions. To look at him happily being feted was sickening and maddening. Many photographs contained the gangster shaking hands with his late father who seemed to struggle with maintaining a smile for the pose. It was obvious in Davenport's pictures with "Big Bill," too. Craddock then located the photo of Danko with his two unnamed lieutenants that he noticed on Gwen's desk. His eyes pierced the photo hoping that he could burn through it like a magnifying glass through paper on a sunny summer day. Gwen interrupted his train of angered thoughts when she returned to his car fumbling with the door handle.

"I'm positive those are the same guys I saw at the police station this morning. No doubt about it!" Craddock swore before the reporter sat down. "I just saw Davenport go by while I was looking at the pictures. I think I'm going to ask him about why these two were at the station this morning and why they would break into your house, Gwen!" Craddock grew incensed. Feeling the rush of blood to his head, he felt certainly that the two had murdered his father and the Chief was mixed up in it. He punched the dashboard of his car, scooped up the incriminating photo, and vaulted from the Toyota. He paced heavily down the hill to confront the Chief despite Gwen urging him to stop. The Chief was in the midst of being educated about the chase and the outcome with Corporal D'Antuano and other officers involved in the chase.

"Hey you, Davenport!" The group stopped and focused their attention on Milton Craddock in a rage of heat storming down the slight embankment. "I'm talking to you, Chief! You mind telling everyone why those two punks in the El Dorado were in your office this morning? I'm sure as hell they weren't turning themselves in!"

The Chief stunned by the irate counselor's
announcement stood ready to defend himself. The ranking
State Police investigator standing near the El Dorado
overheard the commotion and walked closer to the scene
wanting also to hear the Chief's explanation who couldn't
respond to the outburst quick enough. In the midst of his
fellow officers, he stumbled and stuttered his reply
inaudibly. The State Police investigator intercepted the
young counselor.

"Sir? I'm Captain Trevor Bellows of the Maryland State
Police. I'm handling the investigation. Is there something I
can do for you?" he asked discretely motioning for
Craddock to walk with him to an out of earshot location of
the crime scene.

"I want you to arrest that weasel over there and charge
him with complicity in the murder of my father! I have
proof that the punks in the car match this photo in my
hands. They were in the Chief's office this morning!"
Craddock handed the photo over to Bellows who instructed
him to calm down. He studied it as Craddock stared down
the nervous and embarrassed Chief of Police who was
eliciting laughter from a few of his officers by gesturing
with his hand that Craddock had been drinking.

"Hmmm. There is a similarity. We haven't made a
positive ID on the deceased due to the condition of their
bodies, mainly from the multiple wounds to their faces. We
are going to have to wait for a positive ID from the Medical
Examiner with fingerprinting proof of who they are. So I
ask you sir to be patient and let us do our work here
mister uh?"

"Craddock. Milton Craddock. My father was Mayor
Stanley Craddock. I have other photos with them in the
company of Bill Danko." When the State Police Captain
asked of the origin of the photographs, Craddock pointed
to Gwen Blasingame and identified her to the investigator.
He motioned for her to join the discussion with the lawyer.

"So, you are Gwen Blasingame. It seems like all this
commotion was about a break-in at your house. I am going
to have to see your files and of course the photographs you
have. Of course that will require a warrant and I strongly
advise you not alter or shall we say *lose* this information or

I shall have to arrest you for tampering with evidence in a criminal case. Do you understand me?" he intimidated peering into her wide eyes.

Gwen gulped from the steely stare from the stoic investigator and nodded her head. Craddock patted her on the back to assure her she would be fine and protected. Chief Davenport still joking with his rank and file officers glanced occasionally towards the State Police Captain's brief interrogation.

"Chief Davenport is it? I advise you not to leave town until we settle this matter. I would advise you to get a lawyer... rapidly. I assume Mr. Craddock is not an option for you. I would advise somebody who doesn't have an axe to grind with you. You will be served as soon as I meet with the District Attorney."

Craddock growled his displeasure of the Chief. "I'll see you get life for this *Chief*! Mark my words!"

"That'll be enough, Mr. Cradddock. Your Chief of Police is in deep trouble. Let the justice system do its work. You stay cool! Understand?" Bellows inflected his tough no nonsense warning to the obliging lawyer. "I will need a statement about what and who you saw at the Police station this morning with plenty of details."

Davenport moped to the top of the embankment and made his way to his car under the scrutiny and speculation from his policemen. His popularity celebrated moments before had waned drastically. Just one look at the slinking sulking figure indicated he was guilty. There was an air of denial about the Chief that had once secured unity in the force, but as the years went by the Chief knew he was losing control.

Rumors of his involvement with Danko surfaced and he would ignore them, usually laughing them off. The charade was not working and the more he failed to openly repudiate the stories, the more dissension rose in his ranks. This episode all but iced the force's suspicions about his illicit activity. The Chief appeared devastated and lost as he returned to his vehicle. Slowly, he maneuvered his car through the hostile stares of his police department. He radioed for his assistant to take charge. He was going home.

CHAPTER 37

The ride home to Baltimore was a quiet one for Ted Minnis and Octavia Bledsoe. Octavia tried to engage in conversation with Minnis, but his mind was elsewhere. His thoughts were locked on replaying the haunting screams of the Donovan family and how they must have suffered. Mr. Donovan must have been a great father, a real man. Minnis was unsatisfied by his self-assessment. He envied a man like Michael Donovan. Here was a real hero; a man devoted to the end for his love of his family risking his life to save the family pet. Minnis was ashamed of his playboy life style. This event would be the turning point in his life and he decided then on the ride back to Baltimore to be more giving to his wife, Anna. It would be a life altering moment that he could refer back to as the moment that changed his life.

"I'm sorry, Tavia for not being chatty, but I can't shake the image of that family on the boat. It has really hooked me. I can't think of anything else!"

Tavia's attention was fixed on the sunset in front of them as the sound of the steel grates roared as they passed over them on the Chesapeake Bay Bridge. Her hair flew backwards as the deafening breeze drowned out Minnis's apology due to the convertible top being down. Below, skipjacks and smaller boats were concluding their outings and returning to port. The hot breeze turned cool as the sun descended. An occasional launched bottle rocket would burst in the distance providing a brief distraction from the lack of conversation. "Ted, I'm hungry and I need to use a restroom," she exclaimed gently grabbing his arm. "Mind if we pull over?" Ted acquiesced and turned off into the lot for a barbecue restaurant a mile down the road. Tavia darted into the restaurant as Ted stayed behind to put the top back up. Once the BMW was secured he entered the restaurant requesting a table for two. The hostess seated him in a booth near a window overlooking the westbound holiday traffic from the shore. He gazed and his mind drifted again back to the stormy night.

"Great choice, Ted! I'm in the mood for some brisket!" Tavia, refreshed, slapped her hands in delight for her meal. She sat grinning hoping her friend would snap out of his funk. "Ted? What is it? Have I done something to upset you?" Ted held up his index finger noting that a waitress was nearing the table to take their order. Both Ted and Tavia requested draft beers to refresh them from the rigors of driving in heavy holiday traffic back home. The waitress showing the signs of a long day turned rudely back towards the bar area. She would rather be someplace else and by now didn't care about impressing anyone for a gratuity. She was a tall white woman in her fifties with heavy make-up and bleached white hair.

"Tavia. Baby, you haven't done anything to upset me. I keep thinking about that family last night. I can't think of anything else!" Ted explained stroking her arm.

"Me too, Ted. I keep wondering if we really saw it, if it really happened."

The waitress returned with two chilled pilsner glasses of draft beer, the foamy heads cascading over the rim of the glasses like a beer ad in a magazine. She roughly put them down on the table causing them to spill on the table. Not apologizing she uttered in a boorish manner, "Have you decided yet? Ted's face reddened.

"Ted. I'll handle this." Tavia intercepted Minnis's hostility. Grabbing the menu she paused and took her time making a selection. The waitress started to turn back in a rude haste but Tavia told her to wait. Purposely she asked what the ingredients were to the hottest hot sauce and asked the waitress for a comparison with the other four sauces. Ted swigged his beer knowing what Tavia was up to. Now the waitress's face was showing signs of outrage. Her face was reddening as she explained the comparisons through gritted teeth. Tavia was playing this scene like a pro. "I see you offer ribs in different styles. What's the difference between Kansas City style versus North Carolina? Are the ribs bigger?" She chuckled at her question as being naïve to the barbecue experience. The waitress needed just one more push of the button to explode and Tavia was ready.

"If I get the North Carolina ribs will I get Texas toast with it? Doesn't North Carolina have its own toast?" That was all it took. The waitress erupted what was really bothering her. "Look here you! I know what you're doing and I'm not going to take this crap from you or your race traitor husband!" Minnis covered his mouth in a mocked expression of disbelief. She stormed to the back tearing off her apron, tossing it on the floor, her manager on her heels. Ted held up his glass toasting Tavia.

"Well done my dear! Jolly good show! Jolly good!" he imitated in an English accent. "Tavia extended her waffling hand as to indicate it was a so-so performance. The manager rushed to the table apologizing profusely as he garnered the stares of all the diners in the restaurant.

"I am so sorry for that! Look I will give you whatever dinner you want on the house."

"I don't think so. I don't want to any *special items* added to my food from the kitchen. I think we are going to leave. You will be hearing from my lawyer in the morning, sir! Here's five bucks for the beer." Minnis reached into his wallet and threw the five dollar bill on the table. Both Tavia and him had enough and walked out the door to applause by the tables who endured the same *courteous* service from the same waitress. The manager plopped into the booth and cradled his head in his hands.

"Thanks, Taves. I needed that!" Minnis congratulated her as she proudly walked to the car. Impressed by her epic performance, he opened the car door for her and royally bowed. As the BMW attempted to exit the driveway, they noticed the waitress leaning on the outside wall smoking a cigarette. Ted honked the horn and waved his stretched left arm from the window. The waitress stood and returned the one finger salute. Minnis and Tavia roared in laughter at the scene. It was the most memorable part of the weekend. The final leg of the trip was joyful with them breaking down in laughter as they recalled the restaurant scene. "You know Taves. You did bring up an important item. Why doesn't North Carolina have its own toast? I mean Texas has it! France has it! Melba has it!"

Minnis arrived in the front of Tavia's apartment building. He opened the trunk to get her baggage.

"Taves. Miss Bledsoe. I know it wasn't the weekend you expected, but it ended special for me. You are really deserving of someone who can be devoted to you full time. I can't be that guy. I hope you understand."

"Miss Bledsoe?" she smirked. "Ted. I was hoping you would feel that way. You are right. You belong to your wife. I had a great time. I got to see your rich white snobby friends get bombed by a flock of birds. I threw up all over your boat. I got to see the most horrific scene in my life, of which I'll have nightmares the rest of my life. And I showed you how to push back without losing your temper. For me, I will always remember this weekend." Her sincere brown eyes looked deeply into Minnis's eyes and they embraced and kissed. "See you around, Minus." she joked as she walked up the stairs to her building.

"See you, Taves!" Minnis grinned as he started his BMW. His thoughts now focused on surprising Anna in Somalia. This would be Step One of his life changing plans and promoting a more positive image of himself.

CHAPTER 38

I t had been a gut wrenching day for Carl Davenport
that day. The reality of the past had collided headlong
into him reducing him to a rambling and mumbling
paranoid. He turned down his police radio in
deference to the recurring images playing loudly in his
mind. His stomach ached from the constant flipping
on how he was going to be perceived in the
community. So in tune was his guilt that he ran a red light
tuning out the blaring of swearing and car horns. Now, HE
would be a hunted man and put on trial. It would take a
really good lawyer to get him out of this darkness. Maybe
the Lawson and Kramer billboard at the crash scene was a
sign of who would successfully represent him, he
pondered. Suddenly he found himself pulling up to the
front of his house. He sat amazed on how he could drive
the thirteen miles from the crime scene and not recall any
details of the drive. It was if he was beamed to his
residence from some supernatural force.

One force that Davenport was well aware for was the
power of Jack Daniels who awaited his presence inside his
modest home. The Chief had always counted on his alcohol
of choice to render him free from the tyrannical grasps of his
work. This afternoon would be no exception. He unlocked
the door jiggling the door knob with his bulky key chain and
pushed through the entrance to a bee hive of inactivity.

Inside his teen-aged son interrupted his zombie like trance from his video game to say hi. His daughter was talking on the phone with her best friend and briefly waved to him. Brenda, his wife was stowing away the groceries that she had just brought home. She stopped to see that look in her husband's face that told her to not interfere with his stroll to the liquor cabinet. Knowing he wasn't supposed to be home for two more hours coupled with the weight of the world in his face, she smiled comprehending the stress of his position as Police Chief. Davenport grabbed the fifth along with an old fashion glass and made his way to the serenity of his study. He returned to the kitchen and filled an ice bucket with cubes from the ice maker compartment in his refrigerator. Without a word, he strode to his den and closed the door sealing him inside alone surrounded by recent recurring voices that pierced his guts. He removed his utility belt and holster, placing them in the open safe then closing the door spinning the combination dial on the front for security. His tie already loose was yanked around his collar and flung to a chair nearby. He pulled his shirt from the waist and sat in a recliner kicking off his black shoes. The Chief was now ready to forget.

After gulping three full glasses of whiskey to drown out the voices of Milton Craddock, the State Police investigator, and the murmurings from a suspecting group of officers, Davenport turned on his stereo to the sounds of relaxing music. He then unlocked the top drawer of his desk and twisted off the cap of Xanax pills when the voices didn't subside. Taking a random amount that happened to spill in his hand, he tossed them in his mouth followed by a half glass of whiskey and sunk back into his recliner. The effects were instantaneous and the Chief was out cold. Unlike the uneventful drive home from the crime scene, his next trip would be life changing.

***

Carl Davenport awoke to the slicing of his back from a muscular bald man wielding a cat o' nine tails who cursed his inactions. "Row, you miserable piece of shit!" Again he

flailed the whip sending blood from his torn flesh splashing
onto the rowers behind him. He immediately pulled the
roughened oak oar back heeding the command from the
sadistic punisher. The Chief in a state of shock and pain
did manage to survey this odd scene. He was shackled to a
galley ship. The odor of a foul stench caused him to gag
instantly and when he looked to his right he immediately
knew the reason. The sea was a literal cesspool littered
with excrement and body parts enhanced by the choking
effects of ammonium, sulfur, and methane. He heaved
violently onto the wooden deck below him and realized that
this was not the first time somebody had gotten sick due to
the stains and remnants of vomit oozing around him. He
raised his head trying to get a whiff of fresh air but to no
avail. This was the atmosphere all would have to adapt to
their frail lungs. The sky was a swirling mass of green,
orange, red, yellow and gray clouds. Suddenly, an immense
section of a rapid red sky would open to reveal a
voluminous grid of long black rectangular chutes followed
by the falling of silhouetted figures... human figures as if
they were discarded laundry. The figures would free fall
into the chum filled river and immediately be swarmed
upon by awaiting frenzied serpents that ripped into their
defenseless bodies; their wails of torment, deafening. It
seemed to the gaping Davenport that this was the ultimate
processing of Death. The sounds of moans were deafening.
A loud hum drowned out any effort to hear the movement
of the boat's strenuous progress through the sludge. The
hum was punctuated by audible cries for mercy especially
from a man battling the pulling effect of the sickening thick
sea yards away.

   The man clung to a square life preserver trying in vain
to pull up out of the sea and to use the life preserver as a
raft. As the galley ship neared the man, the crew sighed as
a possible break from rowing was imminent. The crew
tattered in rags consisted of men and women. All heaved in
unison to catch their breaths as the command was given to
stop. As the ship slowed, the man showing the effects of
his ordeal stretched his arm for someone to haul him
aboard. Davenport watched in horror to see that the man
was not clutching a life preserver. It was a hairy human

torso! The voice of the man sounded familiar to Davenport and as the ship drew closer he recognized his face. He was a popular comedian who had died recently, Harv Lester. Lester was a comic who regularly chastised religious leaders and blasphemed any religious denominations. He went out of his way to make obscene remarks as part of his comedy routine to heighten his popularity. Controversy was welcomed by the network of which he was employed so there was nothing sacred. His followers grew and with that came a hatred towards those that did believe. Now here he was adrift in a chunky thick river of shit clinging to a human torso with his left arm. A freshly bloodied stump of his right arm rested wearily on the other side of the improvised raft. The boatman stood near the side as the boat neared the drowning man.

"Just one word gets you a seat on this boat, *funnyman*. Have you thought about it since we last passed?" "MERCY!!" the comic cried out struggling and reaching towards the barnacled hull of the boat "For the love of God, MERCY!!" Lester craned his neck to see an immensely long figure slithering through the sea pulling other mercy pleading drifters into the depths of doom. Some called for their mommies. The wailing and futile splashing had no effect on the serpent's hunger for flesh. Their bodies would be dragged violently and moments later parts of his or her body would float to the surface. A leg here, an arm, a head and lots of torsos littered the sea. Obviously that was how Lester lost his right arm. Competing for the carrion were blood stained vultures perched on partially consumed corpses ripping and tearing entrails from body cavities.

The tattered man next to Davenport whispered the magic word. "Amen. All he has to say is the word 'amen.' Remember that if you find yourself in the sea."

"Amen?" Davenport returned staring ahead.

"It means... I believe," the tattered old man stated under his breath.

Davenport wondered. He felt that would be the last word that Lester would ever utter on Earth due to his stout penchant for the denial of God.

The boatman howled with laughter at the comic's instant devout turnaround.

"I wish I had a dinar for every time I heard 'mercy.'"
Looking down a glint in the murky waters caught his
glance. Attached to a severed hand was a gaudy golden
watch... a Rolex encased with diamonds. Then using the
end of an oar, he fished the hand out of the sea and
removed the watch tossing the hand back into the sea
unceremoniously. He then ordered the crew to row leaving
the atheist adrift in the sea behind. He strutted back to his
perch in the rear examining his new prize and reading the
inscription on the rear of the timepiece ignoring his rowers.

"R.W. E. Esq. Guess he won't be needin' this anymore,"
he grimly surmised wrapping the golden band around his
own wrist while wiping the detritus from the timepiece on
his centuries stained pantaloons. Seeing an opportunity to
chat with his rowing mate, Davenport needed answers.

"Were all those people atheists?" Davenport asked
looking ahead.

"Mostly, but now we have been receiving a lot of suicide
bombers, mass shooters, and that scum. You know takers
of innocent souls. Can't blame the Gyrotuprans for that
kind of justice. Now shut up and row!"

Inside the boat, there were men and women attired in
dirty tatters of clothing. All had felt the lashings and
maintained their rowing. Nobody uttered a sound or dared
to unless he or she wanted to feel the sting of the whip. An
old man perched on the bow robotically banged out a
monotonous cadence on a worn ancient drum to keep
everyone's rowing in sync. The sea was burgundy in color
and every once in a while a red-orange glow pierced out
from under the surface. Something dark was slicing
through the water revealing a gashed trail resembling a
lava flow.

There were serpents and eels meandering their ways
through the current in quest to satisfy a perpetual hunger.
To quench his thirst for his sadism, the whip wielder
patrolled up and down the center aisle looking for someone
who was losing strength and not rowing to his liking. A
man near the bow was his target. He loosened the man's
shackles as the wretched man pleaded for mercy trying to
bribe his tormentor with money he didn't have. It went to
no avail and the punisher heaved the man overboard as a

swarm of eels descended on him drowning out his screams and pulling him under the sea. The enforcer smiled at the bubbling frenzy on the side of the boat and leered at the propellers of the ship. "Who will be next?" He shouted. The rowing increased its intensity as if moved to a higher gear mechanically. This effect spurred on the rowers better than being flogged.

Off in the distance Davenport could see the silhouette of land laying on the horizon and it appeared the ship was on course for a landing. The Chief entertained the notion of escape in his fresh mind. He was still stronger than the others to accomplish this feat since he was the rookie on a ship with those who had long been unwilling passengers. Oh, to be free on land again! Then, he finally pondered after his initial and rude introduction to this strange scenario. "Where am I and how did I end up here?" He spoke these words hoping that the man next to him would respond. The man staring straight ahead and sure that the punisher was in the stern area by the location of his voice answered.

"You are in the Milbo Sea headed for Gyrotupra for sentencing. Shut up and row!"

The Chief not knowing how to respond regained his rowing intensity to match. He shook his head as if to jar something in his brain to jog free of any knowledge of these places in his mind. The punisher returned down the aisle peering into each row left and right to inflict another lashing on slackers who weren't pulling their weight. He cursed them as dogs and randomly flailed the whip. The blood and scars on Davenport's back were his first and hopefully his last. The punisher noted that these wounds were fresh and doused his back with a bucket of salty sea water sending the chief writhing from the sting. "Row or I'll feed you to the eels, you mangy cur! They love fresh meat!" He pressed his toothy gritty face into the Chief to display he wasn't kidding. His breath smelled of internal decay from hundreds of years.

The land loomed large on the horizon. The ship was close about less than a mile from shore. The old man in the front stopped drumming. The Chief mused that this must be his minute break. The rowing stopped to the appreciative gasping of breaths from the enslaved crew.

"Is this Hell?" Davenport asked rhetorically staring ahead.

His rowing mate to his right had heard the same question asked before from many a *guest* aboard the galley. Scanning around for the enforcer, he answered his worried mate in a raspy harsh voice so as not to be heard.

"Heh! Hell is at the end of the five rivers. We just sent two guys down the River Lethe a guy named Evergreen and one named Danko. This is paradise compared to that. At least here, you may have a chance to end up in Gyrotupra over there. That guy who was just thrown over. He'll be back on the boat and if he doesn't row, then he will be thrown back in again. We all face the same fate hoping we get a reprieve. But once you go down the River, you can kiss hope goodbye forever."

"Who are you?" Davenport asked. "Do I know you?"

The enforcer finished his sloppy gulping from the fresh water tub. He threw down the ladle and stormed his way to the front of the galley stomping his feet deliberately.

"I hope you can swim!" whispered the man to his right.

The punisher strutted down the aisle. He tugged at the shackles of the Chief, loosening them.

"STAND!" IT"S FEEDING TIME AGAIN!" He guided the Chief whose legs were shaking badly to the side and thrust him into the sea as if he was a disloyal mutt. He could hear the man laughing aloud as the Chief splashed in terror scanning the surface for the eels; his heart thumping out of his chest, his eyes pushed nearly from their sockets. Using the ship's barnacle laden hull as a wall, he launched himself towards the shore like an Olympic swimmer. From behind he could hear the punisher yell, "Faster! Faster! They're coming!" The sadist punctuated his urgings with the usual harsh laughter. The Chief set his sight on the palm tree laden shore ignoring what may be looming behind him. The thick crud had given way to clear warm hospitable waters and the eels or serpents would be repelled by the tropical like sea surrounding the island. He continued swimming at record speed to get to the shallows and away from the eels. Once in shallow water he would run. As he closed in on the shore, a figure waved to him frantically from the beach.

"Over Here! Hurry! Over Here, Mr. Davenport!"

The Chief directed his swimming to the figure on the shore now noticing the coral riddled sea floor below him. The current drove his knees into the razor sharp reef sending crimson clouds of blood to trail him. He righted himself and gingerly walked to the shore where the figure, a native looking individual, clad in khaki shorts and a flowing plaid cotton shirt, holding a long bamboo cane, trotted out to retrieve him.

"You made it! You are safe now. The serpents don't come after you on your sentencing day." The Chief now on the sandy beach leaned over pressing his hands on his lacerated knees and gasping violently. His soaked torn uniform pants dragged below his legs weighted down by sea salt that had accumulated in his pockets. His back stung from the lashings and his knees spewed blood as he bent them. It took minutes for him to regain his breath and he turned to watch the slave ship sail off into the distance. He was elated that he escaped.

The sun darkened native allowed the Chief to regain his strength and to catch up on a normal breathing pattern.

"Mr. Davenport. You must follow me. They are waiting for you." The native spoke in a British island accent.

"Do I know you? How did you know my name?" the Chief exhaled exhaustively.

"I am Elroy Strange and you are in Gyrotupra where we know everything about our guests. We really must be going. They are waiting for you." Suddenly the sound of girlish giggling interrupted Mr. Strange's instructions. Down shore about fifty yards stood four island enchantresses scantily clad in island vegetation barely concealing their assets of allure to man. The nymphs beckoned for the newly arrived to join them. Davenport could not resist.

"Well Mr. Strange I'm not going anywhere and I am not FOLLOWING you!" The Chief feeling confident that he could fight the native if he presented any resistance to his escape plans took off running down the beach and disappeared into the tropical brush in pursuit of the fleeing

native women. A path had already been worn where he
exited the beach. Not hearing Strange's pursuit of him he
slowed his pace and limped along the trail shaded by the
canopy of the tropical forest. He constantly had to stop and
brush off the spiny and prickly items deposited from the
various jungle trees on the path from the soles of his bare
bloody feet. He came to a circular opening where the path
diverted in three different directions. He chose the one
across from him that seemed to go where the sound of the
native girls was loudest.

Suddenly from the other two directions he was
surrounded by people; non-tropical people speaking
English and cursing him. They descended on him beating
him with fists, pelting him with rocks, spitting on him,
gouging his eyes, biting him, and kicking him. A
grandmother with brass knuckles delivered the worst blow
sending the Chief down holding his groin from a
strategically placed upper cut. They were going to tear him
apart until a breeze whispering unintelligible ancient words
dispersed the mob. The Chief pulled himself up wincing
from even more pain causing him to cry out in a primal
scream of hopelessness.

"Will you follow me now, Mr. Davenport?" the native
requested in proof that it would be a safer option.

It was Strange in an impatient told you so stance. The
Chief hands on his knees weathering the fresh blows
assented to Strange with a weak 'yes'. He limped behind
his guide down the trail of his first intention, bruised and
bloody. Strange held the bamboo cane high in his right
hand as to drive out evildoers who lurked in the dense
green jungle.

"You know Mr. Davenport I go through the same thing
almost every time with newcomers like yourself. That's why
I didn't chase after you. It is better for one to experience
the hostility of Gyrotupra in order to entertain any notion
of escape. With me you are protected from these unsightly
elements. I tried to warn you."

"Who were those idiots, anyway? Why are they so
angry?" Davenport paused to collect himself bending over
to rest. He was still reeling from the blows and now he was
faced with the reality of experiences that were not of his

world. Blood streamed from his nose which was broken during the assault.

"Consider them as a welcome wagon, Mr. Davenport. If you deviate from your assigned path you will encounter them again. I advise you not to wander or try to escape. They will find you and I might not be around to save you the next time," his guide warned his aching tourist.

"I hate to see what they do for a bon voyage party!" The Chief stood upright and motioned for Strange to continue to lead him through the dense jungle.

"Bon voyage? That's funny Mr. Davenport. We are near our destination. Try to keep up! We are late."

"You look familiar, Strange. You sure we haven't met before?" Davenport inquired to establish a friendly connection in this hostile land.

His guide's countenance tightened. He was repulsed by the Chief's attempt to befriend him. Strange held back the generous urge to respond to his guest's inquiry. Instead, he ignored him and increased his stride through the brush causing Davenport to rush behind him to catch up while peering over his shoulder for the mob's next opportune chance to get to him.

In a distinct clearing carved from the center of the rain forest lay a majestic and impressive cluster of temples. There was a sixty foot statue of Solon, the ancient Greek law reformer on one end of the lawn while, a statue honoring the wisdom of King Solomon stood at the opposite end. Men with white robes and flowing beards carrying thick tomes were seen entering and exiting the stone and columnar buildings discussing issues of the law and precedents of the law. The Chief overheard one man citing the case, "Talleyrand vs. Bonaparte" as a precedent. The Chief was led up an imposing flight of steps to a judicial type of structure. Each door to the front was guarded by stone carved lions and torches illuminated the expansive hall where courtrooms were holding session. Strange stopped and peered at the sign outside one of the doors.

"This is where we go, Mr. Davenport. Follow me."

"I'm not exactly dressed if I am to appear before a judge, Mr. Strange," the Chief admitted trying to stall his destiny. Again his guide ignored him and urged him to keep up while waving his cane. Davenport looked at the black sign with white lettering outside the door of the courtroom. It read:

Dillon, Craddock, and Gleason v. Davenport

The door swung open to a small courtroom. All in attendance turned their attention to Strange and Davenport as they strolled up the aisle to the defendant's table. Davenport looked over curiously to the plaintiff's side. Dillon sneered his anger toward the Chief as to say, "Give me five minutes with you!" Gleason also directed a spiteful stare towards him. Stanley Craddock sat in the audience section clad in the same tattered garments that the Chief wore. His ruddy complexion and whip induced stripes on his body indicated he too had been an unwilling passenger on the slave ship.

"Your Honor. I am sorry we are late and kept you waiting. I hope we haven't inconvenienced the Court," Strange addressed the judge who was examining documents relevant to the trial of which he was presiding.

"I assume our guest took off running from you like the spineless coward he has been portrayed in these statements," the judge conjectured holding up the documents. "I think we all in attendance today would have been shocked if he *didn't* run from his obligations!" the judge stated to intimidate the defendant eliciting a stifled laughter from the plaintiffs table. "I hope you weren't harmed in any way, Mr. Strange," he conceded. Davenport stood humiliated in front of the court facing the judge in his ragged pants and bare chest.

"No, your honor. I did my duty as much as I could discharge considering the element I was entrusted."

"You may go Mr. Strange," the judge generously commanded. "Your services are appreciated by the Court and noted. Keep up your good work! It looks like your promotion is near."

"Thank you, your honor. I am in your debt, sir." Strange turned grinning ear to ear. He looked towards Terry Gleason at the plaintiffs table who gave him the thumbs up gesture. A familiar looking man in a gray pinstriped suit approached the dumfounded defendant.

"Mr. Davenport? I am your counsel, Declan Stockyard, appointed by the Gyrotupran Government to represent you during these proceedings. I have read your file and I will do my best to represent you. You are being charged with conspiracy and complicity in the murders of Terry Gleason, and Officer Ken Dillon. We are going to plead 'Not Guilty'. Do you agree?"

The defendant still confused nodded his head. Afterwards a bailiff led him and his lawyer to the defendants table. "I don't mean to sound disrespectful Mr. Stockyard, but I don't feel like I'm going to get a fair trial with the way I have already been prejudged," the Chief confided in a whisper.

"It is my advice to you as your appointed lawyer, that if you utter one syllable of your feelings about the sanctity of this preceding, you will find yourself aboard the vessel that brought you here to Gyrotupra in the blink of an eye. Do you want to risk that? Let me know now and I'll plead guilty as charged. I have other cases than yours and they were lucky to find somebody to defend you." Stanley Craddock sitting rows away leaned in to hear the context of the discussion between the defendant and his counselor. After explaining the options to Davenport, he looked back at Craddock and nodded assurance that Davenport would plead not guilty.

Davenport gulped. He surrendered his will to his attorney. "Plead not guilty, I'll behave."

The judge, a stocky dark man in his forties with thick black eyebrows seeing that Davenport and his lawyer had made their pact directed his inquiry to the defendants table.

"Mr. Stockyard. You have advised your client on the charges. How do you plea, guilty or not guilty?" the judge smiled acknowledging Stockyard's last minute volunteering of his services to the court.

"Not Guilty, your honor on both charges," declared the defense attorney. Another trace of familiarity gripped Davenport as his counselor stood and stated his client's position. He looked back and glanced briefly at Stanley Craddock in the audience. A conflict developed in his mind.

His lawyer reminded him of Stanley Craddock in the way
he addressed the court.

"Enter as not guilty. We will begin these proceedings
now. Mr. Del Lonkin for the prosecution please commence
with your opening argument," directed the judge to the
court reporter.

"Your honor. We will prove to the Court that Mr.
Davenport as Chief of the Police of Seaside, Maryland
participated in the outright corruption and conspiracy that
led to the deaths of my two clients. We will prove that he
aided in the planned executions of my clients, Terrence
Gleason and Kenneth Dillon, and the cover-up that
ensued. We will prove that he was under the control of Bill
Danko who masterminded this conspiracy and corruption.
And, we will push for the ultimate penalty he deserves; a
permanent position of rower aboard a slave ship in the
Milbo Sea!"

"Mister Stockyard?"

The lawyer had explained to the Chief why there was no
jury in Gyrotupran law as Lonkin presented his case. The
Judge was the jury and the lawyer reminded him of the
dire consequences of griping and complaining to the court.

Davenport's lawyer stood and addressed the Court." My
client is innocent of these charges. He was under duress
from not only Mr. Danko but by his boss, Mayor Craddock.
Mr. Craddock, by the way was found guilty for his
railroading of Mr. Dillon which ended in his death in
prison. My client had no involvement in that matter and we
will prove that today. My client had nothing to do with Mr.
Gleason's death also. His death was reported as a random,
but tragic accident and I will show you the documents
supporting that finding."

The trial progressed with the testimony from both
Gleason and Dillon. Both clients had to be reminded to
contain their tempers when addressing the court about
their relation with the Chief. When the investigation report
was presented to Gleason by the defense counsel about his
fatal accident, he raved. He strongly maintained that he
had his brakes serviced and equipped with new pads only
two months before. The mechanics who worked next door
to his burger establishment claimed that it was highly

improbable that both brake linings would fail at the same time and there was no evidence of worn brake linings when they inspected the brakes. It was a clear case of sabotage to silence his truthful testimony at the Salvano trial, he concluded.

Del Lonkin produced the report for the Court. He revealed to the court that he had a Gyrotupran hand writing examiner look at the report from the mechanic while comparing it to the Chief's handwriting. The expert concluded that the Chief had forged the report. Lonkin called for Ken Dillon to take the witness stand.

Dillon recalled his past testimony from the Salvano trial and his testimony in Gyrotupra which resulted in Mayor Craddock's sentencing, pointing to him in the audience. He informed the Judge of the about face position his boss, Chief Davenport, had taken a week before he was to testify on behalf of Dillon. While he was in prison, his days were left wondering why the Chief changed his mind about him. He indicated that the Chief was just as guilty as the Mayor in his railroading leading to his eventual death in prison.

Stanley Craddock was summoned to the witness stand next. Craddock had made a deal with Supreme Council to qualify for a special exemption to his status if his testimony would be beneficial to implicating the Chief for his involvement. What was revealed to the Court was that he had met a week before with the Chief.

"The Chief was angry about the way Officer Dillon would always harp about dysfunction in the office and the Chief's lethargic and care less way of dealing with them. This would drive the Chief crazy and would result in many sleepless and hate filled nights. He was going to testify on Dillon's behalf, but he confided in me his reluctance to do so due to the volatile exchanges they would have over work issues. When Danko came to me, he goaded me to push the Chief to act on his reactive hate of Dillon. It didn't take much of me selling the idea. The Chief perjured himself and sealed Dillon's fate. I admit my complicity, but if the Chief had truly testified, then, yes, Officer Dillon would be alive and at home with his family now! A point that I sincerely regret because of what I did to his family and my own. I will never be the same," Craddock said lowering his head in shame and remorse.

Stockyard had only one question for Craddock in his cross examination. "You stated in your testimony that the Supreme Council will review your testimony in this case to reduce your sentence, correct?"

Craddock thought and responded loudly, "Yes."

Now it was time for Davenport to be on the hot seat. Lonkin drilled into him on the matter of his discussions with Mayor Craddock prior to his testimony in the Salvano case. He worked the Chief down without objection from his lawyer. He produced a pad of paper for the Chief to write on and handed over to the Judge to examine the handwriting. The Chief tried to take his time to disguise the writing but was urged by the Judge to write as if his life depended on it. He tried and failed to conceal certain elements of his writing style. The judge was sold on the similarity of the writing sample compared with the evidence of the doctored accident report for Terry Gleason.

Lonkin brought up numerous actual detailed scenarios from the office as described by Dillon to see how the Chief would handle them, or if he remembered them. The Chief failed in both cases and now his temper and frustration surged from the effective needling in recreating the atmosphere at the office.

"I IGNORE THEM! OK! THESE THINGS DON"T MATTER! THEY WILL TAKE CARE OF THEMSELVES! I'M GLAD I SENT HIM TO PRISON!"

The room reverberated with his words. Lonkin looked towards the Judge and waited for a reaction. Stockyard threw down his pen in disgust. The judge banged his gavel as the revelations of what just occurred were whispered between Dillon and Gleason. A bailiff in the wings was directed to the stand and placed Davenport in custody awaiting the sentence when the judge went to his office to decide the Chief's fate. The court room recessed. After forty five minutes the litigants returned to the courtroom to hear the sentence.

"The Court does NOT find evidence that this man, Chief Carl Davenport, was DIRECTLY involved with the deaths of the plaintiffs. Therefore, it does not warrant the maximum sentence. However, I do find that Mr. Davenport's actions are consistent with the evidence of complicity and cover up. I am evoking "the Hell on Earth" statute which will require the defendant to return to Earth and confess his actions to newspapers, television, radio and other forms of media both national and local. You will also devote your time to charity functions and activities to help others on a full time basis. I will be personally monitoring these actions and if you fail or if you *incur* a self-induced death, then you will be dragged back down here and assigned to an eternal voyage on the Milbo Sea! Don't think you are getting off easy Chief! You will be despised and hounded by everyone you come in contact with. It's going to be difficult to show your charitable side! My main purpose is to try and stem the increasing moral decay of society on the Earth by making you a *shiny* example of redemption."

"There exists now an audacious theology that Man is the master of Earth and he controls his fate and that there are no consequences after one dies. Just ask a Holocaust survivor why they still believe in God after their horrid interment in a death camp or why Christians held to their beliefs even as they were fed to the lions. Consider yourself a vital agent in this task! Personally, I think what you have done to these men and their families is both vile and reprehensible! You are Judas without the thirty pieces of silver! You should be sentenced to an Eternity adrift in the Milbo Sea, devoured by sharks and re-experiencing the horror over and over. In fact I hope you do violate the terms of your ruling just to satisfy the hunger for revenge of the court. Just be thankful that there are historical precedents that prevent me from doing so, because you are weak and indifferent and not greed oriented."

"In the case of Stanley Craddock, I find that your testimony was helpful in this matter and you will be recommended for a position in Gyrotrupa." The mayor sighed. "That will be the responsibility of the Supreme Council to decide. You are hereby remanded to a holding facility on Gyrotrupa until the matter is concluded. Court is adjourned!"

Davenport froze in disbelief at how rapid the case against him was resolved. His stunned look caught the attention of his lawyer who was busy garnering his paperwork and placing it into his brief case. He peered over again to the plaintiffs table. Dillon and Gleason vanished into thin air. He looked at Stanley Craddock who was being escorted out of the courtroom in chains.

"I hope you violate the decision Carl. You deserve the hell of the Milbo Sea!"

"So, how did you feel about the verdict?" the preoccupied lawyer inquired passively.

"I feel like I was railroaded," the chief replied trying to imply his displeasure with his representative. His lawyer winced and looked over as Del Lonkin approached the defendant's table.

"Hmm *railroaded*. That's an interesting word, Mr. Davenport. My client says he was railroaded, counselor. What do you think?" he asked his legal counterpart who stood nearby.

Lonkin glared at the defendant. "We have a term for how he feels, Mr. Stockyard. It's called Justice!"

CHAPTER 39

The twenty-seven foot Boston Whaler churned south through the choppy green surf off the coast of Seaside, Maryland. The morning sun reflected off the hull of the sparkling white craft and the wording in blue trim around the cabin, Department of Justice. On board, the USERTs anticipated the final moments where they would be deployed in locating the mysterious missing boat, the *Donovan's Pride*. The compass computer bells chimed with the coordinates that had been entered prior to departure alerting the pilot of the boat of their precise location. The boat bobbed wildly as it came to stop hovering above the site of the sunken boat. The agents converged curiously inside the cabin to learn of the findings of the boats scanning of the ocean floor.

"Sonar indicates there is something down there. It could be our subject boat or something else," the lead agent announced. "We better lower the R-O-V." (The R-O-V stands for Remotely Operated Vehicle which is a robotically controlled search device which uses lights, cameras and manipulators in the retrieval of submerged evidence). Since the ocean conditions were not favorable for a scuba search of the area, it was determined to prepare the ROV prior to its arrival at the site. Utilizing the davit on the aft end of the boat, the crew lowered the ROV gently into the rocking water lapping at the hull of the Boston Whaler.

Inside the cabin, technician Ross Graninger switched on the television cameras and lights. Using his monitor he then guided the vehicle through the plankton infested cloudy green water to the desired depth that the boat's sonar had registered at 12.375 fathoms. Nearing the ocean floor, the technician scanned an area in a 360 degree search until he found an ominous looming dark object beckoning his curiosity at 83 degrees. Using the thruster control, Graninger propelled the ROV through the tumultuous ocean current towards the suspicious but familiar looking silhouette nestled on the sea floor roughly thirty feet away. It was a boat.

The thrill of discovery was short lived by the technician as he guided the ROV closer to the boat. Graninger could see that the boat had been pushed by the current to its port side. The bright lights revealed a faded green hull with evidence of decay from the harsh undersea elements. On instinct the technician switched on the record button to tape the discovery. The ROV now within five feet of the sunken craft surveyed the length of the port side for some indication of its identity and the tech dispatched it to the stern hoping to see if the registration numbers were still legible. To his delight, most of the black vinyl numbers remained intact and he jotted them down on a legal pad. The next task for the ROV was to comb through the boat's cabin and areas below deck if possible.

Noting a tight squeeze through the broken front windows of the cabin and the possibility of jagged glass cutting the control lines of the ROV, the cautious tech manipulated the search vehicle to the aft side of the cabin, hoping that the cabin door was open. The lights of the ROV darted around the entrance to the cabin to the disappointment of the technician. The force of the ocean current had sealed the door and any effort to use the manipulators to open the door would be futile. As he accepted this fact from previous encounters with identical situations, he reversed the ROV from the cabin. Suddenly an image appeared that aroused the tech.

It was a wooden life preserver hung outside of the
cabin. On it read the broken words, "Do v n's ride." Now it
was a certainty. The odds of this boat not being the object
of the search were infinite. This was the long lost vessel
that had disappeared eight years ago. Adrenaline surged
through the veins of the technician and his loud
proclamation of discovery did not go unheeded as the other
USERTs rushed inside.

"We got the registration number, the color of the hull
and now the name of the boat! It is the *Donovan's Pride!*"
he reveled gleefully. "I still have to examine the rest of the
exterior of the boat for evidence of sabotage," he explained
to his excited team members glancing at the images on his
screen. "We're going to need that life preserver and I don't
think the manipulator on the ROV can remove it
delicately," he implied to his mates wary that a dive was
imminent. The two left the cabin, realizing that once the
ROV was hoisted back on board, they would be descending
to retrieve at least the faux life preserver.

As the two left the cabin, the technician directed the
ROV to search the aft end of the boat. Again he was floored
by the images that appeared on the monitor. The aft end of
the boat had deteriorated much more than the rest of the
boat which remained remarkably intact. It looked as if
something had eaten the back end of the craft and the hull
appeared brittle at that point. He lowered the ROV to peer
into the rotted section and focused on an object mounded
over by silt and sand on what would have been the aft
floor. Using the thrusters he swept away the loose deposits
to reveal a container, a glass bottle of some sort. "Why
would there be a bottle under the engine compartment?"
he wondered. He summoned his two fellow agents back
into the cabin to support his suspicions.

"What do you make of that?" he pointed to the screen.

After a short pause, the senior of the two agents Agent
John Eubanks recalled a case in Tampa, Florida. That case
involved finding a glass container similar to the one on the
monitor. It too was located near a sunken boat. "Judging
by the strong condition of that glass bottle versus the
fragile section of the boat, I suspect an acid of some sort.
Probably sulfuric. There is probably a pivoting device that

was installed just above that bottle that permitted spillage of acid when the boat encountered rough seas. See if you can move the ROV to a position above the bottle," he suggested to his awestruck mates.

The lights of the ROV pierced through the harsh darkness of the aft engine compartment revealing hoses and pipes that dangled in disarray. It then illuminated an area on the port side where a steel flange was bracketed and welded to the hull. It rose and fell continually in a rhythmic and noticeable pattern. The top and bottom of the flange consisted of four curved arcs, two on top and two on the bottom, of metal harnessing. The arcs on the bottom had weakened and showed signs of erosion and whatever was housed in between the harness had fallen out, like a rounded bottle. The agent's hunch was confirmed that a pivoting device housing a bottle of some sort of acid sank the *Donovan's Pride.*

The ROV was recovered after a thorough examination of the boat. The two agents now clad in scuba gear plunged into the depths armed with side scanners and evidence retrieval brags. One agent would handle the recovery of the bottle and life preserver while the other gathered sections of the aft portion of the hull to confirm traces of acid. After surfacing with the retrieval bags, all three inspected the evidence. The senior agent smelled the bottle. Despite resting on the ocean floor for nearly eight years, the pungent odor of acid caused his olfactory sense to burn from the inhalation of the foul fumes. The technician held the life preserver in his hands. It was mounted to the exterior cabin wall by two wood screws and the agent responsible for its extraction took great caution in its removal. Now convinced that the boat had positively been identified by its registration number, the hull color, and now the tangible wooden life preserver, he contacted his base with "a mission accomplished" notification.

All that was left was the removal of the pivoting device which would link Danko to the sabotage of the boat and the homicides of the Donovan family. The two divers waited a day before their next dive which would require the use of acetylene torches in extricating it from the hull. Jimmy Castro's wait for confirmation from Greg Harding was interminable.

CHAPTER 40

Seaside had held its annual fireworks display on Saturday, but that demonstration would pale to what would occur Monday July the Sixth. This day would go on the record as Seaside's Independence Day. The Danko control of the tiny coastal resort was finally over. Over the past weekend, Danko died in prison. His two contract men, now positively identified by the State Medical Examiner, were killed in a shootout. And, the biggest event was about to happen. Seaside Police Chief Carl Davenport turned himself over to the State Police requesting reporters from all over to hear a statement about his involvement in the corruption that occurred during his tenure. He admitted that he informed Sebastiani and Molinaro about Gwen Blasingame's files. The day before his statement he acknowledged receiving a death threat from both as a reminder that Danko though dead was still in control of Seaside. The envelope contained a glossy graphic crime scene photograph of Mayor Craddock.

The story erupted with Gwen Blasingame at the epicenter. Rob MacElroy from the Baltimore Sun arrived just in time. News agencies from all over flooded her office and home for details of this story. The FBI sent agents to her home to examine the evidence she had accrued over nine years. The Seaside Daily newspaper reversed its pro-

Danko stance to keep up with the frenzy as its competitors were out selling it. Gwen's face was everywhere on the major networks explaining the scandal that had enveloped her town. She was featured on 60 Minutes. There would not be a town in America that was uninformed of the Seaside Scandal or as the media dubbed it 'Seaside-gate.' Gwen' dreams of Pulitzer were becoming a reality as she compiled every fact in the case to publish her book, "The Sandals Scandals: The Seaside Conspiracy."

Calvin Blasingame was singled out for his heroic chase of the villains. He was honored at an Orioles game, the Dover International Speedway (in which he drove his '51 Mercury on the oval as a pace car). He received endorsement deals from the Miller Brewing Company and he appeared in local commercials for Drummond's Used Cars parading around the lot with a bass drum strapped to his front.

"Hi, I'm Calvin '51 Mercury Blasingame. I'm drummin' for Drummond Used Cars out here on Intrastate 594. Why not come by and buy?" (The ad took over 50 takes: the Miller ad took more.)

The FBI lab confirmed the USERT's hunch on the presence of sulfuric acid on the areas removed from the hull of the *Donovan's Pride*. The manufacturer of the glass bottle was traced to a plant in Rochester, New York. They provided the bottles for a chemical firm to fill the acid in New Jersey which transported it to a distribution warehouse outside of Philadelphia. That is where the sulfuric acid was purchased or stolen since no records could be found with a link to Danko; even though Danko operated from Philadelphia. Local police records did indicate several break-ins of this particular warehouse around the time of the sinking of the *Donovan's Pride*. One of the items stolen was a 1.5 liter bottle of sulfuric acid. The shade of paint on the hull of the missing boat corresponded to paint that Jimmy Castro had saved after he painted the hull of the *Donovan's Pride*.

The wooden life preserver correlated with the one photographed on a Donovan family picture that the FBI was able to obtain from the Seaside Daily News. The lab recreated the function of the pivoting device that was mounted in the aft hull area of the *Donovan's Pride*. After exhaustive testing utilizing a wave pool at a naval model ship engineering facility, the technicians concluded that the pivoting device did indeed work and led to the sinking of the boat. The file on the disappearance of the *Donovan's Pride* was changed to homicide. After seeing the earlier mug shot pictures of Sebastiani and Molinaro displayed in the Seaside Daily News following the shootout and subsequent police chase, Jimmy Castro identified them as the two men who were assigned the welding job on the *Donovan's Pride*.

Ted Minnis and Octavia Bledsoe were cleared of any involvement of the sabotage of the *Donovan's Pride*. The FBI concluded that the two were psychics and that they were guided to the site by forces unknown. The word *ghosts* or *ghost ship* never appeared in the official reports. Ted Minnis has rededicated his life to supporting his wife, Anna and her charitable causes. His relationship with Octavia over, Minnis regards July 4th, 1992 as the turning point in his new life when he abandoned his lustful and material urges.

Mrs. Maria Louise Craddock succumbed soon after the story broke on July the 8th. Milton was by her side promising her that he would fulfill her wishes to restore the family name to Seaside. In the years to follow, Milton chaired every committee to bring community awareness to issues of all matters of cancer, multiple sclerosis, cystic fibrosis, muscular dystrophy, heart disease, and autism. He was recognized by chapter presidents, sponsors, and President George S. Bush for his endless and selfless dedication and sacrifice to the causes he chaired. The community rallied around him and respected his heartfelt desire to his tasks. He was honored by the various Seaside Civic Clubs. As the years passed with a new generation embracing Milton as a hero, the reputation of Stanley Craddock faded. His mother's dying wish now accomplished what she had hoped and even more. Somewhere beyond, Stanley Craddock has been rescued from the dark eternity of the Milbo Sea and serves as a lowly clerk in the Gyrotupran Judiciary system.

Carl Davenport now sentenced to twenty five years in the State penitentiary for his role in the Seaside conspiracy, conducts his ministry everyday trying to evoke a change in the lives of hardened criminals. He is allowed to speak his messages to the prison population and has gained a faithful following. One is a blonde female Corrections Officer who stands above him patrolling on the second floor behind a chain link fence looking down on him hanging on every word. She has been seen by other guards; but has never been seen up close.

Davenport is part of the Scared Straight Program to divert youngsters from a life of crime and imprisonment. His family has long forgotten him for the shame he imposed on them. His estranged wife and his children have long erased him from their memories and currently lead their own lives. When asked about their father they respond with a terse reply of "he's dead!" This is the same response that Dillon's sons utter about their father, but provoking a sympathetic reply from those who question them.

Mrs. Pamela Evergreen reaped the windfall of her late husband's estate. She converted her husband's law firm to indoctrinate a less intensive policy of cultivating their clients. There were those clients and employees that detested her polite stance, but they were in the minority and they gradually left the firm. It was a welcome change and an air of relief and prosperity hovered through the once dank and dungeon-like atmosphere of Evergreen and Carlson. To demonstrate her desire for positive change, she had the statue of her late husband removed from the lobby and donated to a shooting range used by the NYPD. With her new found fortune she established a Parkinson's Research fund in her husband's name. The name Evergreen now became synonymous with philanthropy as she dispensed generously her husband's estate to charity, knowing somewhere he was cringing from her actions.

There was however one haunting image that would remain for her to her dying day. When the limousine was raised from the sinkhole, the bodies of her husband and limo driver were not inside. Investigators had informed her that there were large puddles of blood and tissue splattered throughout the vehicle that were consistent with the DNA of her late husband. Evergreen died a violent death inconsistent with the limo's fall into the sinkhole. Oddly there were no traces of the limo driver. Background checks on the driver at the Coastal Charm Condominiums proved fruitless. He didn't exist and fooled the intensive security checks at the complex. Again investigators were confronted with an unsolved mystery. But the one item that really had everyone stymied was the etching scrawled into the back door of the limousine. In large letters read the word, "VIM." Those religious in nature who had the unfortunate pleasure of being in this monster's company knew the meaning. VIM was a message from God. Vengeance is mine!

And in a remote part of the state, Ben Jacoby emerged from the confines of the State Psychiatric Center a vindicated and soon to be wealthy man.

CHAPTER 41

Life at the Castro home is now at peace. As promised Jimmy returned to the location of *The Donovan's Pride* bringing along Sunny, Danny, and a retired naval chaplain he met at the local VFW. Sunny utilizing her Polynesian craft knowledge from her life on O'ahu had sewn together a beautiful floral lei consisting of flowers of green, white, orange and red flowers. It was to be meaningful. Jimmy had helped with the concept. The lei,of course, was to resemble the Irish national flag. She assembled orange poppies, white orchids and appropriately Bells Of Ireland for the green portion of the lei. For each member of the Donovan family she wove in five red roses including one for Paddy, the Irish setter. Jim Stevenson the retired USN chaplain wore a silver cross around his sports shirt. He commenced the ceremony. After each mention of the names of the deceased, Jimmy clanged a brass bell that he held in his hand with a small hammer.

"Unto Almighty God we commend the souls of the Donovan family, Michael, Joanne, Kathleen, Michael Junior, and Paddy the Donovan's pet and we commit their bodies to the deep; in sure and certain hope of the Resurrection unto eternal life, through our Lord Jesus Christ; at whose coming in glorious majesty to judge the world the sea shall give up her dead." He nodded for Sunny to toss the lei into the ocean. Danny somberly waved.

"We miss you all and we hope you are at peace at last!"

Sunny hugged Jimmy and Danny as they watched the lei float out towards the horizon with the tide. Mr. Stevenson offered his mournful condolences to the Castros. Their thoughts drifted with the lei just as a youngster watches a helium balloon disappear into the upper limits of the atmosphere. To the left of the drifting lei the splash of a leaping dolphin emerged from the depths. It was joined by more dolphins which were intrigued by the flowering ring in the ocean. They were Atlantic White Sided Dolphins, a common sight in the summer. Their black satiny backs glistened in the sun. The lead dolphin managed to catch the lei on his dorsal fin as the others imitated his joyful jumping.

"Look at them! There must be ten of them!" Danny shouted.

Sunny grabbed the binoculars on the console. "No. It's five. Five." She grinned in exuberance hugging her husband and draping the binoculars around her neck. Jimmy smiled at her rubbing her back while he looked at his son proudly.

"Danny. Your prayers are answered. The Donovan's are at peace at last!"

CPSIA information can be obtained at www.ICGtesting.com
Printed in the USA
LVOW01s2043160415

434884LV00031B/1638/P